T0147135

THE LAIRD'S VOW

Despite her pride that screamed at her to again fight him to gain her freedom, Glenna stood still, her hands at her side, her gaze now on his throat. This was all for a greater purpose.

"Go on, then," she commanded.

But he was quiet for so long that Glenna looked once more to his face. Something smoldered in his eyes that stilled Glenna's impatience. She could feel the beating of his heart against her breast, and her own seemed to answer his, knocking against the tender, mortal wall that separated them.

"Would you submit to me?" he whispered, lowering his head until his face hovered over hers. "As my wife?"

"Nay," Glenna whispered against his lips. "I will never submit to you."

"Never?" He kissed her bottom lip, then her top, barely pressing her flesh. "What about now?"

Glenna tried to shake her head, but it was still held in his large hand. She became alarmed at the sudden weakness in her own legs.

"I think I could persuade you," he murmured. "Aye, I think I could." And then he kissed her fully, deeply, as she lay in his arms stupid and helpless to deny him, deny the powerful, unexpected feelings coursing through her body...

Books by Heather Grothaus

THE WARRIOR

THE CHAMPION

THE HIGHLANDER

TAMING THE BEAST

NEVER KISS A STRANGER

NEVER SEDUCE A SCOUNDREL

NEVER LOVE A LORD

VALENTINE

ADRIAN

ROMAN

CONSTANTINE

THE LAIRD'S VOW

HIGHLAND BEAST
(with Hannah Howell and Victoria Dahl)

Published by Kensington Publishing Corporation

The Laird's Vow

Heather Grothaus

LYRICAL PRESS
Kensington Publishing Corp.
www.kensingtonbooks.com

LYRICAL PRESS BOOKS are published by

Kensington Publishing Corp.
119 West 40th Street
New York, NY 10018

All Kensington titles, imprints, and distributed lines are available at special quantity discounts for bulk purchases for sales promotion, premiums, fund-raising, educational, or institutional use.

Special book excerpts or customized printings can also be created to fit specific needs. For details, write or phone the office of the Kensington Sales Manager: Kensington Publishing Corp., 119 West 40th Street, New York, NY 10018. Attn. Sales Department. Phone: 1-800-221-2647.

Lyrical Press and Lyrical Press logo Reg. U.S. Pat. & TM Off.

First Electronic Edition: September 2019
ISBN-13: 978-1-5161-0707-0 (ebook)
ISBN-10: 1-5161-0707-1 (ebook)

First Print Edition: September 2019
ISBN-13: 978-1-5161-0711-7
ISBN-10: 1-5161-0711-X

Printed in the United States of America

Special thanks this time around to:

The publishing team at Kensington, particularly John Scognamiglio and Rebecca Cremonese.

My incredible agent, Evan Marshall.

My friend Amy Blackthorn.

Prologue

January 31, 1427

Northumberland, England

Thomas Annesley was a dead man running.

He felt rather than saw the large slabs of rock thrusting out of the frozen ground as he stumbled past them, the black winter night hiding scores of the treacherous obstacles that littered the land beyond the manicured gardens of Darlyrede House, his childhood home. Thomas staggered and gasped as his wounded shoulder caught the jagged edge of one such monolith, spinning him on his feet and throwing him backward onto another slanted boulder. He lay against it, shaking, his eyes squeezed shut but his mouth open wide with a silent scream of pain. Every reedy breath of frigid air sliced his parched, bruised throat.

Thomas opened his eyes with a whimper to look up at the sliver of moon, its image blurred by tears held behind the frozen crust along his lashes. It was little light, but the trail of blood would make him easy prey for an expert hunter such as Hargrave. Thomas couldn't go on much farther any matter—he'd pulled two arrows from his own flesh, and the cold had stolen most of the feeling in his extremities. But the most distressing indicator of his rapidly declining state was each painful, whistling breath confirming that the ball from the arquebus had damaged his right lung when it had exited the front of his chest. Hargrave's boasting of the expensive new weapon's accuracy had been warranted, it seemed.

Hargrave would find Thomas and kill him, or he would bleed to death. Either way, Thomas Annesley, third Baron Annesley, Lord of Darlyrede, recognized that his life was already over even as he fled through the wild winter night.

He was eighteen years old.

Thomas tried to push himself aright and heard a soft riffle of sound; his clothing had begun freezing to the rock. He was wet from his bare head to his boots with sweat and blood, as though he'd been so full of fear and death that when he'd fallen onto the stone he'd burst like a dropped wineskin.

Cordelia. Cordelia's blood. Rivers of it, the stone floor flooded so that his boots splashed...the walls around him gummy and black...

He wanted to scream and scream; the atrocity he'd seen burrowed in his chest and in his soul just as deeply and permanently as the stone he collapsed onto once more was sunk into the earth. There would never be any true escape for him—he was trapped in his own mind as surely as in the wide-open land of his own demesne.

Cordelia's wide-open eyes, staring up at that dank, dripping ceiling, the once-blue irises now a thin gray ring around gaping pupils, her pale, perfect heart-shaped face unmarked save for the tiny prickling of purple around her eyes...but below her bare, graceful neck, her alabaster skin slashed, ripped into bright ribbons, the body he'd worshipped in secret now ruined and mauled, her abdomen...

Thomas shook so hard with fear and cold that his head nodded wildly. Cordelia was dead—horribly, violently dead. *Dead.*

The rocky scrape of hooves on frozen track elicited a pained whine from Thomas's scorched throat, and he cringed into the rock, as if it might animate and enclose him in a stony, protective embrace. He stopped breathing to listen in the crystal-cold night, and indeed the horse—horses?—was drawing nearer, and he heard the rumble of a masculine voice.

But it wasn't *his* voice. It wasn't Hargrave. It wasn't any of Darlyrede's men, Thomas was sure of it. Oh, God, please...

Thomas lurched from the stone and staggered toward the sound, toward the narrow track of road that wound past Darlyrede House and to which he hadn't known he'd been so close. There should have been no one traveling so remote a path in the middle of the night, especially during the coldest January Northumberland country had endured in generations. But as Thomas pushed himself from stone to stone, the shadowy images of two mounted riders approaching became clearer.

Help, Thomas tried to call, but the wheezing from his mouth was barely audible even to his own ears. He staggered toward the road, stumbled over the toe of his boot, and clutched at his shoulder as he went down. He heard the men's exclamations of surprise, but Thomas did not wait to see if they would dismount to come to him. He dragged himself to his feet once more, lurching into the road, starbursts appearing behind his eyes as he fought for breath.

He swayed to a stop in the middle of the track, flinging his left forearm in a pathetic arc.

Help...

He braced his hand on his thigh and let his head drop as the horses halted. Thomas willed his chest to expand, his lungs to fill with air. Dizzy...

"Great ghost, boy! What think you to be about on a night such as this, and frightening our—" a voice demanded near his ear, and then strong hands around his arm pulled him upright, and Thomas somehow found the breath to give a whistling scream before his vision went gray and a loud buzzing erupted in both his ears.

"My God, what's happened?" the man amended, his tone now one wholly of alarm.

"Who is it, Kettering?" a second voice called out from a distance.

"It's a young man—he's injured. I don't believe I know him. Come, Blake, bring my horse—I daresay I shall require your assistance."

Thomas collapsed against the man, who took his weight easily.

"There now, lad—I say, you're all but frozen. Fortunate we came along just now." Thomas was jostled, and then this saint, Kettering, eased him away to lean against a solid, warm, breathing wall of horseflesh. "Hold there a moment. Blake, take under his hip—with care. I believe he's suffered injury to his shoulder and side—perhaps elsewhere, also. All right, we're going to lift you onto the saddle, lad. Here, bite down on this." Thomas felt a thin wooden rod pushed between his lips to settle between his teeth. "Steady, now. All right, Blake."

Thomas would have cried out again at the pain in his chest and shoulder, but he had no breath left in him, and so he merely tried to cling to consciousness as his teeth sank into the wood and the warm seat pressed his ribs into the muscles of his chest like blades. He lay limp across the beast, tears building up once more in his eyes, his stomach pushing into his throat.

"Fortunate we came along, indeed," the second man—Blake?—was saying, his voice seeming to echo queerly in the wide expanse of the night. "And good thing we're so near Darlyrede House."

"Just so," Kettering said. "I'll lead him so as to disturb him as little as possible. Blake, you follow behind with vigilance—the criminal who beset this poor lad may yet lie in wait for us. Darlyrede shall be our haven."

Darlyrede.

The word rang rings around Thomas's head as he felt the horse beneath him begin to rock and turn. They were delivering him back to Darlyrede, that abattoir, that place of death where Cordelia lay in the river of blood. Delivering him into the stained hands of Hargrave…

Thomas somehow pulled his right leg up and over the horse's back, leaning heavily upon the beast's neck. It took all the strength remaining in his legs to hold on.

"There he is," Blake said from somewhere behind Thomas. "Taking to it well enough, I say—upright before I can even mount. Fear not, my boy; we shall have you in the care of Lord Hargrave's house soon enough, and then we shall most certainly get to the bottom of who has done you so ill a turn."

Thomas dragged his hand to his mouth, removing what he thought must be the carved wooden pin from the brim of Kettering's hat and gripping it in his fist. He took the deepest breath he was able, and then stabbed the wooden pin down into the horse's side. The animal screamed and reared, causing Thomas's vision to gray again, but it must have pulled its reins free from Kettering's hand, for in an instant the horse was thundering northward into the darkness, away from Darlyrede.

If Thomas Annesley must die, it would not be in that house of the damned.

* * * *

"Damn it all!" Blake shouted as his own horse jerked free and bolted into the black, frigid night after its companion. "Kettering, look what your good deed has done to us. I knew we should have stopped for the night in Alnwick."

"Well, that was most unexpected," Kettering lamented. "I wondered that the lad had enough life left in him to persevere unto Darlyrede; I never thought him capable of absconding with our horses. Forgive me."

Blake went stamping about the road for several more moments, cursing and peering into the night while his companion stared contemplatively down the road where the young man had disappeared.

"I say," Kettering at last mused. "Speaking of Darlyrede, should I not think better of it, that lad bore a keen resemblance to young Lord Annesley himself."

Blake sighed and came to stand near his friend. "That's more than a bit unlikely. Isn't Annesley to be wed on the morrow?"

"Indeed," Kettering murmured. "To Lord Hargrave's own Cordelia. You must be quite right, Blake. Whoever he is, he shan't get far, I'll warrant.

He's gravely injured. Even with such a brief encounter, I'm covered in the poor fool's blood."

"Well." Blake sighed again. "Let's you and I get on to Darlyrede any matter and warn Hargrave. Someone of the house is bound to be yet awake with such a happy ceremony so soon to take place. Perhaps they'll ask us to stay on, or at least lend us a pair of mounts; I'll offer my prayer book as a pawn."

"Oh, Blake, look—here comes someone now. I'll wager it's a guard of the house in search of the lad. Ho, there," Kettering called out, waving his arms toward the black-shadowed rider. "There's an injured man who's only just stolen my horse and frightened away my companion's. Perhaps you—"

Kettering's words were cut off as the whine of an arrow ended in an abrupt *thunk* in the man's chest.

Blake stared mute at his friend as Kettering looked down at the stub of arrow protruding from his cloak, then crumpled onto the frozen road. He turned his horrified gaze to the steadily approaching rider and began backing down the road, stumbling, reaching into his fur-lined robe for the costly leather book he carried over his heart. He held it out in both hands like a small shield as the click and scrape of mechanism echoed across the cold expanse of frozen track.

"I mean you no harm! I mean you— No, no! Don't! Please!"

The twang of the crossbow sounded again.

Chapter 1

March 1458

Edinburgh, Scotland

"'Tis beautiful, Tavish."

Miss Keane looked up through her eyelashes as she ran her fingertips over the striped silk folded on the bench between them, the refined lilt of her voice just as smooth as the imported cloth she admired. Her hand drifted to the edge of the silk where Tavish's hand rested and grazed his skin. "Just what I was hoping for. I think I should like to have all of it. And even more, if your voyage was a profitable one."

Tavish felt his lips quirk as he looked down at the daughter of one of the wealthiest merchants in all of Edinburgh. Redheaded and pampered, Audrey Keane was alluringly beautiful. But, even if she and Tavish hadn't been friends since they were little more than children, it was well known that Niall Keane hoped to elevate the station of his only child with a distinguished and titled match, and Tavish Cameron was neither. And so regardless of her coquettish banter, Audrey would remain nothing more than a good friend and a good customer.

Except for this day—there could be no indulging of Audrey's games with barrels of illegal French wine behind his bench and a stranger about the shop. Tavish glanced over at the black-clad man for what must have been the hundredth time; the stranger's back was currently turned to the bench as if he were merely biding his time while waiting for attendance, inspecting the stacks and bundles of oily wool lining the shop floor. But Tavish caught sight of his straight jawline, could all but see the man's ear cocked toward the conversation being carried on over the bench.

A spy, if ever Tavish had seen one. And seen more than one, he certainly had.

"I'm sorry to say that's all I have this time, Miss Keane," Tavish said, his cool tone causing Audrey's eyebrows to rise. "Shall I have my mother wrap it for you?"

The man in black was obviously not the only one whose ears were paying close attention to the business being conducted, as Mam appeared at Tavish's elbow just then, reaching across him and pulling the silk from beneath Audrey's hungry touch.

"I've a fine flax that shan't snag a'tall, Miss Keane," Harriet Cameron said.

Audrey gave his mother a brief, tight smile before looking to Tavish once more. "Naught else?" she cajoled pointedly. "But you said there would be—"

"Ah, aye!" Tavish interrupted and caught sight of the man in black turning his head ever so slightly toward them. He reached into the wooden barrel behind the bench and withdrew two bright spheres, presenting them to Audrey as if they were Scotland's crown jewels. "Forgive me. Here you are."

"Oranges," Audrey said stiffly.

Tavish smiled and then indicated with his eyes the stranger now turned fully toward them. "From Spain."

Understanding dawned at last in Audrey's eyes. "Oh, *oranges*! How lovely! Thank you, Master Cameron—father will be so pleased."

"Perhaps you might return later in the day to see if I've any left," he suggested. "It's all the *Stygian* returned with on this latest voyage. Silk. And oranges."

Audrey Keane nodded smartly and then dared to give him a wink as her maid took the tied bundle from Mam. "I will most certainly do that. I do hope,"—she paused a moment, met his eyes and lowered her voice—"there are...*more*."

"Good day to you now, Miss Keane," Mam said pointedly through her smile.

The redhead only glanced at Mam. "Mistress Cameron." Then she turned and left the shop, trailing her expensive skirts and her young maid behind her through the open doorway and up the stone steps to the bustling spring street above.

"She wanted one of those filthy books you promised her, nae doubt," Mam hissed low at his side as she rewound the hairy twine she'd cut. "I doona ken why you'd waste space on such rubbish. She canna even read, I'll wager."

"'Tis nae filthy, Mam," Tavish murmured. "'Tis a single volume of poetry, easily carried among the bottles. You know as well as I that Audrey reads quite well, much to Master Keane's dismay. You're only salted because you canna read such stuff yourself." He watched the man move to the other side of the shop.

"Och, *Audrey* all the day now, is it?"

"That's her name." Tavish felt beneath the bench top for the familiar smooth handle of the baton he kept, his eyes never leaving the stranger while his mother's mumblings about the dangerous wiles of Audrey Keane faded into the hum of the street noise beyond the shop walls.

Tavish guessed the man in black to be approximately his own age—a score and ten, perhaps a few years more. His profile revealed a high, sloping forehead with prominent brow and cheekbone, a Roman nose above a noble looking chin. Certainly, the man's grooming was impeccable, his long, black hair tied at the nape with a dark-colored silk ribbon, both of which nearly disappeared against the plush quilting of the man's fine gambeson. He was successful—or wealthy, any matter—considering his black suede leggings filling the shining leather boots. The stranger's belt was wide and equipped; long gauntlets hung from his right side, his weapon on his left—a lengthy arming sword with shining silver pommel, its leather-wrapped scabbard stretching from hip to mid-calf. This was no home-forged, crude weapon.

Nay, this was no ordinary stranger.

So the burgess had hired a foreigner to do his dirty work for him, had he? Tavish took firm hold of the baton and slid it silently from its hiding place, holding it down by his leg.

"—Audrey Keane since she was in braids and you'd think Captain Muir and yourself would—" Mam broke off her hushed tirade. "Tav?"

Tavish's eyes followed the stranger as he ambled ever closer to the bench, his eyes still seeming to peruse the bundled wool.

Mam wrapped her fingers around his arm, seeking his attention, but all he would allow her was the slight angling of his ear toward her.

"What are you thinking you'll do with that?" she whispered, shaking his arm for emphasis. "Is it your plan now to beat those who come to hire you?"

"He's nae here to hire me, Mam."

"And how would you be knowin' that?"

"Only look at him," Tavish said. "Nosing about the place, eavesdropping on my business with Audrey. Someone's sent him." Mam's silence told Tavish he'd no need to explain his meaning. "Perhaps 'twill deliver a clear message to the burgess that I'll have no more of his threats and his thieving, do I send his hired man back to him with a glen in his skull."

Now his mother's fingernails dug into his arm. "You hush, now! Hush! Doona speak of such things! The burgess will jail you and take everything we have—everything you've worked so hard to build. *To keep!*"

"I've a revelation for you, Mam—'tis the burgess's intent to take it all any matter. The *Stygian* canna so much as anchor at Leith—as if I were no better than a common pirate." His mother gave him a look from the corner of her eye, but he ignored it. "I'll have nae more of it, I say."

"And I'll nae have my only child hanged!" She pinched the inside of his elbow hard enough to make him wince, and then, before he could stop her, Mam had shoved past him and was gone from behind the bench, approaching the stranger.

"Good day to you, sir," Mam called out, leaning at the waist as if to draw the man's attention.

He turned and gave Mam a short, courteous bow that took Tavish a bit by surprise—usually those sent by the burgess possessed little in the way of manners. "*Bonjour.* A good day to you, Mistress. Forgive me for not greeting you sooner; I had no wish to encroach upon a private conversation."

Any good will kindled by the stranger's courteous French greeting to Harriet Cameron was quickly extinguished by the remainder of his address, spoken with a proper, clipped accent.

An Englishman.

"Oh," Mam cooed, causing Tavish's bad temper to increase. "Well! How verra kind of you! That's only my son, though."

Tavish had the suspicion that, had he been able to see his mother's face, she would be looking up at the stranger through her eyelashes, much as Audrey Keane had looked at Tavish.

"What I mean to say is, he's the master of the shop but he's also my—" Mam clapped her hands together once gaily and then held them against her matronly, aproned bosom. "Have you come to collect goods from the shipment? Perhaps some"—she paused, her turning and nodding head indicating she was looking the man over thoroughly—"cloth for your...your fine"—she reached out a finger and almost touched the man's chest—"self?"

A faint smile cracked the stranger's proper façade and he gave her another short bow. "Thank you for your kind offer of assistance, but I believe I have located what I seek—you *are* Harriet Payne, are you not?"

Tavish's heart stuttered in his chest.

"My, my!" Mam murmured, and Tavish was glad to hear a bit of caution creep into her tone. "I've nae heard that name in an age. Aye, I'm Harriet; Payne was my da."

The stranger nodded. "Mistress Cameron now, of course. I knew you by the lovely mark there on your upper lip."

Mam's fingertips fluttered at her mouth, where the perfectly round mole she was known for lived, but this time when she spoke, all traces of coquettishness were gone.

"Have we met, sir?" she asked.

"Forgive me," the man said and bowed again. "I am Sir Lucan Montague, Knight of the Most Noble Order of the Garter of His Majesty King Henry of England."

Harriet turned wary eyes to Tavish, whose fingers tingled around the handle of the club he still held beneath the bench top.

"What reason have you to seek my mother, sir?" Tavish asked quietly, his heart galloping in his chest as the barrel nearest him crowned so deliberately with a pyramid of orange fruit seemed to become exponentially larger in the room.

Why was an English knight in his shop?

Lucan Montague's gaze, blue and cold, at last found Tavish. "In truth, I seek the proprietor of this works, and the owner of the merchant ship *Stygian*." His accent was clipped and cool, but also completely at ease. He seemed to examine every detail of Tavish's face before meeting his eyes again, and his face once more betrayed a secret mirth. "I believe you are he. You may retire the weapon you're holding in your right hand; I vow upon my honor that I mean you and your mother no harm."

Tavish felt his brows raise, and he couldn't help but glance down at the baton in his hand—for sure, the man could not have seen it from where he stood.

"In fact," the knight said, stepping to the door and kicking away the wooden wedge that held it open, "I've come bearing what I suspect you will consider to be very good news, and all I ask in return are answers to some few, concise inquiries."

A pair of ladies drew up short before the doorway as Lucan Montague began to close the stout shop door.

"*Désolé*. I do apologize—a matter of great urgency, you understand. So sorry. Good day." He closed the door and looked up and down the frame before engaging both intricate locks, while Mam stepped backward quickly to join Tavish behind the safety of the bench.

Tavish laid the club atop the wood, still firmly in his grip. When Lucan Montague turned around, the knight's gaze went immediately to it, but he didn't seem disturbed in the least.

"Your shuttering my business without my leave is not endearing me to your request. You have a short amount of time to explain yourself, knight or nay, before I make use of this baton," Tavish warned. "Now, I'll only ask once more: What do you want?"

"A fair request," Lucan Montague said with a gracious nod. "I believe your mother may possess some knowledge that will assist my efforts on behalf of the Crown to investigate a series of murders that took place in England."

Mam gasped. "Murders?"

But rather than cause him further alarm, the knight's admission prompted Tavish's shoulders to relax. "You have been misinformed, sir; my mother has not been farther south of Edinburgh than Peebles the whole of her life."

"They've lovely wool," Mam added, her smile returning. She laid her hand upon Tavish's arm. "Tav takes me each year for the festival. Have you been, sir?"

"I've not yet had the happy fortune," the knight said, and to his credit, Tavish could not detect even a hint of condescension in his tone. His gaze met Tavish's directly. "Indeed, it was not my intent to insinuate that your mother was in England when any of the crimes were perpetrated, nor at any time before or after, Master Cameron. My questions for her are wholly concerning your father."

Tavish's jaw grew tight, and a pair of moments ticked by in the silence of the shop. "My father is dead."

The knight nodded. "Oh, yes, likely he is hanged now. But he was very much alive a month ago. I interviewed him myself."

"You are mistaken. *Sir*." Tavish spoke in a low, measured voice. "Dolan Cameron has been dead for fifteen years."

Lucan Montague's gaze never wavered. "Forgive me my bluntness, but I don't believe it is a secret to any here present that Dolan Cameron was not your true sire."

The shop was as still as a calm sea at midnight.

Tavish forced himself to swallow while he tried to think of a reply. He had only discovered the fact of his bastard status fifteen years ago, the very day his stepfather had died. And he was fairly certain Mam wouldn't have admitted it even then if Tavish hadn't been intent on surrendering himself to the constable that terrible night.

And it was Mam who came to his rescue again.

"Perhaps," Harriet Cameron said quietly, "you might agree to keep such an idea to yourself, sir. Tav has inherited this shop and his ship from his…from Dolan Cameron. Dolan claimed Tavish as his own son, and all of Edinburgh knows him as such. If rumor was started that…" Harriet paused. "We could lose everything we have."

Lucan Montague pressed his hand to his chest and gave another bow. "Upon my honor, Mistress, I'll not reveal such to anyone in this city." He rose, and his eyes once more met Tavish's. "Although, if what I suspect is contained in yonder barrel is true, and my suppositions regarding your tenuous relationship with the city's officials are confirmed, it will be you who reveals the news I carry. And gladly."

"I do doubt I would be glad to announce to all Edinburgh that the man who sired me was a wandering ne'er-do-well who got a teenage girl with child and then abandoned her to the spitefulness of her family. And then you said he was hanged, didn't you? A bastard is bad enough—the bastard of a criminal might as well hang himself and save the magistrate the trouble."

"Tav," Mam whispered, looping her arm through his and patting his shoulder with her other hand.

Lucan Montague looked at Tavish and his mother in turn with an almost curiously pleased expression. For so long, in fact, Tavish was tempted to brain the man after all.

"You will proceed how you think best, of course," the knight said at last. "My oath will stand, regardless. All I ask in return is that Mistress Cameron answer my questions with candor. Then I shall leave you both. Never to return, if that is your wish."

"Never?" Tavish pressed.

The man bowed again, and Tavish couldn't help but roll his eyes. "Upon my honor."

Tavish looked down at his mother who, rather than mirror what Tavish was certain was his own worried expression, looked wistful and even sad.

"What say you, Mam?" Tavish asked.

She held his gaze for a moment and then turned to the knight. "Go on."

Tavish wondered that the man didn't carry a perpetual aching head with all the bowing and nodding he did.

"You have my deepest gratitude, Mistress. Now." His demeanor seemed to change in an instant, his actions becoming clipped and efficient as he reached into his thick, quilted gambeson and withdrew a flattened roll of parchment, tied with a black ribbon. He looked to the bench and then Tavish pointedly, one black eyebrow arched. "May I?"

Tavish nodded, and the man stepped to the smooth slab of wood, placing the parchment near the baton and then withdrawing a shortened quill pen and small glass phial of ink from his gambeson. After setting up his supplies in a tidy display, the man returned his attention to the rolled parchment. Undoing the package efficiently, he cleared his throat in a remarkably knightly manner and then looked once more to Harriet.

"As one sworn into service of the Most Noble Order of the Garter and also as special emissary to His Sovereign Majesty King Henry, I, Lucan Montague, do proclaim this inquiry to be both lawful and binding. Do you swear before God that you are Harriet Cameron, born of the family Payne?"

Mam nodded. "Aye. I do."

"Did you meet and have relations with a man in the late winter of the year fourteen hundred twenty-seven, known to you as Thomas?"

"Tommy," Harriet repeated quietly. And then, louder, "Aye, sir. He said his name was Thomas."

Lucan Montague's quill scratched on the parchment even as he spoke. "And he was in fact an Englishman?"

Tavish's head whipped around to look down at Mam, but she was paying him no heed, her pursed lips hinting at the strain she felt.

"Aye. He said he hailed from Northumberland. By the darling reeds, although I never could ken what he meant by that, as he seemed greatly afraid of the place to give it such a pet of a name. It had nearly killed him."

This was not part of the tale his mother had told Tavish. "Mam?"

Mam hesitated, and her eyes held what appeared to be old sorrow. "He'd been shot several times. Once with an arquebus. If it hadna been so cold as to have frozen his wounds, he'd a'bled to death, for certain. He was in a dead faint on his horse when I found him."

"He'd been shot. That is new information. Thank you." Lucan Montague's gaze had flitted between Mam's face and the parchment beneath his hand during her explanation, and he was ready immediately with another question. "Do you recall when you found him, Mistress Cameron? The date, as closely as you can recollect?"

"Oh, I wouldna have ken such a thing if it hadna been for the feast day. Imbolc night, it was."

"You're certain?" Lucan Montague, his quill paused above the page. "First February?"

"Aye. I had come to the barn to lay the bed and table for Saint Brigid."

The knight nodded. "And do you vow before God that this man standing before me, known heretofore as Tavish Cameron, is issue from your relations with that Englishman, Thomas?"

For the first time in his life that Tavish could remember, Mam blushed for an instant, but then her chin lifted. "Aye, sir. I knew no other before Tommy. I already carried Tav when me da trothed me to Dolan Cameron. Although neither can give their own oaths to it as they're both long dead, thanks be to God."

"I see." Lucan Montague scribbled on the parchment for several moments before he turned the page toward Mam and dipped the quill daintily before holding it toward her. "If you will sign to your testimony, Mistress. Just here."

Mam took the pen and scrawled her name in careful, stuttering lines while Tavish skimmed the words over her shoulder. She handed the quill back to Montague. The knight laid it aside with a murmur of thanks and then reached inside his gambeson once more to withdraw another rolled decree, this one tied with a green ribbon. Although his words were apparently for Mam, his frosty gaze locked onto Tavish.

"Because Master Cameron is, by yours and Thomas's own vows, quite illegitimate—my apologies—there is little hope that he could claim Darlyrede House even if it weren't being held under guardianship in perpetuity of a trial."

"Beg pardon—what?" Tavish said with a frown.

"It can't be bequeathed because its rightful ownership is already in question," Lucan Montague said in a patient tone, as if clarifying something that should have been painfully obvious. He must have realized his mistake, for he pressed his lips into a thin line and gave a twitch of a bow. "Forgive me; of course you wouldn't know. Tavish Cameron, your father was Thomas Annesley, third Baron Annesley, Lord of Darlyrede."

Tavish felt the floor tilt ever so slightly beneath his boots, but before he could think of a response, Lucan Montague continued.

"He is accused by the English Crown of the murder of his betrothed, Cordelia Hargrave, on the eve of their wedding. Also for the murder of a vicar and a deacon, both belonging to Lindisfarne, as well as the theft of two priory horses. He is suspected in the deaths of several commoners, reportedly abducted from towns and villages nearby to Darlyrede House, as well as some as far away as London. Also, a noble couple, some years after his escape into Scotland, where he did manage to evade capture these past thirty years."

Tavish swallowed hard, while at his side, Mam whispered, "'Twas all true." And then, louder, "Sir, Tommy didna kill anyone—especially nae that sweet girl."

Sir Lucan looked to Harriet with the sternest expression Tavish had yet seen of him. "I do not doubt your confidence in the man, Mistress. However, the evidence I have collected thus far has failed to exonerate him. I must conduct my inquiry thoroughly in order to justify the sentence that has been carried out. Forgive me."

Mam nodded, but her face paled. They had already killed Thomas Annesley, after all.

Tavish's father was truly dead now.

The knight looked to Tavish once more. "As I was saying, Darlyrede—its title and lands—can never be yours." Lucan held out the rolled parchment bound with the green ribbon toward Tavish, and it stayed suspended between them for several heartbeats before Tavish could find the sense to raise his right hand and take the parchment in his grasp.

The paper felt stiff and smooth and waxy and fine. Finer than anything he'd ever legally held in his hands.

He could feel his nostrils flaring, feel his heart crashing against his chest, but outwardly, Tavish struggled to show no emotion as he stared at the rolled proclamation. His entire life, everyone had expected things of Tavish Cameron—to pay what was demanded, cow to the meagerest nobility, beg permission to purchase goods with his own coin. The common people loved him, feared him a little, whispered about his surely questionable trade, but even as one of the wealthiest freemen in all of Edinburgh, Tavish had little more privilege than the basest citizen. He would never be more than that, never good enough.

And it was Thomas Annesley's fault.

Lying, no account, dead bastard! It wasn't enough that he'd abandoned Mam to the shame of bearing his bastard child, but the reprobate had been a criminal as well, to the extent that King Henry had sent one of his own lackeys to hunt down the poor woman for further humiliation and—what? Certainly Lucan Montague had come to demand compensation for Thomas Annesley's victims. What would Edinburgh say about his kind mother, should this gossip leak?

Could Tavish be imprisoned for his devil sire's debts? The burgess would gleefully impound the *Stygian*, along with the shop, their home, and all its contents.

Mam would be turned out with nowhere to go and no way to support herself. He never should have allowed her to sign that damned document!

"I doona have enough at hand this moment," Tavish at last said through clenched teeth. "Mayhap only forty or forty-five pounds, and I doona dare hope that would satisfy sending a man on such a long journey. But I have business to conduct later in the day, which should bring enough to content the accusers. Come again on the morrow, later in the morn, when my mother should be about the market. I'd prefer it if the two of you didn't meet again."

Lucan Montague's eyes narrowed the slightest bit. "I beg your pardon?"

"I'll give you the damned coin," Tavish growled, anger and humiliation and fear causing a stabbing pain in his stomach. It didn't matter that he was a respected merchant of the city, that his shop flourished, that he owned the *Stygian* outright, that he dressed his mother in the best his coin could buy. Tavish Cameron was still common, still a bastard, still at the mercy of the nobles who ruled Edinburgh, and now he always would be.

Tavish continued, pointing the rolled parchment at the finely dressed man. "Whatever sum you require. But when I do, you'll put your mark to my own contract that will mean the end of it. I've leeches enough hanging from me. And my mother has suffered more than her share because of that bastard."

Lucan Montague appeared nonplussed. "Master Cameron, I've not come seeking remuneration from you. On the contrary, I'm here to inform you of your inheritance."

Tavish had opened his mouth to demand the extorting prick cease the useless denials and come back on the morrow, but he closed it as Montague's words worked through the red fury clouding his reason.

"My...what did you say?"

"It's all right there, in your hand."

Tavish began unrolling the parchment and dropped his eyes to the finely scrawled words as Montague continued.

"There was a holding bequeathed to Thomas Annesley when he was yet a boy—a property in his mother's family that cannot be disputed, and cannot be touched by the English Crown. A titled property located wholly in Scotland, and left to his firstborn child by the maiden Harriet Payne."

Tavish's eyes scanned the terms on the parchment as Lucan Montague's dry tone summed up the meaning of the thin banner of the future Tavish held in his hands.

"*You* are Thomas Annesley's firstborn child, Master Cameron."

Tower Roscraig and associated village and industries...Firth of Forth... Sworn before God...

Lord Thomas Annesley, laird of Roscraig.

Tavish dragged his gaze from the paper in his hands, which had taken on a slight tremble. "What does this mean?" he asked in a hoarse voice, troubled at the vulnerability, the uncertainty in the words.

Lucan Montague's mouth quirked. "It means that your father's property and title now belong to you, Master Cameron. Or, should I say, laird?"

Tavish frowned. "You should call me Tavish, I reckon."

"Very well." Lucan Montague nodded. "Tavish Cameron, laird of Roscraig."

"Roscraig?" Mam gasped, and grasped his arm seeking his attention. "Tav, 'tis where Tommy was going the night he left me! To Roscraig, he'd said. It must be a bad place—as bad as that Darlyrede."

"Why would you say that, Mam?"

"Because," Harriet insisted quietly, fervently, "he never came back, Tav."

"Whatever happened after he left you, it was through no fault of anyone at Roscraig, I'd wager," Tavish said quietly. Tavish looked down at the parchment in his hands, forced himself to swallow before speaking again, struggling to keep the tremor from it as he met Montague's gaze once more. "I don't have to pay for it? Roscraig?"

"No. Although you will be responsible for any debts belonging to it accrued through the years of your father's absence, of course. Liens, taxes, etcetera."

"I don't have to receive permission for it—from the king? The burgess?" Tavish looked back at the knight's face.

Montague's eyebrows rose. "The king must be informed of your claim. But you were bequeathed it from your father. I do doubt James shall have any argument. It's yours, Tavish."

Tavish looked back down at the parchment in his hands, but the words there were little more than blurry knots now. "Tower Roscraig," he whispered, trying the name on his tongue. He looked up once more. "It's mine—*now*?"

Montague smiled. "A month ago, in fact."

"And I can go there, with this paper"—he rattled it toward Montague—"and claim it. And the burgess can't…no one can stop me."

"Correct."

"When?" Tavish cleared his throat. "When can I claim it?"

"Whenever you like," the knight allowed, and Tavish felt in that moment that he had misjudged this man twice, for now he could sense that Montague was happy for him. It was a strange circumstance for Tavish to have one of his betters sincerely wish him well.

But no—Lucan Montague was not Tavish's better now.

Tavish was a laird. The laird of Roscraig. He had just inherited a stone hold on the Firth of Forth, allowing him to escape Edinburgh and the burgess forever, allowing him to at last give his mother the life she deserved. All the humiliations, hardships, anxious waiting and hiding, sailing the gauntlet of Leith custom officials every voyage, being forced to carry illegal goods to keep the *Stygian* afloat with the outrageous tolls levied against him. All gone in the moment Tavish had unrolled the parchment in his hands.

And then there was the lovely Audrey, whose rich father wished for a titled match. Captain Muir would surely now curse Tavish for a devil.

Tavish read the words beneath his gaze again, thrice, while Sir Lucan Montague waited patiently.

Mam still hung on his arm. "Well? What else does it say? Is there anything more?"

"Aye," Tavish murmured, turning his face toward his mother's, fighting the constriction of his throat. "I suppose it says that Thomas Annesley did care for you in his own way, Mam." He swallowed at his mother's teary smile and confident nod.

"Oh, Tav. I already knew that."

Chapter 2

Glenna Douglas sat atop her grave and looked out over the gray, flat water of the firth. With the small stone hermitage hidden in the viny fringe of wood behind her and the wide expanse of open water before her; the moist, freshly turned earth beneath her seat and low, dense clouds above, it was a comforting, quiet cell and the only place in the world she could let her mind be still.

The cool, humid air raised gooseflesh beneath the pitifully thin fabric of her gown, the old shawl she'd donned before leaving the Tower little protection from the sharp spring breeze. Spiral strands of her blond hair whipped at her eyes, often tangling in her lashes or catching in the crevice of her pressed together lips, but she didn't bother raising her arms from her bent knees to remove the offending locks—she had a meager amount of heat caught in the tent of her skirts and moving would only shoo away the warmth.

Glenna wasn't surprised when the weak shadow lengthened before her, though she hadn't heard anyone approach—Dubhán was almost silent in all of his movements, and she'd known he would emerge from the hermitage sooner or later to find her there.

"Any better today, milady?" his smooth, low voice queried.

She merely shook her head, loathe to break gaze with the hypnotic monochromatic scene before her eyes, washing her consciousness blank, blurring the pain and fear she felt. But Dubhán did not press her, and she felt she owed him more than such a dismissive gesture after all he'd done for her and the village in the past fortnight. Her entire life, really.

"He yet lives," she said at last.

Glenna couldn't help but catch the movement of the overly large man as he came to sit beside her atop the fresh grave, but he still made no sound—as though his robes were enchanted with a special magic that ensured the keeper of the graveyard allowed the dead to rest in peace. His unique, sweet scent bloomed, and Glenna thought he smelled of great pools of warm beeswax and sweet incense.

"I wish you would allow me to see him." It was as close to a rebuke as Dubhán would give her. "Have you been long away? I could go to him now."

"Nay—not long. I wanted to visit the doocot. See if there were more eggs."

"I should take over the duties of caring for the doves again. Perhaps it would be best not to draw Frang Roy's attentions by insisting—."

"I'm the lady of Roscraig, and I wanted to visit my doocot. I'm nae afraid of Frang Roy." Glenna stared at the firth for a long time more while she waited for her heart to cease its wild pounding. When at last she could draw an even breath, she turned her head to look at the monk directly. "Forty-seven, Dubhán. Nearly the rest of the village this time, and right at the planting."

His brown gaze was gentle on her face, his sympathetic smile warm in the exotic dark smoothness of his skin, framed by the black, wooly hair and beard. "Forty-seven," he agreed.

"Forty-seven," she repeated in an incredulous whisper. "All the children."

"Aye," he acknowledged. Glenna knew he waited patiently for the question she couldn't resist asking again.

"Why?" she demanded. "Why would God do that to us again? To me? And take my father as well, before it's all said and done, will he not?"

Dubhán shook his dark head. "I still have no answer for you, milady. I am naught to him. A bug. A worthless fly. He would not share such knowledge with the likes of me. But"—he nodded once, slowly, deliberately—"it is for our good."

Glenna huffed and turned her gaze back to the flat water of the firth. She hadn't really expected a different answer.

"God has sent sickness—again and again—to Roscraig, killed all but a handful of the village, would see us starved, for our good," she muttered darkly. "Our neighbors call us cursed, and I have little choice but to believe what they say is true. I'm sitting atop soil meant to cover my da and me when we died; instead it covers a pit filled with good people I knew all my life."

Dubhán nodded mildly. "I know. I dug the pit. But God didn't send the sickness, Lady Glenna."

Glenna didn't bother to turn her head to look at him as she huffed in frustration. "You can't have it both ways, Dubhán. If God didn't send the sickness, who did?"

"You know who sent it, milady. Your father knew, as well, when it came." He paused, letting the merry birdsong fill the space between them. "'Twas the devil."

Glenna felt the hated tears swell against her eyes, her jaw push forward. "Da's right; in my mind now, they are one and the same. Good day, Dubhán." She pushed to her feet and half slid down the soft, rich, brown earth mound, leaving deep impressions as she departed the plot where she should have been buried, if not during the last fortnight, then years into the future.

She would never rest there now. Glenna felt her own remaining hours as Lady of Roscraig running away like the little crumbles of earth that chased her descent down the mound.

There was little to plant, and even fewer hands to harvest. They would be fortunate to produce enough to feed themselves; there would certainly be nothing to sell and no coin to pay the king. And once Iain Douglas was dead and King James learned of the latest plague that had all but finished the village, he would have no qualms about removing Glenna from Tower Roscraig and building the artillery he longed for on the firth. Then where would she go? She had no distant family with whom to seek refuge—the secluded clans in the Highlands were rough strangers to her.

I would be better off had I died with Mother, she thought as she strode past the short stone obelisk marking the place Margaret Douglas was buried, its intricate engraving softened by moss. Her mother had never been forced to deal with the loss of her home, her friends, her family—she had left them all behind to grieve her passing and left her infant daughter in the care of a father and lord who was perhaps too kind to be very successful.

And now even kind Iain Douglas would be taken from Glenna.

Glenna stopped on the woodland path that wound around the coastal cliff to duck inside the squat stone doocot, whose domed stone roof peeked up through the branches like the rounded head of a mythical gray bear. She reached into each cubby but came away from the aviary with nothing more than filth-streaked hands. No eggs again.

By the time she reached the edge of the village, the stiff, cold breeze had changed directions and now swelled with the clammy warmth of an exhalation. It raised the hairs on Glenna's neck, and she squinted up into the bright gray glare at the roiling clouds that tumbled ever closer to the double turrets of Tower Roscraig. The approaching gale was screaming over the firth, lashing the placid gray waves into foamy spray and blowing Glenna's thin skirts tight against her legs.

She looked over her shoulder as she rounded the village and saw one of the men pushing a cart from the river; she raised a hand to him, but his head was ducked away from the squall, and he did not see her hailing. Thankfully, there was no sign of Frang Roy, the coarse farmer who had outrageously suggested that the two of them should marry after her father's death. The idea of it was ludicrous, and the memory of Frang's rough, dirty hand trembling against her sleeve caused her face to heat.

Glenna walked up the footpath that met the wide, dry moat and followed it to the bridge. Her footsteps were hollow sounding on the wood, and she frowned as she saw that the unexpected and forceful winds were repeatedly sucking open and then slamming closed the door she'd left unbarred. She wondered if it had been enough to stir her father.

The gale waxed again, this time snatching her veil from her head and dragging her already disheveled blond curls from what remained of the twisted knot at her nape.

Glenna gave a cry of dismay as the small piece of linen disappeared like a seabird around the curve of the east tower, and she stretched out her arm as if she might catch it. Her skirts billowed and flapped like sails, and she looked to her right, where the beach and the now foamy, black waves were in view. Scraping her hair from her face, she looked up at the edge of a dark blanket of storm clouds, roiling just over Tower Roscraig.

The rumble of thunder purred against her eardrums and temporarily took away some of the sting of losing her only veil. It was good to feel something, even for a moment, that wasn't dampness or cold or hunger.

But then the thunder seemed to change, vibrating more in her feet, her backbone; gooseflesh came to her skin once more and she wondered if she was soon to be struck dead by a bolt from the heavens. But the sound only increased, coming from behind her now, and so Glenna turned and she did receive a shock, but it was not birthed from the storm clouds above her head.

A small group of riders cantered toward Roscraig on the Tower road. Three of them, Glenna thought, and their mounts were not the tired nags of traveling merchants; they bore no cart, towed no extra horses.

Hadn't they seen the signs warning them away?

Perhaps they were envoys from the king, who had somehow learned of Roscraig's dire straits. Frang Roy had warned that the king would soon know, but that couldn't be possible—no one had left the village to send word.

Glenna backed toward the door, her gaze never leaving the ever nearing group even as the wind dried her eyes until they stung. She felt behind her for the sturdy wood and slipped inside the opening.

* * * *

'Tis a fortress, Tavish whispered to himself as the wind roared in his ears and he leaned over and patted the neck of his horse, trying to calm the nervous mare and prevent her from racing the black thunderheads to Tower Roscraig. His own stomach clenched, mimicking the ripples of white lightning twisting through the roiling clouds rushing in from the firth, but it was not from alarm.

Tavish had only ever seen Tower Roscraig from the deck of the *Stygian,* and when he had, he'd not given it more than a cursory appraisal, as one who briefly admires some rare and costly jewel that they know can never be theirs. And so as he now approached the double-towered keep on horseback for the first time, he wanted more than anything to stop and simply stare.

Light tan stone turned muddy in the fading light, the tall, round east tower connected to a shorter western turret by a one-story range, which boasted a single door across a bridged moat, as well as a low sweep of battlements between the two keeps that gave Tower Roscraig its name.

I have a moat, he realized to himself and nearly laughed aloud from excitement and pride.

Tower Roscraig. It was his. It belonged to Tavish Cameron.

Laird Tavish Cameron.

Tavish hadn't realized how much he'd slowed his mount until the blasting wind threw the first cold raindrops against his warmed face. He blinked and urged his horse on, once more riding alongside Mam and Lucan Montague.

"Tav," his mother began again in a worried voice. "The signs—"

He looked at the edge of the wood where yet more shredded flags snapped taut in the gale and large faded X's seemed to glow like weak ghosts on the rough bark of the trees. "It's fine, Mam."

"But there are more of them," she insisted. "What if it's the plague?"

"Probably a ruse meant to keep people away, is all. Sir Montague found no record of a lawful claimant residing at Roscraig since Thomas Annesley inherited it. I have faith in his thoroughness."

Lucan straightened even further in his saddle. "While I appreciate your confidence, it is improbable such a desirable location would be neglected. At any rate, someone has paid the taxes."

"Neighboring lords?" Tavish suggested.

Montague's expression was unfathomable. "I suppose it's possible."

Tavish allowed the idea to ride along with him for several moments and then silently decided that he didn't care if King James himself had taken up residence at Roscraig. He'd been ready for this moment—had been preparing for it in his discontented mind—his entire life.

"Again, my thanks for accompanying us to Roscraig, Montague," Tavish said at last. "That you are here to vouch for my claim means a great deal."

The knight gave a shrug. "I do doubt the word of an Englishman will carry much weight. But perhaps any occupant can put forth a word or two that I can add to my investigation as I proceed. I still say it would have been preferable for you to have arrived with your captain and hired men."

Now it was Tavish's turn to brush off the comment. "Anyone we might find surely has expected the rightful family to one day claim Roscraig. As it is, we have shared the ever-narrowing road with no other travelers. The settlement appears deserted; the fields are overrun. Where are the villagers?"

"They're probably all dead," Mam muttered, and then she hurriedly crossed herself as they came around the corner of the nearest derelict cottage.

Indeed not even sheep nor goats roamed the dirt tracks of the town; no colorful banners flapped on the stone walls beneath the battlements of the keep; the torch brackets to either side of the bridge and entry hung void.

Tower Roscraig seemed to be waiting—empty—for Tavish Cameron.

They came to the bridge now, so narrow as to allow only one rider across at a time, in single file. Tavish's mount shied and tried to back away from the suspended passage. He took a moment to quiet the mare and then looked over his shoulder.

"Mam, wait for me here." He then nodded to Montague as he passed the knight, urging his horse onto the narrow wooden bridge first.

A fortress, indeed, he thought as he encouraged the mare across the deep, rocky ditch below. The hoof falls were amplified exponentially, the party announcing itself to the hold as Tavish and the English knight made themselves vulnerable in procession. There wasn't even room to turn around, and he could feel his mount gathering anxiety beneath him.

He was very aware of the height of the bridge and its narrowness as he pulled the mare to a stop and slowly, carefully dismounted against the single rickety railing. Montague was doing the same. The beasts were nervous, and every shuffle of hooves sent echoing barks through the moat to ricochet off the thunderheads that were now dropping thin threads of light farther down the beach.

"Shh." He reached up to draw the reins over the horse's head and then led her to the door. A granite boulder of thunder rolled across the rocky sky, causing the horse to roll her eyes and pull up. "Shh. Just a bit of rain." The beast reluctantly moved forward once more.

Tavish raised his gloved fist and pounded on the entry. He glanced at Montague and then looked more closely at the door, which appeared to be covered with fresh gouges and deep cuts to the wood. Tavish leaned his ear nearer but could hear no sounds above the wind and the pounding surf around Tower Roscraig.

Had the place been looted and abandoned?

"Hello?" he shouted, then pounded on the door again. Tavish stepped back to look up at the tapering walls of the keep, the arrow slits and higher, narrow windows, the battlements. All empty.

Tavish came into the slight shelter of the stone doorway once more and tried buffeting his shoulder into the wood near the iron handle. Although it appeared that someone had attempted quite recently to hack the thick plate from the door, the handle held firm. He braced himself more firmly and dealt the wood two more firm blows, the give in the frame indicating the door was most likely barred from within.

He leaned back once more and looked left and right—he could see no postern gate at either side of the keep to indicate an alternate entry past the moat. Unless whoever had barred the door had departed via boat on the Forth, someone must be inside.

"Hello!" he shouted again. "Master of the hold! Guard!" He sighed in exasperation as he struggled briefly with his horse once more. "Scullery!"

To his surprise, he heard a scraping of wood, a thud, and then the door creaked open a pair of inches, the telltale rattle of chain drawing taut filling the blackness within from where a woman's voice also sounded.

"What do you want, then?"

Tavish cleared his throat. This woman was perhaps one of his own servants—he wanted to make a good, lairdly impression.

"Good day," he said in a grave tone, although the howling wind took away much of the solemnity he sought to convey. "We have traveled from Edinburgh to seek the guardian of Tower Roscraig. Would that you admit us and announce us to him."

"There is no guardian. Go away." The door began to shut.

Tavish stepped forward and placed his foot into the opening. "No guardian?"

The blackness within the keep was silent for a pair of heartbeats. "The *laird*—if that's who you mean—is not accepting visitors. We're not buying anything, either. Didn't you see the signs? There is sickness here. You should leave while you can." The door squeezed Tavish's boot for a moment before the woman half growled, "Move your foot."

Tavish left his foot where it stood and braced his shoulder against the door again for good measure. "Laird, you say? Laird who?"

"The laird of Roscraig, imbecile. Move your foot."

"Please," he said, lowering his voice. "I understand our arrival is unannounced. But as you can see if you'll only open the door"—here, Tavish turned slightly to point down the length of the bridge—"my elderly mother accompanies me, and it's already started to rain. You must believe that we have come at the behest of the old laird himself—Annesley, he is called."

"Och, for certain." The woman's eye roll was audible. "That's why I've not heard the name Annesley in the whole of my life. Move your foot, or I'll cut off your toes."

Tavish dug into his doublet for the decree, even as the downpour increased. "It's right here—with the royal clerk's own sigil. Look." He unrolled the parchment and held it up, not bothering with what part was revealed—it was likely the girl couldn't read any matter. He only needed inside the keep. "It's all right here."

"I don't care what it says—it's mistaken. Iain Douglas is the laird of Roscraig, and always has been. I don't know this Annesley."

"Tavish?" Harriet Cameron called through the roar of the rain in a warbly voice. When he turned to look at his mother, she appeared to be nearly soaked through already.

He appealed to the blackness again. "Perhaps we are wrong. But, please… my mother. Wait, here…" His hand dived between shirt and doublet again for the loose coins he carried and fished them out, holding them toward her. "For the trouble of sheltering us. Please."

After a long moment, a slender, pale hand emerged from the opening, and Tavish readily placed the coins into the palm, worried that such a pittance that he would give to beggars along the road would not be enough to satisfy even a simple servant in a country hold, but he daren't withdraw from the door to attend to his purse.

The blackness was quiet again, this time for several moments. "Move your foot," the unseen woman repeated.

"I can't do that, maiden," Tavish said in a low voice. "The sun will soon set and I—"

"If you don't move your damned foot, I can't loose the chain."

Tavish hesitated. She could be tricking him—it was what he would try to do, after all. But he slid his boot free from the narrow opening with some difficulty and stepped back from the door as it slammed.

The obvious rattle of chain sounded through the thick wood, but Tavish was unsure in that moment if it was being loosed or doubled. A moment later, however, the door began creaking open again, and Tavish gave a silent breath of relief as he turned to hail Mam.

"My thanks, maid—" he began, but his words fell off abruptly as the woman who had denied him thus far came into view.

She stood framed by the tall, dark rectangle of the interior, one hand still hidden behind the door, perhaps holding fast to the handle in consideration of yet denying Tavish entry. The fingers of her other hand clutched at the dingy gray shawl knotted across her chest and covering the faded stripes of her kirtle, which at one time might have been colored burgundy and deep green but now held only the worn hues of an autumn leaf still clinging to its twig in the midst of winter's icy assault. The finest part of her costume was the delicate golden chain around her waist, boasting several keys at its dangling end. Her hair was unveiled, a riot of blond, springy curls parted in the center of her head and falling over one shoulder. Her eyes were narrowed, pale green like a cat's, appraising Tavish as he stood there staring dumbly at her, the rain now running in a stream from the end of his nose.

She appeared wild and wary and dangerously beautiful—like the very striations of cliff and wood holding Roscraig poised above the Forth.

Tavish felt a sharp jab in his back and started, giving the woman a short bow. "I thank you for your kindness, maiden." He began to step forward but was drawn upright at the sudden appearance of a sword tip from behind the door, pointed in the general direction of his throat.

It wasn't the door handle she'd been holding, after all.

"Your name," the woman demanded.

"Tavish Cameron," he supplied immediately. "Of Edinburgh. I've a shop there, and merchant ship, the *Stygian*."

Her cat eyes darted pointedly behind him.

"Sir Lucan Montague—he's English; I do hope you'll forgive him that. My mother, as I've already said, Harriet Cameron."

The woman met Tavish's gaze once more, and her eyes narrowed even further, examining him openly. "Are you well?"

Tavish thought the polite inquiry was delivered with more than a bit of hostility. "We are weary from the road and rather wet at the moment, but aye, I am feeling fit. Kind of you to ask."

Her lips thinned. "Have any of you been *ill*?"

Tavish paused, thinking of the abandoned village, the fallow fields he'd seen. Was he risking his life in entering this stone hold?

"I think we run more of a risk of the ague are we to stand about in the rain," he answered pointedly. If he was going to die, it would be in his own home. A home he had been owed for many years.

"I'll give you shelter for the night—naught more than a chamber. But I'll first have your word that you'll take your leave at first light, and I don't care what your *decree* says."

Tavish opened his mouth, but hesitated.

Lucan Montague came to his aid at just the right moment, stepping forward with a bow and declaring, "Upon my honor, dawn shall witness my departure, *mademoiselle*."

The woman nodded warily and then stepped back into the blackness, swinging the door open with her. Tavish handed the reins of his mount to Montague before dashing halfway across the bridge to hurry Mam's horse over the moat. The storm chose that moment to release its full fury, ushering the party at last into the safety of Tower Roscraig. Their hostess pushed the door closed against an explosion of thunder as the horses danced and shook and threw water onto the stone floor of the wide entrance passage that appeared to divide the hold in half. A large, square opening at the far end was illumined by the storm, and through the black grid of a half-lowered portcullis Tavish could see a long finger of land disappearing into the deluge, the black shadows crouched at its sides hinting at buildings.

The maiden did not reengage the chain through the thick brackets set into the mortar of the walls, nor did she drop the hinged bar into place to secure the door. Instead she turned to the group, the weapon that was obviously too large for her still at the ready, and Tavish marveled that a girl so slight could even heft it, much less hold it aloft with one hand.

"I am Glenna Douglas," she said at last. "As I've already told you, my father isn't entertaining visitors. You may see to your horses in the stable." She pointed toward the storm through the far end of the passage. "And then I will show you to a chamber." Her gaze flitted from one to the other in Tavish's party. "Again, a chamber and no more—I'll not feed the lot of you. So take what provisions you would have from your packs."

The silence hanging around the woman's words seemed to grow louder than the fierce storm as the three travelers stared at the blond woman in the wake of her announcement. Her frown increased as the moments crawled by.

Tavish at last bowed to cover his shock. "As you wish, mai—*my lady*."

If anything, Glenna Douglas's gaze was still distrustful. "I'll fetch water while you tend your mounts—our well isn't tainted. You'll be staying in the west tower." Her blond curls inclined toward the doorway behind her, and Tavish recalled that was the shorter, wider of the two turrets. The great hall and the family apartments must be in the taller, east tower. He itched to take off and explore every last corner of the keep.

The lady stared at them pointedly as they all continued to drip on the stones. "The rain'll get no drier the longer you wait. If you're not returned by the time I've fetched the water, I'll have a mind to lower yonder gate and leave you to the stables. You'll have plenty to drink there." Glenna Douglas then lifted the hem of her skirt while still wielding her weapon and turned to disappear into the dark doorway of the west tower,

"My thanks," Tavish called after her, but his genial air was quickly fading as the reality of the woman's claims settled around him. He turned to help Harriet dismount. "I should have known she was noble by her spiteful tongue."

"Can you blame her? A wee thing like that, minding the door for strangers on her own?" Harriet said. She limped to the doorway, her hand on one rounded hip as she stretched her other arm up to brace it on the doorway. "I'd've likely nae had the courage to open it in the first place. We've given her a bit of a surprise, is all."

Tavish looked to Lucan Montague, and the two exchanged a silent thought as they each took charge of the horses—Glenna Douglas was in for a much deeper shock than the arrival of unexpected guests.

He looked back to his mother. "You'll be all right here, until we return?"

"Aye, aye—go on," she said, waving at him briefly. "I'll loosen up the old joints a bit and follow the lady. She might need my help."

"You stay there and rest, Mam," Tavish ordered. He glanced around the passage and then lowered his voice. "You're no servant. You don't fetch water any longer."

"There's nae shame in fetching one's own water, Tav. Heaven knows I've done so all me life, for man and beast. Including you. Go on," she insisted with another flap of her hand.

Tavish grinned at his mother's scolding, and then he and Lucan Montague led the mounts through the wide entrance hall to the rear opening. The men broke into a trot as they ducked beneath the portcullis into the rain once more and dashed toward the stable.

Tavish's grin widened even as the lightning flashed around him and the storm bore down on Tower Roscraig.

My stable.

* * * *

Frang Roy waited until the old woman had pulled her girth into the blackness of the west tower doorway and he could hear her breathy exertions descending the stairs before he stepped into the passage, returning his belt to his waist.

He was angry. Angry that Glenna had opened the door to the travelers. Angry that she had granted them entry. It was careless, even with her childish display of the old man's derelict sword—it could have been anyone at all come to the tower. At this very moment, he should be putting his terms to Glenna once more, forcefully if need be, and with whatever discomfort necessary for her to accept his will.

She would not have refused him this time.

Then Frang recalled hearing the jingle of coins placed into Glenna's hand by the pushy stranger at the door, and his frustration dissipated like the smoke from an extinguished wick. He was a patient man. He'd waited all these years; another night would make little difference.

He walked to the door and let himself out, closing it carefully—soundlessly—behind him.

Chapter 3

Glenna's arms strained with the effort of pulling the thick rope through the pulley suspended over the well until at last the bucket appeared from the depths of the dark hole set in the stone floor. She wrapped the rope in a figure eight around the stay, but before she could reach out to take hold of the bucket, the old woman from the entryway hobbled into the cellar and stepped to the edge of the well.

"Allow me, milady," she said and removed the handle from the hook with a grunt, her thick arms taking the weighty bucket down with ease and without spilling so much as a drop.

Glenna had soaked her skirts each time she'd drawn water.

"Thank you," she said stiffly.

"The set's a bit high up for a wee thing such as yourself."

"I don't usually draw the water," Glenna answered immediately and then regretted her words. Even though she'd taken her son's pitiful payment readily enough, some strange manner of her pride didn't wish the old woman to know that the few servants Roscraig once boasted were now all dead or had fled the hold. Her mind filled with the memory of the Tower's gouged door, the pounding and shouting from beyond...

"Hmm" was Harriet Cameron's only response. But the old woman seemed to be studying Glenna's flushed face in the gloom of the cellar. "You look familiar to me, milady. Do you travel often to Edinburgh?"

"Nay." This time it was Glenna's turn to be noncommittal. "Thank you." She reached out to take hold of the bucket, but the woman turned it just out of her reach.

"Milady, I couldna allow you—"

Glenna cut off the old woman's protests by striding forward and seizing the bucket handle, pulling it away as she passed to the stairwell. "This way."

The bucket was heavy—much heavier than when Glenna usually carried it. She tried to measure her breaths without obvious strain as they gained the first level and continued to climb up the spiral corridor.

"O' course, you would know if you'd been to the town or nae, but I do vow I've seen you before." They arrived at the upper level, and Glenna stopped before the chamber door nearest the stair to catch her breath and wait for Harriet Cameron to hobble toward her. "Forgive me, milady; the journey astride has fair crippled me. Biggar, perhaps?"

"What?" Glenna asked with a frown, the word still breathy, to her dismay, from the exertion.

"Perhaps I caught sight of you at the shearing in Biggar."

"I'm afraid not," Glenna replied and then turned to open the door as the clatter of boots on the stone steps beyond grew louder. She gestured through the doorway.

Glenna followed Harriet Cameron inside and set the bucket down inside the room, waiting with pounding heart for the two men to join them, berating herself for leaving her father's sword in the cellar. She felt very vulnerable with such strangers in the house, one of whom had been able to talk his way inside before Glenna had even known she had decided to open the door, it seemed now.

Tavish Cameron entered without any trace of wariness, a pair of satchels slung across his wide, rain-wet shoulders, the Englishman garbed head-to-toe in black strolling at his heels. His gaze found Glenna at once, and she noticed that she caught hold of her breath in her chest as his blue eyes boldly took in her appearance.

"Ah, my...lady," he said while reaching inside his short cloak to retrieve the parchment he'd shown her earlier that was tucked between his shirt and doublet. He was unrolling it even as he approached her, causing Glenna to bring a hand to her throat instinctively, her feet to carry her back farther against the door behind her.

"I understand that your father is refusing visitors, but if you will show him—"

Glenna scrabbled for the door handle at her back while she interrupted the large, frowning man. "I already told you; I don't care what your decree says, and neither does my father." Tavish Cameron stopped short, and his eyebrows raised as he once again pinned her with his bright gaze. Glenna swallowed and gathered her bravado for a final display.

"You'll leave on the morrow. First light," she reminded them, her eyes going to the black-clad Englishman, who seemed infinitely safer to look upon. She stepped through the doorway, pulling the door shut after her and then scrambling with her shaking hand to seize hold of the chain about her waist and fit the correct key into the lock before she could be challenged.

She stepped back from the door and waited, her chest heaving, cursing herself for a fool. What had she been thinking, granting them entry? Harriet Cameron seemed kindly enough, but it was clear that her son had ulterior motives. Glenna had little in the way of defense if he wished her harm or to rob her. Not that there was much to steal in the whole of the keep, save the few coins Tavish Cameron himself had given her.

She knew that Iain Douglas would have offered them his own bed had it been he who had greeted them.

The truth of it shamed her, and so, when no one rushed the door with pounding demands for release, Glenna turned and escaped down the stairs, wondering how one might manage to sleep after having imprisoned three people in one's guest chamber.

* * * *

Tavish saw Lucan Montague's movements freeze from the corner of his eye as he stood and stared at the now closed chamber door. The scraping of metal was unmistakable.

"Have we been incarcerated?" Montague hedged.

Tavish nodded. "Aye."

The English knight came forward as a flare of light blossomed behind him—Mam had managed to ignite a stub of candle she'd found, bringing at least an illusion of warmth and brightness to the cold stone room.

Tavish held up a palm. "Wait," he advised quietly.

"Wait?" Montague repeated. He began to rant in a stream of fiery French, but then seemed to realize that his efforts were wasted in a foreign tongue. "I'll be damned if I shall acquiesce to being held against my—"

"Shh." Tavish held up a finger before creeping toward the door and leaning his ear against it. After several moments, he straightened and began searching in his clothing and among his various pouches again. "You'll not be held against your will anywhere. Especially"—he withdrew a ring of small iron rods of varying shapes and lengths and began to flip through the cluster—"not in a keep that belongs to me."

Tavish crouched to one knee and inserted a likely candidate while Mam went about the chamber singing under her breath. She slid thick coverings from the conspicuously few furnishings in such a large chamber, sending up clouds of thick dust that made her swat the air and cough.

"Good heavens," she gasped. "None's slept here in an age, I reckon! Tav, there's neither wood nor peat."

Tavish withdrew the first rod and flipped through the ring again even while he glanced up and around the room. "A moment, pray, Mam." He inserted a second, then a third. On the fourth rod, the mechanism inside the door scraped, and the door pulled inward of the jamb.

Tavish gained his feet and tucked his tools away before inching the door open and looking into the corridor. Both the stairwell and the passageway to the right were black, and not a sound could be heard above the crashing of the ocean waves and the roar of the wind beyond the stones. Tavish ducked back inside the room and pushed the door closed.

"There you are, Montague," he said as he crossed the floor and went to a pair of small tables against the inner wall. "You may go where you please now, although I would recommend you wait until after we've had our supper. Mam's brought meat pies." He bent and examined one of the dainty, round-topped tables, then picked it up by a leg and turned it this way and that.

"That I have," Harriet confirmed. "Lamb."

Lucan Montague brightened. "I do fancy lamb pie."

Tavish took two table legs in hand and looked up at Montague with a wink. "As do I." He swung the table against the stones of the hearth where it broke apart into tens of pieces with a crash. Tavish tossed the now dismembered legs atop the pile. "There you are, Mam."

"Oh, you're a dear," Harriet said. "I'll just warm them up a bit and they shall be quite lovely, I think."

Tavish looked up to find Lucan Montague regarding him with raised eyebrows. "What?" he demanded. "'Twas my table. Now it shall heat my supper before I venture out to find out exactly who is running my house, regardless of what the Lady Douglas commands."

"*She's* lovely," Mam offered as she laid the fire.

"Quite so," Montague agreed, to Tavish's surprise.

But Tavish kept his own counsel: *She's lovely, aye—and quite panicked, the stiff woman dressed like a maid who still managed to look down her nose at me.*

While Mam unpacked the foodstuffs and built up a small fire, Tavish and Lucan Montague finished setting the chamber to rights. There was little to work with, and so it didn't take long to determine that Mam would sleep atop the single bedstead in the large room, its mattress so thin and pitifully old that he worried his mother might fall through the rotten tick and stuffing. Tavish and Lucan would sleep on the bare, dusty floor.

The only other sizeable furnishing was a tall-backed chair, its thick wood carved in intricate, deep design and its back and seat upholstered in now rotting, threadbare, rose-colored fabric. Tavish didn't count the other small table—a candle stand, really—for it would eventually be fed into the fire as surely as its twin. Perhaps the queer old chair would meet the same fate in the night.

He walked toward the hearth now as Mam was positioning the pies close to the fire and noticed another item draped in a dingy, time-singed cloth, hung upon the chimney stones. Tavish reached up and pulled a corner of the sheet, dragging the cloth free in a cloud of dusty years.

"Good heavens, Tav." Mam choked and waved her hand. "Mind the supper!"

But Tavish had no reply as he stood and stared at the portrait that appeared through the swirling cloud. He heard Lucan Montague step to his left side; Mam gasped again, this time not from the choking dust, and rose to flank him on his right.

It was a painting of a family; a man and woman, their pale profiles facing an open window and a view of what was possibly the firth beyond the very walls that sheltered them. Before and between the couple stood a little boy, perhaps four or five years, with curling blond hair beneath a rounded red cap. The child was facing the artist, his blue eyes bright on the canvas, his bowed lips unsmiling and yet somehow still merry and mischievous, as if he had plucked the peacock feather gracing his cap himself. His mother's hands curled over the boy's shoulders, while his father held a hooded falcon atop his left fist. They were all three dressed richly, their jewelry and slit sleeves speaking volumes about their status.

Mam's voice was hushed. "'Tis as if I'm lookin' at you as a bairn." He turned to look down at his mother in surprise, and she continued. "It must be Tommy."

Tavish turned his eyes back to the portrait as a strange feeling sank into his stomach. "My hair is dark," he protested lamely.

"Aye, but you were fair as a wee lad," she answered, a smile in her voice. "Fair with curls, and your mouth set just so—as if you'd again stuck your finger into the honey when you thought I wasna watching."

Tavish swallowed, his gaze going first to the pale woman with the pointed chin, her dark hair smoothed beneath an ornate headdress, and then the man whose jowls and coiffed hair bespoke his wealth and security.

"Who are they?" he asked with a jut of his chin. "Could they be my... grandparents?"

"They must be," Mam answered. "I doona know their names—Tommy never told me."

Tavish had all but forgotten the English knight still stood at his side until Lucan Montague spoke.

"Lord Tenred Annesley and his wife, Lady Myra."

Tavish turned his face toward Montague in surprise. "How do you know?"

"There are other paintings of the family hung at Darlyrede House. I've become well familiar with the hold...over the course of my investigation," he added anecdotally as he continued to study the portrait. "Roscraig was a gift to Lady Myra from her family upon her marriage. Lord Annesley moved the family here for approximately a year at his wife's behest, so that young Lord Thomas could know of the land of his mother's kin. The spring of 1413, I believe."

Tavish looked back at the painting of the three, and his voice was unintentionally gruff. "'Tis a bit awkward that you seem to know more about my family than do I, Montague."

"I daresay I'd better," the knight quipped and then clapped his shoulder good-naturedly. "I've been studying them all my adult life; you only found out about them last week."

Tavish thought the comment strange, but let it go as it elbowed for room in his brain with the idea that he was currently looking upon his blood kin—his noble kin—in his own castle. *Tenred and Myra—my grandparents; Thomas, my father.*

"Och, I've burnt the pies!" Mam cried from near the fire again. Tavish hadn't noticed she'd left his side, so transfixed had he been.

Indeed, Lucan Montague had also taken his leave to recline on a blanket he'd spread before the small fire. Mam was already portioning the meal. Not knowing what else to do with himself, he joined them.

The food was delicious, as all of Mam's offerings tended to be, and did much to dispel the storm's chill. While the silence of the meal was not exactly tense, the cold, damp chamber had acquired an atmosphere of melancholy propagated from the painted images watching over the repast, from which Tavish was eager to shake free. He rose from the blanket with a stretch and a sigh.

"Well, I'm off," he said, crossing the floor toward the door.

"Where's off?" Mam called out warily.

"Glenna Douglas was not keen for giving me a tour," he explained as he reached the door. "I'd know the lay of the land before tomorrow's battle, so to speak."

"What if you should encounter her?" Montague queried, although his tone conveyed little true worry. "Or her father? Either is likely to run you through."

Tavish opened the door then patted his doublet atop where the decree of his inheritance rested. "I am well prepared to defend myself." Then he stepped into the dark corridor, closing the door on Mam's shaking head and Lucan Montague's salute.

Tavish wished briefly for a torch; the uppermost passageway was pitch, save for the weak flashes of now distant lightning, but even that small contrast of light and dark was enough to render him nearly blind as he sought to familiarize himself with his surroundings. The west tower was wide, but the chamber he'd just departed was the only one at this uppermost level. Tavish felt his way to the top of the stairs and then began a careful descent.

There were several more chambers between the top of the tower and the main floor, and a quick duck inside the still and echoing rooms convinced Tavish that none boasted even a single stick of wood. A faint yellow glow from the doorway to the entry hall gave him pause, and he stood motionless on the step for what felt like hours, but he discerned neither movement nor sound and so he hesitantly stepped into the wide corridor.

There was a single torch held in a sconce along the wall, its wrapping and pitch nearly spent. Tavish pulled it from its holder and held it high as he turned around, causing shadows to bulge and dance wildly over the damp stones. The entrance door was not only chained once more, but the long brace had been lowered across a trio of metal brackets; at the opposite end of the hall—toward the now hidden finger of land and the firth—the gate had been completely lowered. Tavish looked down as he walked toward the portcullis, noticing a set of small, damp footprints on the stones.

Had Glenna Douglas lowered the heavy barrier herself? Tavish must have only just missed her, considering the freshness of the prints, and he was thankful she'd left the torch behind.

He looked all around the dark seams where stone floor met stone walls and at last located the rods that locked the gate in its lowered position. He raised it slowly and with great caution, wincing in anticipation of a rusty squeal, but none came. When the portcullis was just high enough, he ducked beneath.

The air outside was bracing and salty fresh, with the faint shadow of a winter in fast retreat. He checked on the horses briefly and found all three sleeping contentedly, but he frowned as he realized theirs were the only mounts in the small barn.

Perhaps the Douglases kept their own animals in a separate shelter, so as not to be tainted by such common beasts.

The next low stone building was warmer inside, and as his eyes adjusted, Tavish noted the tiny red glow of a banked fire in a hearth so big he'd at first taken it for nothing more than an exterior wall. He looked around more closely now at the dusty, empty shelves lining the walls—there were a couple of overturned, rodent-chewed baskets, an empty cloth sack dangling forlornly from a peg. A table in the center of the room was laid with a small, dingy cloth and closer inspection revealed what was perhaps a crumb of gray crust—or a pebble. A wine jug stood at the edge of the cloth, and when Tavish picked it up by its neck and shook it he was rewarded with a watery rattle. He uncorked it with his teeth and sniffed the contents before turning it up and taking the two healthy swallows of wine eagerly. He returned the empty bottle to the tabletop and looked around again with a sigh.

Could this dismal place be the kitchen? Where were the leftover winter stores? The last of the gourds, the dried beans? Where were the barrels of now-weevily oats? The last scraps of a dried, carved haunch? Where was the ale?

His frown deepened as he left the bleak structure and moved back toward the shadow of the tower.

He lowered and secured the portcullis as silently as he'd raised it and moved to the bottom of the stairs of the east tower, his foot resting on the bottom tread for several moments. It was possible that he would encounter a servant, or even Lady Glenna or Laird Douglas themselves were Tavish to breach the sanctity of the family quarters.

But he didn't think he would meet with anyone.

In fact, the idea that Tower Roscraig was all but empty began to grow bigger in his mind with each step Tavish ascended. And when he came to what could only be Tower Roscraig's great hall—its empty length and breadth punctuated by the long, open windows flanking another enormous hearth at the far end—Tavish felt certain his instincts were correct. He crossed the bare floorboards to the gaping hearth and held forth the hand not gripping the sputtering torch.

The stones were blackened, but icy cold—as though the grand opening hadn't seen a hearty blaze in years. Tavish turned to the left, then to the right—the ragged cloths meant to cover the two openings to either side of the stone chimney flapped in long strips into the frigid room along with the wind and the misty rain—the shutters were also missing. He turned once more to look back toward the entrance; no trestle dominated the wide-planked floor, no rich tapestries warmed the walls. Instead, water ran down the stones and dripped from the corners.

No villagers. No servants. No soldiers.

There is sickness here...

From the evidence before Tavish's eyes—even in the shadows of night that were perhaps kinder than the harsh light of day, even before the mysterious illness that supposedly beset the town—it was obvious that Roscraig had not prospered in years.

Tavish turned back to the window and looked out over the lashing black waves roiling beneath the high lightning beyond the shore and realized that, for all the lady's dire threats upon his arrival, there was nothing to prevent Tavish's acquisition of Tower Roscraig, after all.

He'd had to fight all his life to gain and keep everything he had ever called his own, and so when he'd set out from Edinburgh, he'd been prepared to do battle. But in reality, all that would likely be required to take possession of his home was to set the woman and her father—if there was indeed such a person—on the road beyond the moat.

His moat.

Perhaps Glenna Douglas was nothing more than a very convincing imposter. Perhaps she was even quite mad, fancying herself the lady of Roscraig. She had, after all, readily taken the pittance he'd offered her. Tavish's mind went to the other chambers in the west tower, and he wondered in his eagerness who currently occupied his rooms. Perhaps even now, Glenna Douglas was resting her wild blond curls upon his pillow, her willowy body atop his bed.

He recalled the sensual tilt of her eyes, her long, slender waist encircled by a fine chain, and he wondered if she would refuse him if he sought her in the dark...

He shook himself from the fantasy. Let her have her last night of false nobility in peace. Tavish was full of his mother's warm cooking, a nightcap of decent wine, and on the brink of launching his own dynasty.

Or was he merely continuing Thomas Annesley's?

The intrusive thought gave him pause, and his eyes went instinctively to the stones of the chimney. In the torch's dying glow, Tavish fancied he could see a faint outline where perhaps a portrait had once hung.

Chapter 4

Glenna came awake with a start, raising her head from her folded arms and blinking in the pale gray light of dawn. She wiped at her mouth with the back of her wrist and sat up fully in the chair, her stiff, shaking hands moving instinctively up the thick furs and stopping over the slight hump. She held her breath, felt nothing; closed her eyes and concentrated.

There it was, at last—the slight rise of an inhalation.

Glenna opened her eyes and finally dared look upon the face of her father. He was so pale, his skin so translucent, that Glenna could see the network of thin, twisty veins in sharp, blue-green relief. His eyelids were deep lilac, his nostrils and mouth gaping holes. The last of his white hair had fallen out. He'd not eaten in five days. He'd not woken in four.

And still, he lived.

Glenna stood with a hiss as her stiff muscles protested her uncomfortable vigil. She moved to the head of the bed and picked up the rag folded near the wooden bowl, dunking it in the icy water she'd brought last night and mixed with half of the remaining wine in all of Roscraig. She wrung it lightly and then gently wiped the insides of Iain Douglas's lips and cheeks, the roof of his mouth. The liquid seemed to disappear at once, and his throat made no motion of swallowing. She'd hoped to try once more squeezing a few drops of the mixture into his parched mouth, but when she'd done that two days ago, he'd wheezed so weakly and for so long that she thought she had likely killed him.

She folded the rag in half and replaced it near the bowl once more and then leaned over the bed to place a soft kiss on her father's forehead.

"I'll return in a bit, Da," she whispered. "Seeing our guests off."

Glenna left her father's chamber, closing the door silently after her. Once she was free of the room, her stride was swift, her icy feet inside her worn slippers flitting over the familiar depressions of the stairs. She came to her own chamber and quickly washed her face and combed and twisted her hair into tight confinement and then looked down at her dress. Her sense of pride—what little she felt she had left—protested the idea of the strangers seeing her in the same worn gown as they had at their arrival.

Especially Tavish Cameron. She would not have a common merchant looking down upon her so.

Glenna quickly untied her shawl and chain, then slipped out of the striped kirtle, replacing it with the dark gray wool she pulled from the tall wardrobe. It was coarse; a bit too short for her at the hem, much too loose at the waist and bust. But it would have to do. She shook the creases from her shawl before draping and retying it about her shoulders and chest so as best to hide the widening holes in the weave. She once more donned the fine chain.

She had done all that she could with her appearance now, having lost her veil the day before and so, after a quick glance at the brightening window, she quit her room and once more gained the stairwell, feeling as she went for the keys at her waist.

Glenna was passing the wide opening of the great hall when a tawny shape within the high-ceilinged room caught her eye. She stopped, swaying on her feet, and stepped backward.

There was a man in the hall, standing to the left of the chimney and looking out the window, his boots braced wide on the still-damp floor. Her stomach leaped before she realized that it was not Frang Roy who trespassed. She blinked.

It was that blasted Edinburgh merchant.

"What are you doing in here?" she blurted. And then she strode through the doorway even as he turned his head lazily to glance at her over his shoulder, seeming entirely unconcerned at her arrival or the discovery of his escape. "How did you get out of the chamber?"

"That lock is rubbish," he said mildly, looking once more out the window at the firth, its waters beginning to sparkle gloriously in the dawn. "I'm not accustomed to being held prisoner when I've paid for accommodation. In fact, I've a mind to ask for the return of my coin when I complain to the proprietor. Wait a moment—would that be you?"

"I didn't wish to *give* you accommodation," Glenna clarified through gritted teeth. Her heart began pounding in her chest again at his casual threat to recoup his pathetic payment. "Roscraig isn't an inn, and I am no proprietor."

He looked at her at last, one eyebrow quirked. "Ah. That explains the absence of biscuits when the maid didn't come in to bank the fire."

Glenna felt her face heat to the tips of her ears.

But the man wasn't finished. "Lest you be too very embarrassed—I did find the last of some wine in that hovel that might have once been a kitchen."

Glenna's heart plummeted into her stomach. "You drank my wine?"

"I'd complain at the grittiness, but that can't be helped when 'tis not properly decanted."

Glenna felt her shoulders shaking with rage and humiliation. "'Tis time you were on your way. Even were I not offended at your trespass through my private quarters, the sun has risen, and you gave your word that you would leave at the dawn."

"Actually," he drawled, "*I* didn't give *my* word. 'Twas my knightly companion who made that vow and, true to his promise, he has already gone. Ridiculously honorable, that one."

"Well, you're certainly not staying any longer, vow or nay."

"Actually," he repeated, and if Glenna had had her father's sword at hand, she would have run the bastard through, "I am staying. Quite a bit longer."

"I'll have you thrown out," she threatened, but her fear was growing with each crash of her frantic heart. She was completely alone in all of the Tower with this man.

"Aye? By whom?" It was as though she'd spoken her thoughts aloud. "The young man in the village? Or the crusty old farmer? Who I'll be speaking strongly to about stealing eggs from the doocot, by the by. In case he happens to be a relative of yours."

Glenna could feel her nostrils flaring. "I don't require assistance disciplining my villagers. I—"

"My villagers," he interrupted.

"—know exactly—" She broke off. "What did you say?"

"I said, 'my villagers.'" He reached into his vest and withdrew the rolled parchment he'd tried to show her yesterday. "Perhaps you will better understand that I was taken aback yesterday at your denial of a guardian of Tower Roscraig, and by your mention of your father as laird. For, you see," he was unrolling the creamy page now, "although I don't know who you truly are or why you're here, I have indeed come at the behest of Lord Annesley, the rightful laird of this place, whether you know his name or nay." He held the parchment open. "Lord Thomas Annesley was my father, and he has bequeathed Roscraig to me."

There was a loud ringing in Glenna's ears. She glanced at the scrawled black writing on the page and then back into the blue eyes of the man watching her closely.

"So, aye, they are my villagers. And I believe you are the one trespassing."

"You told me you were a merchant," she accused, and was alarmed at the wild trembling of her words. "A merchant from Edinburgh."

"Aye, I am," he acquiesced.

"And yet your father was noble?" she taunted incredulously, but her words held little force. "Were you some gutter bastard of his? A last resort as an heir?"

His lips quirked then, although his eyes fell steely, and Glenna knew she'd at last hit a sensitive area. "Guilty," he said lightly. "But we only have to consider the history of our own ruling families to know that the circumstances surrounding one's birth actually mean very little. Tower Roscraig is rightfully mine."

"You're a liar. Get out of my house," Glenna demanded.

"Read it yourself," the man invited. "Och, but you probably can't."

Glenna reached out and snatched the page from his hand and scanned it quickly. From what she could make out with her throbbing eyesight, the decree looked authentic. She thrust it back to him without finishing it.

"My father has been laird here since before I was born."

The man shook his head. "He never was."

"He is!" She resisted the urge to stomp her foot. "I'll send a plea to the king. You'll be hanged."

"No need for all that," he said mildly. "I've already sent word to him. James shall be my guest over the warmer months." He looked around the hall pointedly. "Once I see the Tower outfitted properly for guests. Or residence. Goats even, really."

She'd hoped to bluff him. But what if this man had actually invited the king to Roscraig? The last thing Glenna needed now was James's personal witness to her and her father's dire straits.

Her heart was so high in her throat that she feared she would vomit it up were she to open her mouth. But she struggled to swallow, thinking of the thin, motionless figure lying unconscious above their very heads.

"My father is Iain Douglas, the laird of Roscraig. He fell ill when the sickness came to our village a fortnight ago. You can't possibly think I would simply take your word for such an outrage when he is too weak to defend his home and his honor. An accusation such as this would surely kill him."

The man rolled the parchment neatly while she spoke and glanced out the window repeatedly, as if only half listening to her begrudged plea.

Now he nodded at her. "I am truly sorry for your troubles, Miss Douglas."

"Lady," Glenna insisted, feeling as though he'd slapped her. She lifted her chin. "I am Lady Glenna Douglas, and you will address me as such."

"Whatever you say, princess. But Roscraig is mine by rights, and I owe you or your father naught. Collect your things and be gone. I have more important business to be about. In fact"—he turned and pointed a long arm toward the window, where a small, dark shape could be seen on the glistening water of the Forth—"that is my ship, just there. I must greet my captain and be about my duties. My home shall require much attention in the days to come, for it's been woefully neglected."

He tucked the parchment back into his vest and seemed to hesitate before he gave her a short, stiff bow. "Good day, *Miss* Douglas. Och, I beg your pardon; *princess*. And good journey to you." He walked away from her swiftly.

Fear seemed to be clawing at her insides now. "I'll bar the door against you!"

"I'll break it down!" he shouted at the ceiling, not bothering to look back at her.

In a blink, he was gone from the room.

Glenna backed up into the stones and then looked out the window. Indeed, there was a small, sturdy-looking cog swiftly gaining on the beach, its sails falling down with graceful ripples, its deck alive with a score of tiny figures.

Roscraig was being invaded.

She slid down the wall until she rested on her hip, her knees falling to one side and both hands shooting out to brace herself against the damp floorboards while her head dropped forward. A wave of dizziness swept over her, and she felt the blood leave her face.

My father has been laird here since before I was born.

He never was.

She raised her head as sounds of footsteps echoed in the large room.

Harriet Cameron had entered the hall and stopped abruptly, her hands going to her bosom with a gasp as she seemed quite surprised to see Glenna.

"Good heavens!" She crossed the floor with flapping skirts—sturdy, woolen garments, but they were bright and colorful and well made, with a crisp, double-bodiced apron covering them. She immediately knelt at Glenna's side and laid a gentle hand upon her back.

Glenna flinched away. "Leave me."

"Tav's never been one for gentleness, I fear," she said softly, and her hand did not move. "Why do ye nae come with me, and let's have a bite to eat, shall we? You're naught but skin and bones, my lady."

Glenna's breath caught on her inhale. "There's nae food," she admitted inanely, unable to think of her pride in this moment. "There's naught."

The old woman's hand moved in a gentle circles on Glenna's back, and she could feel the prominent ripples of her own spine against the woman's plump palm.

"Och, there's plenty of food," she said. "And there will be more to come."

"'Tis nae mine," she said on a reedy whisper. "Please, leave me. My father lies above, dying, and your son has just told me that the only home I've known isn't mine. And never was. Either he is a liar, or my father is. I know not what I'm to do."

"Come," the woman insisted, gaining her feet and tugging Glenna to stand, taking much of her weight against her bosom. "We'll worry about all that later. Nae matter what happens, you'll need your strength to care for your da now, will ye nae? Who else does he have?"

Glenna glanced at the woman in fear, but there was no maliciousness in Harriet Cameron's face.

"No one," Glenna admitted in a whisper.

Harriet nodded. "That's right." She shook Glenna's arm lightly. "Come on then."

* * * *

The bright morning sunlight sparkled over the still-wet stones and grass as if the whole of Roscraig had been crusted in diamonds; the firth was a gray-green shimmer like the rippling robe of fae royalty, and Tavish stopped at the top of the steep, switchback stone steps that led down the side of the cliff of the rear courtyard to the beach, reveling in his triumph. His eyes prickled and he swallowed, closing them for a moment and taking a deep breath in through his nose of the gusting wind, so cool and fresh and free.

He'd won. At last.

He opened his eyes, ignoring the tickle of thought that hinted it had been too easy; his conscience that wanted to remind him of Glenna Douglas's fine features, stricken pale, her thin form standing defiant before him in her rough gown.

You drank my wine?

She was not his problem. He started down the mossy, neglected stairs, not even the tall bank of dark clouds roiling in from the west able to shadow his conquest.

But he was forced to make allowances for the dire state of the prize he'd won and the immensity of the tasks that lay before him by the time he reached the wet, brown beach and saw Captain John Muir slogging through the shallows toward him. The end of Roscraig's dock—mayhap more than half of it—was completely gone, the black tops of ancient, rotted pilings gasping at the surface between waves. Two ships hands were turning the dinghy back toward the *Stygian* when Muir and Tavish met with a clasp of hands.

"They'll take new measurements before we come any closer," John said as a greeting. "The maps we have of Roscraig's shore are old—'tis as though none have traded with the hold in fifty years."

"That I can believe," Tavish allowed. "Had you any trouble from the harbor?"

John Muir nodded curtly, his tanned face stern inside the circle of white created by his close-cropped gray hair and short beard. He was only ten years Tavish's senior, but a more temperate and wise man Tavish had never met, and Tavish was more proud to call John his closest friend than he was the captain of his ship.

"You may tell your English mate that 'twas right of you to leave ahead of us. The burgess had us boarded and searched. He seemed desperate to find you aboard ship."

Tavish's blood boiled. "Did he take anything?"

"Nay. There was little he could say about a cargo of crew and personal goods leaving Leith. I told him where for we were bound, but I expect he didna believe me. We'll be followed."

"Let him follow—he's no power beyond Leith. As soon as Roscraig is outfitted, we'll not drop anchor there again short of a request from the king himself."

"There's more," Muir said. "The night of your departure from Market Street, the shop caught fire."

"What?" Tavish said, his anger chilling slightly.

The captain's face was grim. "Burned to the very cellar, Tav. Naught left but charcoal. Took the two shops to either side of it, as well, before the rain came."

His shop was gone. The place that held all of his childhood memories, both good and bad. The only place before Roscraig he'd ever known as home, and his failsafe if the king decided against him.

Now there was nothing to go back to.

"Was any one hurt?"

Muir shook his head. "Nay. Rumor in the taverns is that the burgess set his lackeys to it. Not that any would stand up with an oath."

"Of course not." Tavish cursed softly and then sighed. "He would have never let up, as long as I was in Edinburgh. Mam will be upset that the place is gone."

Muir turned toward the land to look up at the backside of the stone keep. "Was she abandoned?"

Tavish mirrored the captain's pose, glad to change the subject, and both men admired the rocky promontory jutting toward the firth like the giant bow of a mythical ship.

The captain's query called to Tavish's mind the deep gouges in the entry door beyond the moat; the way Glenna Douglas had sought to lock him in a chamber.

"Not exactly," Tavish said. "Naught I canna bring to heel, though."

"Good," John grunted. "I've brought all you asked from Market Street, and glad I am that we loaded it so soon. Will you be needing more from the town straight away?"

"Aye, Captain—a good deal more. Roscraig hasn't been properly occupied in years. I'll be needing to outfit everything from the hall to the dairy."

John Muir raised his eyebrows.

"And people," Tavish continued. "Your men on leave are welcome here to work; their families to stay on in my employ in their absence."

"It's servants you're needing as well, then?"

Tavish nodded. "Anyone suitable. Even if they're not suitable."

Captain Muir grinned. "I'm not a man to judge house servants, Tav."

"Perhaps you would find reason to pay a call to Master Keane and relay to Audrey my sudden need for domestic assistance. I'm certain she would know exactly what I require."

"And perhaps I could happen to mention, by the by, your inheritance?" Muir taunted.

Tavish felt his neck warm, but found he didn't mind at all. "It's no secret now, is it, John?"

"Nay, but I'll warrant Audrey shall be cross that you didna tell her yourself. Quite."

Tavish grinned. "I'm certain you can convince her to forgive me—she's always listened to you above any other. Do you need my assistance in coming ashore?"

"Nay—we've hands aplenty this short trip. We'll rebuild the dock straightaway."

"Good. Send word 'round that half of them may stay when you return to Edinburgh. I'll pay them their usual sailing stipend with a bonus. I've a roof that needs mending and some walls and paths rocked. Several cottages are in disrepair, and the fields need turned right away, should any have a yearning to play at farming."

"My God," Muir said. "Is it so bad?"

"Naught I can't bring to heel," Tavish repeated. "I'm off to tell Mam you've arrived—she'll be anxious for her hoops and pots." He offered Muir his hand once more. "Captain."

Muir took Tavish's hand but also touched his forehead with his left fingertips and gave Tavish a salty wink. "Laird."

The dark clouds made good on their rainy promise as Tavish bounded up the three flights to the courtyard. He saw the smoke coming from the kitchen building and dashed toward it, knowing that's where Mam would likely feel most at home in such a foreign place. He couldn't wait to bring the news that Muir had arrived with their possessions.

Tavish grabbed onto the doorframe to slow himself as he ran beneath the lintel, feeling the wide smile on his face, the cold rain on his scalp.

"Mam! The *Stygian* is—"

The smile fell from his lips as he took in the scene before him: the previously dusty, abandoned room now scrubbed clean, its shelves set to rights with the small provisions they'd traveled with. A fire crackled merrily in the enormous hearth, encouraging the simmer of a pot of some delicious-smelling stuff that his mother was ladling into a wooden bowl.

"Ah, you reminded me of when you were a lad just now, Tav, dashing into the kitchen to tell me this or that," Mam said with a delighted smile as she hung the ladle on a hook and turned toward the square table in the center of the room. "Warms my heart."

She set the bowl down on the table before none other than Glenna Douglas, who was looking up at Tavish with her green eyes rounded, her hands clasped tightly on her lap.

The two stared at each other for several heartbeats, while Mam shook out a wide napkin and smoothed it over the blond woman's legs, lifting and replacing Glenna Douglas's clenched fists.

"There you are, milady. Careful now—'twill be hot. Come have a bite, Tavish—it's just now ready."

Milady? *Milady?*

"What are you doing here?" Tavish demanded in a low voice, ignoring his mother.

If she had been startled by his entrance, she recovered quickly. Her cat eyes narrowed. "Did you expect me to simply vanish upon your command?"

"Aye," he said with a nod.

Mam tossed him a stern look as she set a wooden cup next to the bowl and filled it from a skin. "Now, let's nae argue over the meal. Milady, here's a good heel of bread."

"Thank you, Harriet."

The subservient tone pierced Tavish's brain like splinters. It seemed like someone else's hand that reached out and wrapped fingers around Glenna Douglas's scrawny bicep; someone else's rage that yanked her from the stool, leaving it to topple sideways with a clatter; someone else that pulled her behind him from the kitchen and into the rain while she shrieked.

"Let go of me!"

She resisted with what little strength she possessed, jerking at her arm, digging her heels into the soft courtyard. But Tavish plucked her up as if she were naught but a weed and pulled her into the wide entry hall, splashing through puddles that were already forming from the downpour outside.

"*Let go!*"

He reached the bottom of the stairs to the east tower and swung her around in front of him before pushing her up the first two risers and at last setting her free. He began mounting the steps, prompting her to retreat up them backward, even though she continued to glare at him defiantly.

"My mother," he said, as deliberately as he ascended each step, "is not your servant."

She nearly stumbled but caught herself and backed up the stairs more quickly as he neared her.

"You don't *have* any servants," Tavish clarified. "Nor have you any food. Nor crops. Nor livestock. Whether 'twas you or your da, someone's run Roscraig nearly into its grave, and so any courtesy I would have shown you for your stewardship of my home doesn't exist. You've no right to be here at all."

She lashed out at him with her fists, her claws. He shouted as he raised a hand to his face, and then his other to ward off the next blow. She turned and stumbled up the stairs as if she would escape him, but Tavish was quicker, seizing her bony wrist and whipping her around to press her against the stones of the stairwell.

"Turn me loose, you bastard!" she screamed up at him, her hands flailing, her knees and feet churning into his body. "You common filth! Thief!"

Tavish managed to capture both of her wrists in what he knew must be a crushing grip, and then he seized Glenna Douglas's chin and jaw, effectively stifling the flow of vitriol from her mouth.

"*Shut up,*" he growled, nearly nose to nose with her as the thunder crashed beyond the stone walls. Their torsos pressed together, and he fancied he could feel her heartbeat trill within her shallow frame, like that of a captured bird. "You gather your things, and the things of your father, and you both be gone from my house. *My house,*" he emphasized. "As soon as the rain stops. If you are so inclined to work for your keep, you may have one of the cottages in the village. *Princess,*" he added with hissing scorn.

He released her jaw and yanked his hand back as she tried to bite him with an outraged shriek. She stumbled sideways and then backward up the stairs glaring at him, her eyes fiery but dry. When she was out of his reach, she stopped, her mouth twisting in a sneer.

"I'll not be your villager," she spat. "You're a common bastard, and you always will be. Words on a page don't make you noble."

"On the next dry day," Tavish repeated. "I don't want to see sign of you before then, lest I lose my temper and teach you a lesson on how to mind the laird of the hold."

"You keep your filthy, beggar hands away from me." She lifted her chin as she turned and left him on the stairs.

Tavish touched his mouth and looked down at the blood on his fingertips. The mad woman had busted his lip. He turned to go back down the stairs and saw Mam waiting at the bottom with a laden tray in her hands and a look of disappointment on her face.

She raised an eyebrow at his pointed glance at the food and drink on the tray. "Nae a word, Tavish Cameron. I'm yer mam and I'll cuff ye as well, laird or nay."

Tavish gritted his teeth as he walked past his mother toward the barbican. He could just see the first of the ship hands carrying crates and barrels into the courtyard.

If he'd had any doubt of Glenna Douglas's nobility before today, her behavior confirmed it without a doubt. She was utterly useless to him. Whatever difficulties she and her father had created for themselves were only Tavish's problems inasmuch as the Douglases had so outrageously mismanaged Roscraig, and it would be he who must rebuild the derelict hold and village.

The sooner she was gone from his house and out of his way, the better.

Chapter 5

Glenna flung herself across the foot of her father's bed, her body shaking, her throat choked with gasps. Her arm throbbed where Tavish Cameron had gripped her. She knew that her flesh was so spare now, dark bruises would testify to his touch.

She felt as though she were either going mad or in the malevolent whirlwind of a never-ending nightmare. Everything in her life was being systematically destroyed. The village was gone, the hold was in poverty. What would happen to her after Iain Douglas drew his last breath?

The chamber door gave its familiar, tired creak, and Glenna whipped her head around.

Harriet Cameron stood in the doorway holding a tray in her hands. "I wanted to bring it before it went cold."

Glenna froze for a moment, her pride warring with her aching, lonely heart. This woman was the mother of the monster who was stealing her home. But she had also prepared her own food for Glenna to eat, and her efforts seemed without rancor.

"Might I come in, milady?"

Glenna didn't trust herself to speak—indeed, she had no idea what she should say to the woman were she to open her mouth, and so she only nodded dumbly.

Harriet entered and briskly crossed the floor, affording Glenna time to straighten from the bed and swipe at her eyes while the woman slid the tray onto the bedside table, jostling the pathetic bowl and rag that had lived there for what seemed like weeks now. Then Harriet faced the sunken countenance of Iain Douglas and gave a quick bob.

"Laird Douglas," she said courteously, as if the man were conscious of the goings-on in his chamber. Then she picked up the bowl of porridge and abandoned napkin and turned, offering them to Glenna.

Glenna took the sustenance and eased down on to the edge of the mattress. "Thank you." She was wary of the woman and embarrassed at the hunger that gnawed at her insides, but as if Harriet Cameron sensed as much, she turned back to the wan figure on the bed, her hands on her generously rounded hips, giving Glenna privacy for her first ravenous tastes of the food.

"How long's the laird been in his state?" Harriet asked, not looking at Glenna.

Glenna swallowed and cleared her throat before answering. "This morn was the fourth day."

Harriet's brow lowered on her profile. "He's nae woken a'tall? Taken nae drink?"

"Nay." Glenna dropped her eyes to the bowl and scooped another spoonful while Harriet stepped to the bedtable. "I…I've bathed his mouth. With spiced wine. 'Twas all I had." She lifted the porridge to her mouth but spoke before taking the bite. "Your son thought it fitting to drink the last of it himself last night."

Harriet turned her head quickly, and her face bore an expression of unabashed surprise. Then her features seemed to calm, steel themselves against emotion. "I apologize in his stead, milady. You are welcome to anything I have to replace it, of course."

Glenna ignored the comment and looked back to the contents of the bowl as she swirled it with her spoon. Her stomach had filled quickly, the few bites settling like thorny rocks.

"It doesn't matter, though, does it? He'll die."

"Have you a priest?" Harriet asked, in one manner ignoring Glenna's comment, but also confirming it by the very question.

Glenna set the bowl aside on the still coverlet and twisted the linen cloth between her hands. "There is Dubhán. The hermit monk who lives along the cliff. He sees to the graveyard. The…the burials."

"Thanks be to God for that, at least. With your permission, I'll send for him this afternoon."

Glenna's throat constricted. "Nay," she rasped. "Da doesn't want that. He renounced all religion after my mother died. He—" Glenna stopped, shocked at how readily she seemed to want to share with the woman the horrible memories bubbling up in her own mind—the pounding on the keep door, Dubhán's voice calling out for mercy the day the villagers began to die...

Glenna took a deep breath. "He wouldn't want Dubhán's blessing."

Harriet winced. "But, milady, his soul—"

"*Nay.* He is still laird here, no matter what your son says. I will obey his wishes."

"Of course, milady. Of course. I didna mean to add to your upset. I'll visit this Dubhán myself soon and take him a basket of food. Beg your pardon, milady, but I'm supposing his supplies match your own?"

Glenna felt her face heat. "Dubhán looks after himself."

"I see. Well," she sighed. "There's likely naught I can do to save your da, you ken, but I might be able to give him a mite o' comfort." Harriet looked to Glenna. "If milady wishes."

"It doesn't matter what I wish," Glenna replied bitterly. "As soon as the rain stops, Tavish Cameron would see us tossed out on the road."

Harriet Cameron looked at Glenna for a long moment while thunder rumbled gently. "It's still rainin', is it nae?"

Glenna nodded dumbly.

"And your da still lives. Let me help you while I can." She paused. "You might think Tav is only hard-hearted and cruel, but he isna. His mind is foremost for business. And for the time being, his business is Roscraig."

Glenna felt her temper flare. "Roscraig doesn't belong to him."

"That isna my argument to make," Harriet rejoined gently. "And I willna play you false by saying I doona think my son deserves what his own father has given him. But I would ask you: if you could choose, right now, between Roscraig and your da, which would you have?"

Tears came into Glenna's eyes, extinguishing the fire that wanted to blaze inside her. "Of course I would have my father."

"Aye. And so, for now, you have the privilege of choosing which battle you fight. Tavish never had a choice."

Glenna lifted her chin. "That isn't my doing. If anyone's, 'tis yours."

The old woman dropped her eyes for a moment, and Glenna felt a prickling of her conscience.

"I've never had much say myself over the path I've traveled, milady. And so I understand a bit of what you're feeling now, and I'm sorry for you. But I canna stay Tavish's hand in what he chooses for Roscraig, even if I had wish to. So if you'd rather I leave you and your da be, I will."

In that moment, Glenna overcame her self-pity and anger to feel shame for the way she had treated Harriet Cameron. If her father had been conscious to witness her behavior, she knew it would have shamed him, too. The woman had been naught but kind and apologetic from the first moment she'd arrived at Roscraig, and she was the only person left who seemed to genuinely care what happened to her and Iain Douglas.

"Forgive me, Harriet," Glenna said quietly. "Please. I…I'm tired. And frightened." She looked up at Harriet, who was tidying the bedside table, piling the bowl and used cloths in the center of the tray. Glenna couldn't help but ask stiffly, "Are you not glad to now have a home such as Roscraig?"

The woman glanced at her with a smile as she leaned over Iain Douglas and slid her palm along his forehead, the sides of his face. "Aye. But I was glad of our home in Edinburgh, too. I will be happy anywhere that Tav is happy. I doona wish you or your da ill from it." She straightened but still regarded Iain with a slight frown. "It wasna plague, then?"

Glenna sighed. "I don't know what else it could have been. He fell ill a week ago, after everyone else in the village who'd been stricken had already died. He took to his bed and slept heavily that night. The next day he was weaker. The day after he didn't wake at all."

"Nae boils? Nae spasms of breath?" Harriet pressed her, reaching beneath the furs as if feeling along Iain Douglas's arm.

Glenna shook her head. "None I was witness to. Why do you ask?"

"'Tis rare that the Death doesna show on the skin or in the lungs. It's been known to happen of the verra old or young—the sickness shuts their insides down before the sign can show." Harriet looked to Glenna. "How many did it take in the village?"

"Forty-seven."

"Mercy," Harriet breathed. "Took all your help, apparently. The signs on the road looked old."

Glenna blinked; her pride wouldn't allow her to admit to Harriet Cameron that there'd been warning signs on the Tower Road for as long as she could remember. And there had been no full staff in years.

The woman shook her head when Glenna failed to answer, but then turned back toward the table and went on briskly. "I'm going to fetch my bags for some freshening herbs and give the laird a good wash, with your permission, milady."

Glenna shook herself. "You needn't do that. It's not your responsibility."

"I know it's nae. I wish to." Harriet picked up the tray and bobbed in Iain Douglas's direction. Then she gave Glenna a quick smile and made to quit the room, but paused, looking back with a wince. "But perhaps milady wouldna mention it to Master Cameron if she should happen to speak with him."

Glenna huffed. "I intend to avoid the man completely. You've my word I shall not speak of whatever kindness you wish to bestow upon us, lest the mighty Tavish Cameron rain hell down upon us all."

Harriet's smile returned. "Just so, milady."

It seemed very quiet after the woman's departure; quiet and darker and colder, with the sound of the steady, heavy rain outside the keep. Glenna looked at her sleeping father and wondered what he would do if he were well enough to deal with Tavish Cameron's invasion of Roscraig.

Perhaps she *should* be glad of the king's visit. James would have found out the sorry state of the village sooner or later any matter. If she was going to be evicted from her home eventually, it would give her more than a little satisfaction to hope that the arrogant bastard from Edinburgh might never call the Tower his own.

But where would that leave her?

She rubbed absentmindedly at her arm where he'd bruised her; then her eyes went to the bodice of her ugly gray kirtle, where the tiny speck of brown reminded her how she'd lashed out at him as if he were naught but a common criminal.

Wasn't he? Hadn't he invaded her home? Laid hand to her?

For now, you have the privilege of choosing which battle you fight. Tavish never did.

Glenna didn't entirely understand what Harriet Cameron meant, but for now she thought the woman's advice was sound: She would stay by her father's side and fight for him for as long as he lived.

And for as long as the rain held out.

* * * *

Tavish was soaked through to his skin as he came into the entry hall from the courtyard. The echo of the downpour beyond turned the corridor into a roaring cave, but he could still hear his mother's strident voice above the cacophony as she stood on the bottom step of the west tower with tray in hand, apparently berating the large man before her.

He was tall and wide, with a head that appeared to be quite pointed beneath the shape of his coarse, wet hood. In one pawlike hand, he carried a basket, and Tavish recognized him at once as the figure he'd seen coming from the cliff that morning.

Tavish slid the heavy wooden chest from his shoulder and let it drop into the crook of his arm with a huff of exertion as he neared.

"...doona care who ye are, milady isna— Ooh, there you are. Thank the Lord."

"What is it?" Tavish asked as he came to stand before the pair, swiping the rivulets of water from his forehead.

Mam's mouth was set in the expression that warned Tavish she had made up her mind about one thing or another. "This man here is demanding entry to the east tower."

Tavish raised his eyebrows and looked—slightly up, to his chagrin—at the hulking villager. "Who are you?"

"'Oo am I?" the man repeated. "That's nae yer affair, stranger. I've come to see Lady Glenna. I know where she stays."

"You do, do you?" Tavish said.

"Aye, I've brung 'er her eggs." He gestured with the basket, and Tavish glanced down to see three tiny ovals rolling nestled in a shallow layer of straw. "'Oo are you?"

"Tavish Cameron. Laird of Roscraig."

"Laird of—wha?" The man snorted a laugh and looked around the hall as if seeking someone to share the joke with. He looked back at Tavish. "You're nae the laird. Douglas—" The man broke off. "The old man's dead?"

"He's nae," Mam interjected sternly. "Lady Glenna doesna wish to be disturbed."

"I'll nae be turned away, old woman," the brutish man said, offense clear in his gravelly, slow tone. He looked back to Tavish, his small eyes narrowing even further. "I'm Frang Roy, Lady Glenna's own man. She wants me."

"Well, now that we've introduced ourselves, you may kindly hand the basket to my mother," Tavish said, "and be on your way until I call for you."

"Bugger off," the man snorted again. "I doona take orders from the likes of you, ye bonny laddie. With those long locks, I'd have me dinker in your crack before I kenned you was a bloke." He broke out into a guffaw that Tavish joined him in readily.

"Oh, that's...that's good!" Tavish said. "That's jolly! One moment while I—" He groaned through his laughter as he set the heavy chest on the stones and then straightened, still chuckling. "Aye, that's much better." He smiled.

Tavish punched Frang Roy squarely in the nose, twice, in blurring fast succession.

While the man was still bringing his hand to his battered face, Mam swooped in and snatched the basket with the pitiful offerings in it as she crossed the entry hall and disappeared down the corridor. By the time

Frang Roy dropped his hand and charged forward with an enraged yell, Tavish had drawn his short sword.

Frang Roy halted, but Tavish could see that he was searching with those small, watchful eyes, waiting for an opening to catch Tavish unawares. If the man did manage to lay hand to him, he could likely break Tavish in two.

"Have I your full attention now?" Tavish asked. At the giant's answering nod, he continued. "Good. You and I seem to have made a poor start, and that's a shame, I say. So here's what we're going to do: You're to turn about and take your smelly, dimwitted self through the door and over yonder bridge. When you've quite remembered how to address the laird of the hold, as well as how to mind your language in front of a lady, you may return and request audience...*with me.*"

"But, Lady Glenna—"

"Lady Glenna no longer has anything to do with the running of Roscraig."

Frang Roy stood there, his shoulders heaving, and Tavish could almost hear the creak of his brains grinding together as he sought to make sense of the situation.

"Who sent—?"

"Nay," Tavish cut him off. Then he gestured with his sword point. "Go."

Frang Roy paused a moment longer, staring at Tavish with dull eyes, and then his gaze went pointedly to the money chest at Tavish's feet.

"Things have a habit of disappearin' at Roscraig. Coin. People. Mind yerself, Tavish Cameron, that someone doona make you disappear." Then he turned and opened the door, leaving it swinging wide after he passed through and began to clomp his way across the long, narrow bridge in the pouring rain.

Tavish let out a sigh and closed and barred the door after the man, thinking once more of the gouges on the outside wood, and the way Frang Roy had identified himself as Lady Glenna's man.

Was it possible the slight blond woman felt kindly toward such a slow beast? Would she have granted him entry into her private quarters with no one else in the hold? He had seemed quite confident in his intentions. The idea of it brought a frown to Tavish's face.

Tavish picked up the money chest once again with a grunt and hefted it to his shoulder. He paused and looked toward the dark, quiet stairwell to the east tower for a moment. Then he turned and began to climb the western steps.

* * * *

Glenna watched from the shadows as Tavish Cameron's wide back disappeared across the corridor, her hand pressed to her chest as if it might quiet her galloping heart.

Nothing would change the fact that she hated the Edinburgh merchant.

But for the first time in weeks, she felt temporarily safe from Frang Roy.

Chapter 6

Two miracles occurred in Glenna Douglas's life following Tavish Cameron's tyrannical demands; the first was that it rained for the next full fortnight. She watched from her chamber window as, day after day, the gray skies hung rippling sheets of silver rain across the leaden waters of the firth. During that fortnight, Tavish Cameron's cog ship arrived and departed on four occasions, on the latest trip finally able to send men over the new dock that had been reconstructed even through the deluge.

Much rain on the firth in spring was no wonder, of course; the miracle of it was that the rain would often stop before midnight, allowing Glenna to catch a glimpse of a brilliant black sky. But when she awoke in the morning, the sunrise was smothered by the choking, watery clouds again, the rain once more drowning the fields, the muddy paths, and ditches of the village, the Tower Road.

There was not one dry day in a fortnight for the Edinburgh merchant to enforce his eviction, and indeed, she had not caught sight of the man except from her window in those many days. And so Glenna had had much time to think upon her situation, which had been further complicated by the occurrence of the second miracle.

Iain Douglas had woken the day after Harriet Cameron had assumed his care.

He was not at all well, and indeed, his wakeful periods were marked by slurred, delusional murmurs. He seemed largely unaware of the strange woman who plied him with strong-smelling concoctions, and pressed thick, muddy toweling to his chest and abdomen. Indeed, he didn't even recognize Glenna herself, once holding out a frail, trembling hand toward her in the still of midnight and croaking, "Meg."

Neither did Harriet Cameron seem pleased by her success in rousing Glenna's father. Her usual kind smile was pressed into a grim line when she warned Glenna that even if he lived, he might never completely recover his nimble mind. Harriet guessed that he'd been apoplectic, perhaps during the night early in his illness, for now his face drooped on the right side, his right arm was drawn up against his body, his mouth seemed unable to stiffen and form words out of his shapeless moans, as if he were trapped in a state of perpetual pain or nightmare.

Glenna was left to consider the realities of her future on those long, lonely, clear nights, contemplating the blazing stars washed sparkling clean by the days upon days of cold rain. She had no idea how she would fend for herself if Tavish Cameron turned her out of Roscraig, never mind if she were to be turned out with an invalid father. Even with the hold undoubtedly in deep debt, Glenna felt she had no other choice but to appeal to the crown. Iain Douglas was still one of Scotland's lairds—surely the king would have some mercy on them both.

Perhaps he would make a match for Glenna. She tried to ignore the logic that told her any husband the king would find for such an impoverished lady would likely be old and hoary; a widower, perhaps, with children to care for. Or her imagined betrothed would be cruel and wicked, taking on the king's charity that was Glenna and her father and paying Roscraig's debts to avoid punishment for some evil.

Without doubt, he would be ugly and harsh; vulgar and foul. There was no dearth of well-off women willing to marry a handsome and landed man, young or old, after all.

The idea quickly brought the image of Tavish Cameron to Glenna's mind. He was certainly not ugly, even if he had been unkind to her. She frowned as she admitted that there would be plenty of maidens eager to come to Roscraig as the wife of such a young, virile laird and take Glenna's place as lady of the Tower.

Then she went very still.

Why should any other young woman need come to Roscraig to take her place? Why should the king have to marry Glenna off to some distasteful stranger? Glenna was already Lady of Roscraig; Tavish Cameron was already sufficiently distasteful to her. It wouldn't take much for her distaste to blossom into full loathing. The bastard would need some credibility to lend to his newfound class status, and Glenna knew more than anyone left at Roscraig, save Frang Roy, about the village and its resources.

Perhaps a rich, bastard Edinburgh merchant was just what Roscraig needed. Perhaps Glenna was what Tavish Cameron needed.

And so, by the time the fourteenth day of her captivity arrived, sunny and clear, Glenna at last had a plan.

* * * *

Tavish sat back in his chair with a contented sigh as the servant took away his dish. He looked down the length of the trestle table, gleaming in the candlelight of the hall, the dry stones flickering with the cheery glow of the hearth mingled with the red wash of sunset coming through the windows behind him. At the other end of the table, Mam picked up her dish and handed it to the girl with unintelligible words of encouragement.

It had taken him four days of pleading to convince her not to clear the table herself.

But now his mother looked very fine, sitting in her embroidered kirtle, wearing the blue stone earrings he'd purchased for her. Even if she was glaring at him once more now that they were alone in the hall again.

"You're still set on it, then?" she asked without preamble. She had done little else but harangue him over the matter of Glenna and Iain Douglas in the time Tavish was not tending to the revitalization of Tower Roscraig.

He sighed. "Mam, please."

"The laird's unwell, Tav."

"I beg to differ," he said, lifting his cup to salute her. "I've never felt better." He took a drink.

"What if you're wrong?" she pressed, leaning forward. "What if the king doesna side with you?"

"He'd be going against a legal inheritance," Tavish reminded her. "You saw the state Roscraig was in at our arrival. James would have to be mad to deny an experienced merchant such a location on the firth. From both military and trade standpoints, my inheritance of the Tower will be an answered prayer for our monarch. And I'll more than welcome his experiments in artillery."

"Perhaps he'll want Roscraig for himself," she sniffed.

Tavish took another sip of wine and then shook his head as he swallowed. "He won't want the tending of it."

"You doona know that," Harriet insisted.

"I reckon I will once he comes now, won't I?" Tavish rolled he eyes as his mother looked toward the window with a hurt expression. "I ken you've grown fond of her, Mam. I feared that very thing. 'Tis why I wanted them out at once."

She still refused to look at him. "'Tis nae right, what's happened to them."

"Perhaps it isn't. But that doesn't change the fact that Roscraig doesn't belong to them." He sighed and pushed back from the table with a screech of chair legs and, carrying his cup, walked to the end of the table to crouch down at his mother's chair. "This is our home now, Mam. The home that Thomas Annesley wanted us to have. Would you let the woman play on your sympathies so as to take the very bed from beneath you?"

Harriet's head whipped back around to pin him with a scolding frown. "Lady Glenna wouldna do such a thing."

"You don't know that," Tavish said, using her own phrase against her. "And you would do well to stop referring to her as 'lady'; I've already commanded that none of the servants refer to Glenna Douglas as such, lest they be immediately dismissed. You're only encouraging confusion."

"I'll refer to *Lady Glenna* however I choose, and I'll thank you to remember who 'tis you're speaking to, son."

Tavish sighed again. "You are too kindhearted for your own good, Mam. Glenna is not some ill, orphan child in Edinburgh's poorhouse."

Harriet pursed her lips. "She may as well be."

"She is a stranger to you, and a desperate one at that. She has been spared by the rain this past interminable fortnight—more time than she was owed. She should have by now resigned herself to reality."

Tavish would have rather perished on the spot than admit that he'd spent many of those interminable nights lying in his own bed, his mind filled with images of the haughty, hostile woman.

Mam looked into his eyes, and Tavish plainly saw the depth of emotion she was holding back. "I think Laird Douglas was poisoned."

Tavish drew his head back in surprise and then huffed a laugh. "Poisoned? When nearly the entire village just died from illness? Did Glenna fill your head with such an idea?"

"Nay—I've nae shared my suspicions with her. But that's just it—Laird Douglas fell ill after most of the folk had died. Once the sickness was realized, he never left the hold."

The gouges in the door...

"You know just as well as I that the miasma can lay sleeping in a man for days before he succumbs."

"But Lady Glenna affirms he had no cough, no boils a'tall. And his fingers and toes..." She glanced around and then leaned forward in her chair, whispering to him. "*Black.*"

"If he never left the hold, the only one who could have poisoned him was his own daughter," Tav reminded her.

Mam shook her head. "Nay. That…that *man*, Frang Roy. *He* was the last one to see the laird before the door was barred from the villagers. He brought the eggs. They were part of the last meal Laird Douglas ate."

Tavish glanced at the table, now cleared of dishes. "We didn't eat the eggs he brought, did we?"

Mam shook her head. "I threw them out straight away."

"Good." Tavish paused. It was possible that Frang Roy could have had opportunity to poison Iain Douglas. But tainting the laird's food didn't make sense to Tavish. "What reason would he have for injuring the laird, Mam? Frang Roy's only a farmer—and a poor one, at that. It's not as if he could aspire to rule Roscraig."

Mam placed her hand atop Tavish's. "He wants Lady Glenna," she said pointedly. "Once her da was dead, there would be no one here to stop him."

"No one save me, Mistress Cameron."

The smooth, accented voice drew Mam's and Tavish's attention to the doorway, where Roscraig's newly installed man at arms entered with a hooded figure at his side.

"Beg pardon, laird," Alec said. "Dubhán said he was expected."

Tavish pushed to his feet. "My thanks, Alec." He looked to the dark-skinned man standing in the long robe. "Good evening, Dubhán. I should have come to the hermitage sooner."

"The rain, laird," the man said, opening his palms and giving Tavish a slow, bright smile as he looked pointedly around the hall. "You have had much more important work to do in bringing the Tower back to life than greeting a lowly servant such as myself." He turned toward Mam and gave a nod. "Mistress Cameron. I am blessed again by your presence."

Tavish felt his brows raise. "The two of you have met?"

Mam nodded. "I took a march up the cliff earlier today—my legs needed it after being cooped up in the keep for so long. I forgot to mention I invited Dubhán, Tav."

"I do hope my arrival is not inconvenient. It isn't often that I come into the village—Laird Douglas is not devout, and I am in truth no vicar."

"Not at all. Please." Tavish returned to his seat and gestured to the chair on the side of the table, between himself and Mam.

"This is a special treat for me, to partake of such hospitality." The monk bowed his thanks before sitting and accepting the cup set in front of him. "Since the village all but dissolved away, I keep to the cliff and tend the dead—what I was sent to Roscraig to do."

Tavish regarded the calm, exotic-looking man with pleasant curiosity. "How long have you been at Roscraig, Dubhán?"

"Oh, the lord sent me here many years ago," he said with a fond smile. "Before Lady Glenna was born. I have watched her grow."

"Was Laird Douglas ruling when you came?"

The black man looked mildly surprised. "Aye."

Tavish couldn't help but glance at his mother, and wished he hadn't when he saw her smug expression. He looked back to the black man, who seemed to be relishing each tiny sip of wine, cradling the cup in both his hands and closing his eyes with a small smile as he swallowed.

"Did you know the laird before him?"

"Forgive my ignorance, but nay. As you might have guessed I was not born of this land. My parents were killed in Tunis when I was a small child, and I was raised by Franciscans. I was sent here after I submitted to the lord, to care for the cave. Here I have remained."

At this, Tavish sat up, his sea merchant ears perking. "Cave?"

"In the cliff below the hermitage. One of the first saints of Scotland is said to have died there. Though I do not receive many pilgrims of late."

"That does interest me, Dubhán," Tavish said, his mind going at once to the heavy chest currently residing beneath his bed. "I would like to visit this cave myself."

"As you wish, laird," the man acquiesced. "It is a dangerous path, though, I warn. Many are rumored to have disappeared from the cliff. Most are never seen again."

"I thank you for the counsel," Tavish said, the monk's words calling to mind the warning from Frang Roy.

Things have a habit of disappearin' at Roscraig...

An awkward silence descended for a moment as the dark monk seemed to be considering his words carefully. "Do not think me impertinent, laird, I pray. But…Lady Glenna has no family to speak of if—" He paused and Tavish saw his pale nail beds go even whiter as they gripped the cup. It was obvious the man was struggling with unexpressed emotion. "Have you spoken to Laird Douglas?"

"I have not," Tavish said, not liking the guilt he felt tugging at a corner of his conscience.

Mam reentered the conversation then. "The laird is still quite unwell, Dubhán. He's only spoken a handful of words, and those are mostly nonsense. He might yet die."

Dubhán gave a solemn nod toward Mam and then turned his doleful gaze toward Tavish. He leaned forward. "Perhaps you will permit me to bless him, milord? While there is still time?"

An exasperated feminine sigh floated on the warmed air of the hall. "We've talked about this a hundred times, Dubhán." A moment later the slight, pale figure of Glenna Douglas stepped from the shadow of the corridor into the room. "You know he stopped believing in such things long ago." Glenna walked toward the table as she spoke, but her attention seemed to be on the room itself, her gaze going about the hall.

The monk stood as she reached his side, and Tavish himself felt the instinctive urge to rise, but kept his seat as he thought of the way she had dared strike him, as if he were no more than a stable boy; her boldness in occupying his dreams the past fortnight.

This was his hall and he would not stand for her.

Dubhán dropped his head in humility. "There is always hope."

"I know," she said, reaching out to take both of the monk's hands in hers. "You have done your best. But I will uphold his wishes. If you love him, you will do the same."

"My first love must always be for the lord," he replied with an easy smile. "And bringing those of unbelief to his unyielding mercies."

"I understand." She let his hands drop and then turned to Tavish, and her lips parted as if she meant to speak straight away. But she closed her mouth and her slender throat convulsed, her nostrils flared.

Tavish noticed that, although she was again wearing the same faded gown as upon his arrival at the Tower, tonight her hair was swept up in a complicated labyrinth of twists that culminated in a regal peak at her crown and adorned with a small sprig of spring greenery that was trembling ever so slightly. Her green eyes flashed at him, suggesting her hatred for him was still just beneath the surface. She was so thin, her skin so pale and smooth, Tavish could see the flutter of her wild pulse in the delicate column of her neck.

"Have you a request, *Miss Douglas*?" Tavish said courteously, deliberately goading her as a distraction from her exquisite appearance. "Directions to the nearest town, mayhap?"

"My first request, *Master Cameron*, is that you not continue to shame your mother by lazing on your haunches like some ill-mannered mongrel when a lady enters a room. I have full confidence that Harriet taught you how to behave."

Tavish was not expecting his barbs to be so expertly returned to him— and with such accuracy. So for a beat of time, he could do nothing more than blink while he recovered the use of his brains. She really did think a lot of herself.

He looked left and right, leaned back slightly to glance beneath the table and then let his gaze rove her leisurely from head to foot and then back to her eyes.

"Forgive me—I didn't see a lady enter. Is she hiding behind you?"

The gibe struck its intended target, for Tavish saw the roundness of her chest rise, her cat eyes narrow even further.

"I will show Dubhán out," Mam piped up brightly as her chair legs squeaked on the floor. "Good night, Tav." She gave Glenna a rueful smile. "I'll look in on your da before I retire, milady."

"Thank you, Harriet," Glenna Douglas whispered, but her hateful gaze remained trained on Tavish, as if she dismissed a servant worthy of not even a glance.

Tavish looked up at her benignly, stretching out one leg and folding his hands atop his stomach. "Why does the close of the first dry day in a fortnight find you yet in my house?"

"Roscraig isn't yours. Besides, even if it were, I have nowhere to go, and well you know it."

"That's not true at all—I gave you your choice of any of the cottages in the village."

"If you think to so easily be rid of me upon naught more than a questionable scrap of parchment, you are as dense as you appear," she said. "It will take no less than the king's command for me to be moved."

"He will be here within the month," Tavish rejoined easily, pleased at the flash in her eyes. "Not long to bide one's time in the village."

"Then you shouldn't mind waiting there," she offered.

Tavish couldn't help but laugh. He glanced up, indicating the portrait once more hanging over the great hearth. "I have a court-witnessed decree from my father—an English lord—that Tower Roscraig and its title belong to me. What proof have you?"

She stormed toward him at last, her skirts swinging against his legs as she stood over him. Her arm pointed behind her toward the doorway. "My proof is my father: the laird of Roscraig who lies above your head, dying! You are a naught but a bastard interloper who doesn't have the decency to so much as pay his respects to the man whose home you think to steal!"

Tavish gained his feet, noticing that Glenna initially flinched at his movement but continued to stand her ground.

He leaned down close to her face. "Insult me once more in my hall, princess, and I shall give you the back of my hand. Test me and know. I have been most generous in giving you this past fortnight. I owe you—and your da—naught. Your time is come. Be gone."

"If you would have a dying man moved," she said to him steadily, "then *you* go above and do it yourself, so that his death can be only on your hands. *You* remove him from your mother's kindness and care. *You* explain his death to the king when he comes to entertain your common groveling. *You* do it, and be damned."

"You didn't come down here only to curse me," Tavish said aloud as he realized it. He let his gaze flit over her face, her hair pointedly. "You want something. You want to deal."

Her eyes widened so slightly that, had anyone else been watching her, they likely would have never have known. But Tavish was alert to every pore and curve of her face, and Glenna seemed to recognize that as she blinked then took a step away from him. "The king could deny you," she said.

"Nonsense," Tavish scoffed.

"Your father was English," she insisted. "And so that makes you half. Posture all you like, but you know as well as I that James hates the murdering bastards. He would be well within his rights to toss you out on your swollen head, and then where would you go, hmm? I'm of the impression that you'd not receive a warm welcome upon your return to Edinburgh."

"I can give James all the coin Roscraig owes—every last shilling. The amount of income I can glean here is limitless, and the king will recognize that."

"If all the king wished for was wealth, many flags would fly across Scotland. When he chooses to fight, you would make a fine trumpet."

Tavish stilled. This woman was no imbecile. As much as he wanted to deny it to Mam and even to himself, the points Glenna Douglas made were valid and entirely plausible. But if she realized their likelihood, she also knew that there was an equal if not better chance that King James would award Roscraig to Tavish rather than an impoverished, ineffective corpse or the corpse's even more impoverished daughter.

What intrigued Tavish most in that moment, though, was Glenna Douglas's heretofore secret agenda with him in the hall.

"I've been in the business of commerce long enough to know when I'm being sold a cargo of questionable worth. So I'll ask you once more: What is it you came down here tonight for? And say it right out—no more dodging. What do you want?"

"Very well." She lifted her chin. "I want to marry you."

Chapter 7

There, she'd said it. It was out in the open now, and all Glenna had to do was withstand this terrible, awkward silence while Tavish Cameron stared at her. She steeled herself not to squirm, not to look away from him for even an instant. He took a quick step back, letting in a rush of fresh, cool air, and Glenna drew a deep silent breath through her nose.

"You want to…marry me?" His brows were drawn together between his eyes like the folds of a drapery.

Glenna lifted her chin the slightest bit. "That's right."

His frown was suspicious now. "But…you hate me."

"I do."

"And I hate you," he added.

"You've made that clear, aye."

"Then why would—" Tavish Cameron broke off, then a smug, knowing smile softened his rugged features. "Of course you'd rather marry a man you hate than try to manage somewhere without the benefit of a title."

She tried to smother the tiny flames erupting from the rippling bed of angry coals inside her before she spoke. "I have nowhere to go, whether my father lives or nae. I was born within these very walls—my mother is buried on yon cliff. I'll not leave, even if it means I must shackle myself to one beneath me, and whose very presence I loathe. I will withstand any suffering if it means my father and I remain."

"Your enthusiasm is tempting," he quipped with a quirk of his mouth. "I do see that becoming my wife would be the best solution for *you*. But what of me?"

Glenna blinked. "What of you?"

"Aye," he insisted with a growing smile as he strolled back toward his chair and lowered himself into it, picking up his abandoned cup and pausing it before his lips. "What benefit would it be to me to take such a shrew for a bride? You've no dowry, I assume." He drank.

She shook her head slightly. "None," she admitted. "But you need me. Marrying me all but guarantees Roscraig will remain in your hands." Glenna could see that she had the man's ear. Perhaps he was a skilled merchant after all, willing to hear the full details of the bargain.

"Go on," he said, watching her intently now.

She steeled herself for the plain facts she must voice aloud. "It would clearly be in the king's best interest from a standpoint of coin to strip my father of Roscraig and grant it to a successful man of commerce."

"Not to mention I'm the rightful heir," Tavish Cameron quickly interjected.

Glenna ignored him. "He would be paid what is owed him and stand likely to receive a comfortable profit from your future efforts. I," she paused but forced herself to go on, "have naught to give him."

"You're not much of a catch so far, I must say."

"Would you shut up and let me finish?" she snapped.

He grinned at her, increasing her fury. Glenna took a quick, calming breath. "Even so, it is said that James is a fair man. It would prick his conscience—and his reputation with his people—more than a little to so oust a son of Scotland, in favor of a common...shopkeep."

"Resorting to flattery, are you?"

"I was refraining from calling you bastard."

"Ah. Courteous, as well. Becoming more and more of a prize the longer you speak."

"If you marry me," Glenna forced through clenched teeth, "James has the best of both worlds—he is paid his debt, has honored his loyal subject—*my father*—and stands to profit from Roscraig's prosperity under...skilled management," she muttered, the words nearly causing her physical pain.

Tavish Cameron's eyebrows rose. "You think I'm skillful?"

She sighed and gestured with her open palm around the hall. "My resentment of you doesn't make me blind. Walking into the hall tonight was like walking back into my youth. I would not have thought it possible to accomplish what you have in only a fortnight. I must admit that I would like to see..." She faltered.

"See what?"

"I'd like to see what you can do for Roscraig in a year," she finished in a rush, her chin tilted even further. "If you are in fact the rightful heir to Roscraig, and you marry me, James could never refuse your claim."

"What of your father?" Tavish Cameron suggested. "What would you tell him?"

"If he recovers…well, we might tell him that we made these arrangements in preparation of his death. So that Roscraig…and I…would be cared for."

"What, I just wandered up the Tower Road past three score signs of plague, fell madly in love with you at first sight, and determined you would be my wife?"

Her cheeks ached they burned so intensely. "There's no need to lie." She paused. "So blatantly. We would portray you as a wealthy merchant in search of a respectable bride."

"But I thought I was to marry you?"

Again, she outwardly ignored his goading, although inside she wanted to brain him with the ornate candelabra on the table.

"We wouldn't tell him I was the rightful heir?" he pressed.

Glenna was close to the breaking point. "I don't know! He's unlikely to recover enough to understand any of what we say to him any matter," she shouted. The silence in the hall pulsated while she reined in her temper. "Marrying me would give your claim to Roscraig unquestionable legitimacy. A characteristic you'd otherwise be hard-pressed to achieve, no matter how successful you are in business."

His eyes narrowed even though he kept his half smile. "And you still managed to call me bastard." He returned his cup to the table and stood, looking her up and down. "Your hatred of me would likely pose a problem."

Glenna frowned. "I don't see how. I'll hate you as much here as I would if I were somewhere else."

His eyes sparkled. "I want children. Lots of children. My own heirs."

Glenna's stomach did a tumble. "I would fulfill my obligation to Roscraig."

To her surprise—and her dread—Tavish Cameron began to walk toward her slowly. "Is that how you would view our bairns? As mere obligations?"

"Most couples don't enjoy each other's company, and yet they have large families," she said stiffly. "I would of course welcome my own children."

He stood before her now, so close that she could feel the warmth of him in the cool air of the hall. She noticed his lips then, quirked in their familiar grin, and she realized that they were actually smooth and well shaped. "As many as I could give you?"

Glenna dropped her eyes to his tunic, made up of tens of red squares of velvet bound together by thick golden embroidery. "I would not wish to be bred to death, like some prized heifer."

"Of course not," he said, his voice lowered, changed in timbre just enough to cause a shock of gooseflesh to ripple up her arms. "Despite our arguments, I do find the looks of you quite pleasing."

She couldn't help raising her eyes to him quickly.

His lashes half hid his gaze as he looked down at her and his left hand came up to caress her cheek. Glenna flinched slightly at the surprising heat that tingled on her skin, but he did not pull away.

"Are you a virgin, princess?" he whispered.

The tenuous enchantment was broken. "What a vulgar—"

But he caught her wrist and held it between them. "Surely 'tis not vulgar to ask after the condition of the merchandise I'm being offered," he said in a low voice still, but this time the gentleness was gone, replaced with an insistent curiosity. "I've a right to know if another has laid a foundation on the land upon which I would build."

Glenna hoped her gaze burned him. "I have known no man."

"That's good, that's good," he said and then tugged her closer by the wrist he still held. "Come here."

She resisted. "Let go of me."

Tavish Cameron opened his fingers immediately, holding out his splayed palm as evidence for a moment before dropping it. But Glenna only saw this from the corner of her eye, since she could not tear her gaze away from his blue eyes. No matter the jesting tone in his words, his eyes held no mirth.

"Come here," he repeated.

Glenna stepped forward a pace—there was but a scant hand's breadth between them. Her face was turned directly up toward him now.

"Closer," he commanded.

She stepped her slippers between his feet and then they were touching, although both their hands remained at their sides.

"Good." Tavish Cameron seemed to be inspecting her mouth with those sparkling blue eyes. "Do you sing?" he asked.

Glenna felt her forehead crinkle. "What?"

"Do you sing? I've heard 'tis a desirable talent in a noble wife."

"Aye. I can sing."

"Dance?"

"Aye."

"Can you read?"

Her confusion turned to irritation in an instant, as it seemed wont to do with him, and she took as step away. "Of course. You're not inquiring for a steward. I—"

His hands were upon her in a flash, at her nape, her waist, pulling him back against him.

"I'm not finished," he said.

Despite her pride that screamed at her to again fight him to gain her freedom, Glenna stood still, her hands at her side, her gaze now on his throat. This was all for a greater purpose.

"Go on, then," she commanded.

But he was quiet for so long that Glenna looked once more to his face. Something smoldered in his eyes that stilled Glenna's impatience. She could feel the beating of his heart against her breast, and her own seemed to answer his, knocking against the tender mortal wall that separated them.

"Would you submit to me?" he whispered, lowering his head until his face hovered over hers. "As my wife?"

"Nay," Glenna whispered against his lips. "I will never submit to you."

"Never?" He kissed her bottom lip, then her top, barely pressing her flesh. "What about now?"

Glenna tried to shake her head, but it was still held in his large hand. She became alarmed at the sudden weakness in her own legs.

"I think I could persuade you," he murmured. "Aye, I think I could." And then he kissed her fully, deeply, as she lay in his arms stupid and helpless to deny him, deny the powerful, unexpected feelings coursing through her body.

Beyond the roar in her ears, she vaguely heard the clang of metal, the echo of hurrying footfalls in the stair and corridor beyond. But she was startled when Tavish Cameron broke their kiss and stood her aright, bracing her briefly with his hands on her shoulders before he turned back to the table for his cup.

Glenna blinked rapidly and brought her fingertips to her mouth as she watched him turn the cup upward, his back to her now.

Did this mean he accepted her proposal?

The footfalls were closer now, but they were not the crash of wide boots nor the stiff soles of the servants. Glenna turned dazedly toward the doorway of the hall as a dazzling image of ivory and green silk floated across the stones, a tall, gilded headdress atop a glut of shining red locks.

"Tavish," the woman breathed and rocked to a stop for a moment at the opposite end of the trestle table. She brought both hands to her mouth, just as Glenna herself had done, and then she picked up her skirts and ran the remaining length of the table, throwing herself into Tavish Cameron's arms and kissing both his cheeks. "I've wanted to do that for ever so long. And now I am free to, whenever I wish."

Glenna could feel the blood draining from her face as the couple pulled apart and the beautiful, splendidly outfitted woman turned a bashful glance toward Glenna.

"Forgive us," she said with a tinkling laugh. "We've not seen each other for some time."

Glenna only nodded, forced herself to swallow. She would not look at Tavish Cameron, even when his richly timbered voice spoke.

"Miss Glenna Douglas, of Tower Roscraig," he said. "Miss Audrey Keane of Edinburgh."

"Soon also to be of Tower Roscraig," the woman said with clear happiness in her voice as she turned her face back to Tavish.

Glenna's lungs froze so that that her "How do you do, excuse me," was stiff and breathy. She turned on her heel and strode toward the doorway, the wood feeling spongy beneath her thin slippers, seeking to escape as quickly as she could.

But not so quickly that she failed to hear Miss Keane's bewildered remark to the bastard standing in the hall with Glenna's pride in his fist.

"Do you address all the servants here by 'Miss,' darling?"

* * * *

"Ho there, Muir," Tavish called out as he came aboard the *Stygian* balancing the heavy trunk on his shoulder. He spotted the captain backing down the ladder from the forecastle beneath the sparkling night sky, the air cold and crisp in response to the balmy, bright day. The firth was high and boisterous after the days upon days of rain, and the *Stygian*'s planks rolled beneath Tavish like the crests and vales of a familiar road.

"Laird," Captain Muir greeted him with a clasping of hands. "I was on my way to the Tower. You needn't have come down."

"I wished to," Tavish replied, setting the chest down with a grunt. "I've been too long away from the *Stygian*. I might sleep aboard her tonight if you have no objection."

At this, Muir's slashing gray eyebrows rose. "She's yours; I suppose you will sleep where it pleases you. A sling upon the waters might fail to tempt even me away from a fine bed in a grand home such as Roscraig, though."

"Audrey has overtaken my chamber."

Muir laughed out loud. "I wondered why you'd brought the chest with you."

"Dammit, John, the invitation was for her father."

"And well aware of it, I am. But Master Keane had important business in a few days' time that could not be put off. Audrey wouldn't hear of staying in Edinburgh." Muir grinned again. "Your inheritance must have motivated the man to a greater extent than you'd hoped, Tav. Not only did he give his blessing for Audrey to journey to Roscraig, he took it upon himself to send along her dowry in anticipation."

Tavish turned his face toward John. "What?"

"Staking their claim on the realm's newest laird. Niall must be eager to be quit of her. I'd be wary, were I you."

"My letter didn't ask for Audrey's hand," Tavish said. "Naught was agreed upon."

"I doona think your protests shall be too great," Muir said, his tone containing just enough humor to suggest he didn't believe a word Tavish was saying. "I've a trunk below with five hundred pounds Scots and the deed to a tenant farm west of Dunfermline."

"Five hun—" Tavish broke off, running his hands through his hair and turning away from Muir to walk to the port rail and lean his forearms on it, looking out over the roiling waves.

He heard the captain's footfalls approach behind him. "I'd planned to deliver the good news to you myself, along with the trunk and a bottle of brandy that somehow escaped its crate. But something tells me you're in no mood to celebrate."

"Five hundred pounds, Muir," Tavish mused.

The captain's tone was incredulous. "Is it not enough?"

Tavish turned his head to look at the older man. "I'd have taken two. It's *Audrey*. Remember when the two of us would compete for her attention? Her father threatened me with the stocks more than once."

Muir chuckled. "Aye. And he threatened to have me thrown from his ship in the middle of the ocean. I believe I was ten and three, the first time."

"You eventually came to sail for me any matter."

"I wanted to carry something other than wool and hides. Niall Keane was too concerned with kissing the burgess's arse to take on cargo worthy of a voyage."

"Always was a bit of pirate in you, Muir."

"Bah. Hauling wool and hides has made Niall Keane fat and complacent. Meanwhile, look at us." Muir reached across and slapped Tavish's flat stomach so that his breath left him in a huffing laugh.

"Fat and complacent, maybe. But most certainly safer. And richer." Tavish stared out over the water with a sigh. "Now he supposes I'm good enough to marry his daughter. A farm, as well, you say?"

"Dunfermline. Three hundred acres. Master Keane is eager to sign it over to you once you've your da's title. There's a small manor house for an overseer, when there is one; mostly families growing wool for Keane. But if it should become a wedding gift for his son-in-law, the laird of Roscraig..." Muir paused for a moment. "I believe he's of the mind that you might wish to go into business with him."

Tavish hung his head. It was a dream come true—everything he'd ever wished for.

"This is all too soon. I can't marry Audrey—I can't marry anyone—until the king comes," Tavish muttered. And Glenna Douglas—he needed time to explain to her. "I do not accept the dowry. You'll have to carry Audrey back to Edinburgh on the morrow, Muir. With Keane's trunk. The man assumes too much."

"Nay, Tav," the captain said on a laugh. "One voyage with the lass was enough—we're nae pups any longer. Her father wouldna be pleased. Besides," Muir straightened from the railing, "you need Audrey to prepare for your guests."

Tavish stilled. "What guests?"

"The guests for the feasts."

"What feasts?"

"The feasts Miss Keane has invited the guests to." John slapped Tavish's shoulder. "What do you say, laird? Shall we seek Poseidon together?"

Tavish waved his hand at his friend. As much as he would like to forget his own troubles in a drunken stupor, he must keep a clear head tonight. "I'm not fit company, John."

The captain squeezed Tavish's shoulder briefly. "With that I canna argue."

As Muir's footfalls echoed on the wood away from him, Tavish turned and leaned his back against the railing to stare up at the twin turrets silhouetted against the night sky. Several round-topped windows in each tower glowed from within.

He now found himself in the midst of a problem he'd not anticipated. Even if he wanted to help Glenna Douglas in her plight, he'd hinted to the wealthiest merchant in Edinburgh that he would soon be looking for a bride, and the man had enthusiastically charged ahead. Audrey was here now. She was his friend, and she *wanted* to be his wife. No matter what had prompted the stiff Miss Douglas to offer herself up to Tavish, no matter the even stranger urge he'd relented to in kissing her and turning the prickly woman—even temporarily—into a warm, pliable pleasure in his arms, he could not accept her offer.

There was no room now at Roscraig for Glenna Douglas, literally or figuratively.

He found himself wondering what it would be like to kiss her again, and then chuckled as he realized that she would likely just try to kill him next time and have done with it. He couldn't allow the Douglases to stay at Roscraig indefinitely, but to appease Tavish's conscience, Iain Douglas could live his last days in his own bed. Tavish would perhaps offer Miss Douglas the manor house at the Dunfermline farm. That would give her a place to live to preserve the illusion of her station and her pride, and would perhaps placate Tavish's mother.

And yet, he could not stop calling to mind the sprig of spring greenery in her hair and how readily she had come to him when he'd not forced her; the way his heart had beat while he'd held her; the sweet taste of her soft mouth.

Tavish shook his head. Glenna Douglas was noble—of course she'd known the right things to say and do to turn his head. It was all a ploy to get what she wanted, nothing more.

Too bad for the princess—it was Tavish's turn to get what he wanted.

Chapter 8

Glenna sat at her father's bedside the next morning, watching him sleep. She felt she'd done nothing else for years now, just sitting there, watching Iain Douglas die while their world crumbled down around them.

Only now, his skin was not quite so transparent, his lips no longer cracked and gaping. His periods of consciousness were brief and few, but it no longer felt like he was slipping into labored, wheezing oblivion when he closed his eyes. His grasp on reality, however, remained tenuous and fleeting.

He slept now, and Glenna was glad that she wasn't forced to pretend a smile, encourage his awareness. She'd never felt so humiliated, such rage as when riding the ugly ocean of feelings that had borne her along through the night and brought her to land on this uncertain and desolate shore of her father's bedside.

Tavish Cameron had led her on, allowed her to make a fool of herself, knowing full well that he was wedding another. He was in fact waiting on her arrival even while he'd kissed her.

Miss Keane. Miss Audrey Keane. A beautiful, stylish young woman, obviously of considerable wealth by her manner of dress, but not a titled lady. And yet Audrey Keane, a commoner, would take Glenna's place at Roscraig. Take her place as Lady at Tavish Cameron's side.

What a grand joke he likely thought it.

She heard the door squeak open behind her but didn't turn. It would be Harriet, bringing the morning supplies to care for Glenna's father.

"Good morn, Miss Douglas."

His deep voice caused her to flinch, and she turned her head slowly, unable to believe that he would show his face here, of all places.

And yet, there he was, pushing the door closed behind him and then standing at the end of the bed, looking not at her, but at the still figure of her father. Glenna's gaze never left him, her eyes narrowing into a glare.

"What do you want?" she whispered through her teeth, trying to forget it was the exact question he'd posed to her the night before.

It seemed to take some effort for Tavish Cameron to look away from her father and meet her eyes. "To apologize."

Glenna continued to glare at him.

"I wasn't expecting Miss Keane last night," he added.

"You weren't expecting her last night. You hoped to have more time to toy with me, is that it?" Glenna hissed.

"Nay," he said mildly. "That wasn't my intention at all."

"Nor was it your intention to tell me you'd asked another to marry you after I'd made a fool of myself?"

"Everything about last night was unexpected. But now that Audrey is here...it would be best that you find other accommodations. We are expecting guests."

Glenna knew her mouth had fallen open, but she didn't care. Did this man have no shame?

He continued. "I know you have objection about moving to the village, and so I can make arrangements for a manor house on a farm at Dunfermline. It's not so very far, and there will be servants to care for you. You may depart this afternoon."

Glenna bolted from her chair at last. She wanted to shout and yet was forced to speak in a hissing whispers. "Look at him! Look at him, you fool! Think you he can be moved?"

"Your father may stay until his end," Tavish said quietly.

She began shaking her head even before she could command her mouth to speak. "Nay. I won't leave him. You can't possibly think—"

"My mother will continue to care for him. I've already commanded my servants to begin packing your things."

"Nay!" Glenna insisted, her voice rising with the hysteria that was building inside her. She stepped toward the door as if to leave and then looked back at her father, her emotions in such turmoil that she didn't know which way to turn, what to say. "You can't simply...eject me! This is my home! Who do you think you are?"

"You will likely be happier at Dunfermline than you would be seeing me in your father's place. There is no role for you here. Audrey will have little sympathy for you when she learns of your...circumstances."

"You mean the circumstances that I am rightful lady? That a bastard's come in and stolen my home?" she croaked, unable to prevent the sob that was building in her throat.

"It will be an easy journey," he said, no longer looking at her. "I will have word sent to you regularly until…" His words trailed away.

Glenna flew across the floor, and he raised his hands to catch her before she threw herself upon him.

"Stop, Miss Douglas," he warned quietly. "Don't make this harder than it must be."

But she didn't fight him—it was pointless. He was so much stronger than her, and Glenna knew it would take very little effort to have her removed from Roscraig. "You can't do this," she repeated, and felt the tears at last course down her cheeks, but she was unable to care as her humiliation was now complete. She had no pride left, no home, nothing. "Please, please. Tavish—laird—please, don't send me from him. He's all I have left."

"Don't cry," he whispered, looking away from her face.

"Why?" she demanded. "Doesn't it please you to hurt me? To wound one of your betters? Aren't I to pay for what your father did to you?"

"You're not my better," he said in a gravelly voice, and yet he still would not look at her.

"*I am,*" she insisted on a hiccough and pounded once on his chest with her fists. "*I am* your better, Tavish Cameron. I was born at Roscraig a lady. And I am lady here still. Last night you wanted me." She sniffed and jerked her hands free and then reached up with both palms and laid them alongside his face to turn his gaze toward her. "You kissed me, and you wanted me last night. Do you want me still?" She raised up on her toes and pressed her mouth to his.

He turned his head away. "Glenna, stop," he whispered.

"You do," she insisted, turning his face back, forcing him to look at her. "You do want me—a lady. Something fine that would otherwise be out of your reach." She kissed him again, with such force that he fell back a step, and Glenna felt his hands come to her waist. She pulled away and looked into his eyes, even as angry tears that still trickled from hers. "I'm not some ha'penny shopkeep's brat who's in awe of you. I'm better than you. And more than you. And—"

Her words were cut off as Tavish kissed her this time. Glenna poured her anger into returning his kiss, wrapping her arms around his neck, pressing her trembling body into his. When at last he pulled away, he was breathing hard and glaring down into her face.

"I do want you," he admitted. "But I won't marry you."

"Then keep me," she challenged, the words out of her mouth before she fully realized the idea. "Keep me here, as your mistress. Live up to your reputation and now your status. I dare you." Her heart was galloping in her chest like a runaway horse—she couldn't think about what she was suggesting, the meaning behind it.

And so she stood up taller on her bravado, pressing him, goading him intentionally. "Or are you too afraid? Afraid to handle a possession so far above you? Afraid that I would outplay your Miss Keane?"

She should have been humiliated, pitting herself against a common wench like Audrey Keane for the attentions of a lying, bastard Edinburgh merchant; a man who was willingly destroying what was left of her life. And yet, she found her stomach clenching in anticipation now that Tavish Cameron was holding her even closer.

"You don't know the rules of the game in which you are entering, princess," he said, even as his hands roved her back and his desire pressed into her stomach. "I need not promise you anything. Should you not please me, I'll have you moved to Dunfermline and there'll be no arguing."

"Or perhaps you'll not please me. Perhaps I shall go on my own," she retorted in a shaking whisper against his mouth.

"It will serve you well, I think," he said between his teeth, "to be taken down a notch while in my *employment*. And so I agree to your offer." He stepped away from her abruptly, bringing a chill of air to wrap around her shoulders and replace his warmth. "Miss Keane settled into my chamber last night; the servants are even now moving my things into yours."

"Very well," Glenna said, lifting her chin and trying to project an air of triumph. "I'll bring my belongings here."

"You shall leave your belongings where they are," he corrected, his eyes burning a fiery path across her collarbone before meeting her gaze once more. "Your employment begins immediately. I will require you to entertain my guests as part of your duties, so perhaps try a bit with the way you dress, hmm? Your other tasks will not require so many clothes."

He left her then, her cheeks still flaming, dizzy with what she had agreed to.

Glenna had sold herself to Tavish Cameron.

* * * *

Tavish wasted no time in leaving the Tower, crossing the tall, narrow bridge and clomping down the mud-slicked path toward the village. He was eager to escape without catching sight of either Audrey Keane or his

mother, and luckily the tasks before him distracted his fuzzied mind away
from the memory of Glenna Douglas in his arms, pressing her hips—

He turned toward the path and made his way around the village to where
the track began to snake up the cliff. He passed the round stone doocot and
decided he liked the look of it very much, ducking inside it for a moment
to admire the cubbies and the fecund quiet of it. It didn't seem a place that
would provide a poisoned medium.

His doocot.

He reached inside one of the indentations and felt a small, warm oval
nestled in the prickly grass. He withdrew the egg and tossed it slightly in
the air before catching it in his palm and carrying it from the shelter with
him. An offering, of sorts, from a pilgrim. Of sorts.

Tavish continued up the path until the trees disappeared from the edge,
and the path widened into a hilltop meadow, punctuated with stone obelisks
and crosses. A small cottage was set back against the treeline, its chimney
releasing a wispy column of sweetly spicy smoke.

As if the man had been awaiting his arrival, the wooden door of the
cottage opened and the dark monk, Dubhán, emerged, pulling the door
closed behind him and crossing the graveyard with a bright smile on his face.

"Laird Cameron, a pleasant surprise," he said. "Good day."

"Good day, Dubhán. I came to apologize for the brevity of my hospitality
last night. My attentions have been spread thin since my arrival." He held
out his hand, revealing the tiny egg. "An offering for the saint of the cave."

"Ah," the monk said, taking the small oval and holding it up between
thumb and forefinger as if to examine it. "It is just the thing." He lowered
the egg with a genial smile. "The path is treacherous, as I have said."

"I'd hoped you would lead me," Tavish ventured.

"Gladly," Dubhán said. "But I have traveled it many times. And the rain
has only increased its hazard. I would not dare to forbid my lord passage,
but it would be a shame for you to give up Roscraig when you've only just
taken it, even if it is for a greater reward."

Tavish laughed. "I've kept my feet upon many an ice-slicked deck in
the midst of a winter gale, Dubhán. I have no fear of a muddy path."

The dark man gave a bow. "As you wish, laird." He then tucked the egg
inside his robes and walked straight toward the edge of the cliff, where the
bright sunlight glinted over the wide expanse of the firth like diamonds
rolling over gray velvet. As Dubhán came to the cusp of land, he turned
back to Tavish. "We begin here."

Tavish looked down. There didn't seem to be a path at all, only a flat
stone jutting out from the cliff a hand's breadth below where the grass
poked out into the breeze. He looked back to Dubhán.

"That's the path?"

Dubhán nodded and smiled. "The way is narrow, laird."

Tavish raised his eyebrows at the monk.

Dubhán laughed. "Have no fear. If it is his will, we will be preserved. Only mind the vines—one slip when the wind blows just so..."

"Only mind the vines," Tavish muttered as he neared the cliff edge and pushed back the heavy curtain of ropy climbers. He saw the water of the firth foaming around the rocks far below. "I think I'll concentrate on not falling to my death."

"Also advisable, laird," Dubhán agreed in an admiring tone.

Tavish took a deep breath and then stepped after the monk, Dubhán's whispering Latin hissing by his ears on the cliff breeze.

* * * *

Frang Roy stood in the entry hall, looking about himself uneasily at the bustling strangers weaving over the corridors and the courtyard overlooking the firth. They all seemed busy and comfortable with their duties—as if they had always called Roscraig their home. No one was paying him any mind, and the nosy old woman who had denied him on his previous visit was nowhere to be seen.

He made his way into the spiraling stone corridor that led to the east tower, his senses on high alert for anyone who might question his presence. At the doorway to the great hall, Frang paused. The room had been transformed into a stately and fine chamber, the likes of which he could never recall seeing in the old stone keep. Shining candelabra, colorful tapestries; there was even a muted portrait of three strangers hanging on the wide chimney—the first painting Frang Roy had ever seen in his life.

He stared at the piece of art for several moments, and his frown increased. Then he continued up the stairs, his intended destination the chamber that lay above the great hall, but Lady Glenna's room was empty. Frang returned to the entry corridor and crossed it, jostling the line of servants descending the western stairs and forcing them to juggle their carefully balanced trunks and furnishings.

The door was open to a chamber on the second floor, and Frang stood a moment in the doorway, watching the woman at the window, her back toward him. Glenna was wearing a fine gown he'd not seen before, one that lent exaggerated curves to her slender frame, and a tall, ornate head covering that hid her curls.

Frang Roy stepped into the room just as she turned.

"Oh!" she said. "I thought you'd all gone." She walked toward him.

It was not Glenna Douglas. This woman was red-haired, with wide eyes and a bow mouth; voluptuously made and dressed. Frang froze.

"I suppose you might as well take that dreadful thing next," she was saying, frowning distastefully at an old, handsomely carved chair.

"Where is Lady Glenna?" he blurted.

The woman's frown turned decidedly more ominous as she looked at him directly at last. "How should I know?" Her eyes narrowed as she looked him up and down, as if at last truly seeing him. "I understand from the other servants that the laird has forbidden anyone from addressing the girl who lives here as lady." She paused. "I don't recognize you; where are the other men?"

"Takin' a rest," Frang said carefully.

"Overexerted already, are they?" the woman said. "I suppose I shouldn't be surprised—father says country servants are lazy. Any matter, stop calling her lady." She looked at Frang expectantly. "Well?" And then gestured to the chair.

Frang stood still. "Where am I to take it?"

The redhead gave an exasperated sigh. "Where am I to take it, *Miss Keane*," she corrected. "For the next month any matter, and then you shall address me as Lady Cameron. Do you understand? *Do you*?" She put her hands on her hips. "Are you slow?"

Frang stuttered. He had the instinctive urge to step forward and twist the woman's head sharply just so she would cease talking.

"Where am I to take it, Miss—Miss Keane?"

"Harriet's hired you, likely," the woman murmured with a roll of her eyes. "It's to go to the other tower. The chamber the laird has taken up." Her tone was so cool, Frang wouldn't have been surprised to see frost come from her lips as she spoke. "*For now.*"

Frang said no more, but stepped forward to heft the heavy chair into his arms. He turned it horizontally against his ribs and left the chamber.

He had to slant the chair up as he made his way down the tight curve of the staircase, and again after he crossed the entry and mounted the steps to the east tower. Each of his footfalls trod more forcefully than the last as he tried to make sense of the woman's words.

He came into Glenna's chamber once more, his breathing labored more by his mental exertions rather than the physical act of carrying the chair. He set it down on the floorboards with a grunt and a crash and soon realized that the chamber was no longer unoccupied. His and Glenna Douglas's eyes met in the same instant, and even as she turned quickly toward the door, Frang reached behind him and closed it, stepping fully between the blond woman and the exit.

She stiffened her posture. "Get out, Frang." Her eyes were red-rimmed, her cheeks flushed, her lips scarlet slashes in the daytime gloom of the chamber that washed her skin to chalk.

"You didna give me an answer, Lady Glenna," he said. "An answer to my offer. And now look at the mess we're all in."

She said nothing, but he saw her throat flex as she swallowed. Then she held out her arms and looked around pointedly, indicating the chamber in which they faced each other. "This is the only choice I have if I am to retain any sort of hold over my home and the laird's health."

Frang frowned. "I s'pose you reckon you've a better lot with that prick what's taken over 'round here, aye?" He began to step toward her. "You his whore now? S'what the redhead woman said."

"Stop right where you are, Frang Roy," she warned boldly, but he could hear the warble in her voice.

"You think he's to let you keep the Tower s'long as you spread your legs for him? What would yer da say? Your mother?"

"What I do as lady of this hold has naught to do with you. If…if you go now, I shan't say anything to him. He'll not know you were here."

"Here?" Frang needled. "In your bedchamber, you mean, where his servants are bringing his belongings?" He stopped now, in arms' reach of her. "I said, that redheaded bitch told me you was his whore now. But I wanna hear it from you."

"Frang, you surely understand that I could never marry you," she said in a breathy voice, as if her throat was being constricted, making the words' escape difficult. "I am a lady. You…you are a—"

"Peasant?" he finished for her. "A common farmer?" He snorted darkly. "If it's coin you think we'll be lacking, I can get you coin."

"Frang," she began.

He stepped closer, lowered his voice. "Oh, my Glenna…there are things I want to say. Things I will tell you, teach you." He raised his hand as if to touch her hair.

She flinched and backed away. "You frighten me when you speak this way. I am waiting for the king's arrival. I will present my case to him, and he will decide Roscraig's fate."

"'Twas my hope that you'd choose me willingly," Frang said, his words cajoling even as he voice tightened with impatience. He stepped closer to her. "I can give you all you wish but for a bit of kindness."

"You canna give me anything," she said, sliding her feet backward. "You would have hurt me had Dubhán nae come along."

"I only wished to protect you. I love you, milady—I do." He followed. "Your cruelty isna comely. I'm giving you a choice yet again. If you again refuse me, you will have nae protection from the piss ant Cameron, the king—nor even the servants what's been brung here and ordered to treat you like dirt. There are worse people than I who would do you harm. And when they are finished with you..." He raised his hands.

The door to the chamber opened with a squeak, and Frang Roy turned his head.

"—enough to wait for—" Tavish Cameron broke off, his hand still on the door latch. Dubhán and a rugged-looking gray-haired man stood behind him in the corridor. "What the hell are you doing in here?"

Frang Roy walked casually toward the door. "Miss Keane bade me carry a chair to this chamber." He made to move past the smaller man, but Tavish Cameron stopped him with a hand upon his chest. Frang reluctantly halted and looked pointedly down at the man's offending touch—like a cat's paw upon the chest of an ox. He then looked into Tavish's face.

"I told you not to show yourself about this hold until you were able to act respectfully. And now I find you in my very chamber."

"Worried I'll steal your sweet?" Frang smirked.

"This is only our second meeting, and I've already had more than enough of you," Cameron said. "Gather your things and join the party leaving for Dunfermline this afternoon. I'll have Alec give you a coin for your work today."

"You're banishing me from Roscraig?" Frang asked with a chuckle. "Do you wish to starve?"

"Laird," Dubhán said quietly from behind him. "Roscraig has been without a strong leader for many years. Frang has kept his own counsel in that time, and it's he who ensures the fields are planted."

"Roscraig's fields have been mismanaged for years, just as everything else in the hold. Gather your things, and get out," Tavish Cameron repeated. "I care not if you go on to Dunfermline, but you'll not stay here."

"I'm nae going anywhere," Frang scoffed. "You've nae right to—"

The laird drew his sword. "This afternoon. The next time I see you on my lands you're a dead man."

"My gracious, all this fuss over an ugly old chair?" a melodic voice called out, and Miss Keane entered the room from the corridor. "What did he do, set it on the bedstead? He didn't seem very clever, I admit. I wondered to myself if he would get lost on the way."

Frang wove his way through the crowd, jostling both Tavish Cameron and Friar Dubhán on his way out. "You'll get what's comin' to you," he growled.

The chamber was filled with awkward silence for a moment, and then Audrey Keane broke in. "I hope it wasn't something I said."

John Muir gave the woman a short bow. "'He may answer, and say this and that; I care not, for I speak right as I mean.' I'm certain your words held naught but the truth, Miss Keane."

She gave the sea captain a grateful smile. "You flatter me with Chaucer, Captain Muir." Her face held a pretty flush when she looked back to Tavish Cameron. "Laird, the guests are beginning to arrive."

Tavish sheathed his sword. "Thank you, Miss Keane."

She stood there a moment longer, her eyes darting to the blond woman whose head drooped, and then she fastened a bright smile to her face. "Shall I help you ready?"

"Nay," Tavish said. "I have assistance, should I require it."

Her smile faltered a bit. "I shall meet you in the hall, then. Good day, Captain. I do very much hope your schedule allows you to join us. 'You're so merry and jocund, that at a revel when I see you dance, it is a salve for my every wound.'"

She curtsied to Muir's bow, then left the room.

"Miss Douglas," Tavish began. "Were you harmed?"

"Nay."

"Very good. You shall attend the feast, as well."

She raised her head and looked at him, and her eyes were wild even as her chin lifted proudly. "Am I to serve you?"

"You are to entertain. I excuse you to ready yourself elsewhere. I have need to conduct some business in my chamber."

"Does this business involve Roscraig?"

"That is none of your concern."

They stared at each other for a moment and then Glenna lifted her chin and turned from him. "Good day, Dubhán; Captain Muir, I must apologize that we have not yet been properly introduced. I wish you farewell until we meet again."

The two men murmured courtesies to her but would not meet her gaze as Tavish held the door open. As soon as Glenna had passed into the corridor, the merchant closed the door firmly behind her.

She heard the bolt slide home.

Chapter 9

After Tavish Cameron had evicted her from her own chamber while he conducted his secret business, Glenna had ascended to her father's chamber, where she had managed to find a faded blue kirtle she'd not worn since she was ten and two in the bottom of a trunk. She'd grabbed up her sewing basket with its few precious supplies, but found no place inside the keep with good enough light where she felt she would not be stared at or be in danger of encountering Audrey Keane. So Glenna spent the afternoon in the courtyard behind the stone kitchen, sitting on a low, splintery stool with an old gown on her lap and a needle in her hand.

The garment was shorter than she'd guessed it would be; the bodice and hips too narrow. It was stained near the waist and frayed at the yoke, evidence of a frock worn by a more carefree and rambunctious girl. Glenna spent the next several hours carefully separating sections of seam and undoing the hem, painstakingly rejoining them at the very limits of their boundaries. She embroidered tiny crosses over the frayed edges, scrubbed at the stain with salt. When she was finished, it looked little better than a large rag, the expanded seams clearly showing a darker stripe of color where it had been protected for so many years.

But, like everything else in her life now, Glenna had little choice but to wear it.

She sat with the finished kirtle in her lap, resting her aching back against the warm stones of the kitchen while the breeze off the firth lifted her hair from her neck. She closed her eyes for a moment and listened to the ghostly sounds of laughter and conversation coming from the mouth of the entry hall. So many voices and sounds—animals and servants; the muffled rattles and chopping from the building that hid her. It seemed over loud to her now, after so many years of tight-spiraling quiet.

Glenna stood up with a sigh and folded the kirtle into a tidy package. She spent only a moment in the kitchen, ducking in to retrieve the slickstone from a shelf and place it in the lined basket to carry with her. She kept her head down and walked swiftly through the entry hall and up the stairs, flattening herself against the stones as strangers came and went through her home, heedless to the fact that they passed the lady of Roscraig. The great hall was already milling with people—guests, she reminded herself—their raucous conversations spilling out and assaulting her as she dashed past.

Glenna paused at the head of the corridor when she saw the man standing before her chamber door. Alec, she reminded herself, in charge of the many sailors Tavish Cameron now employed in the village. She began walking once more, wondering with a growing knot in her stomach if he would refuse her entry, but upon seeing her, he immediately stepped to the side of the doorway.

"Miss," he said, fixing his gaze on the stone wall across from him. "The laird wished me to tell you that he will expect you in the great hall."

Her step faltered only a bit, and Glenna didn't think he'd noticed. "Thank you." She went inside as quickly as she could without throwing herself through the door.

She leaned against the wood with a sigh. Her chamber was again blessedly empty of people, although it had been taken over by several new pieces of furniture. Glenna set the bundled gown and basket on the bed as she looked around, noticing the wide table pushed against a wall and paired with the old, tall chair; four large trunks held closed with great bandings and hasps; a wide, low shelf of sorts, populated like a beehive with a score or more of little square cells, most housing rolls of tied parchment and vellum. A fire had been laid some time ago, it would seem, and the typically cool chamber was warm and quiet.

It smelled different too from when she'd left it only hours ago—before, she'd never thought the chamber possessed a distinctive scent, but now the air seemed imbued with the heady fragrances of leather oil and clove, and even something sweet and floral. Glenna tried to ignore it, but she found herself drawing deep breaths of it, savoring the sensuous atmosphere.

Tavish Cameron had not only taken over her home, but the very air she breathed.

Glenna laid a cloth on the floor before the fire and set to carefully pressing the years-old creases from the blue kirtle with the slickstone until her shoulder ached. When that was done, she quickly disrobed down to her skin then pulled the scratchy woolen work gown back on to cover herself while she pressed her yellowed and frayed underdress. It did little to improve the garment, but it was her only one, and it did look a little better to her eyes after the attention.

The same dented pitcher and bowl and her wooden comb still stood on her own small table, but now there was also a fresh cake of soap and a stack of snowy cloths resting on the wood, and a short, carved cup holding a clutch of sweet violets. Glenna washed thoroughly, relishing the clean feeling of her skin and the scent of the tiny blooms on her wash table. She soaped her hair, scrubbing at her scalp and rinsing it repeatedly until half of the water from the bowl was soaking into the floorboards and the woolen gown was thoroughly wet.

Glenna didn't care. Gaining confidence in her privacy, she removed the old gray kirtle and used it to press the moisture from her hair, and then sat upon the wool before the hearth while her skin dried and she pulled the wooden comb through her curls until they glistened like gilded flourishes. Then she carefully tightened the brittle cords on her old slippers and brushed at the thinning leather with the rough, damp wool.

She stood and pulled on her ensemble, feeling more and more like that younger, more carefree girl who had once worn this same blue gown. Clean of body, with tidy clothing and freshened shoes; her hair shone and bounced as she gathered it atop her head with a scrap of fabric to cascade in a river of curls down her back. The final touch was a handful of the violet blooms to adorn her hair. She inhaled deeply and was satisfied: She had done her best to represent Roscraig as its rightful lady at the first feast the Tower had known in—

Glenna couldn't remember.

But tonight she would show Tavish Cameron that she could serve him better as lady of Roscraig than Audrey Keane could ever dream of.

She took a deep breath and opened the chamber door, but stood there for so long before stepping through the doorway that the guard stationed in the corridor finally turned his head.

"All is well, miss?"

"I believe so," Glenna said with a frown. Then she looked the young man in the face. "Aye. I am well. Thank you, Alec."

The guard smiled. "You look well, if you don't take offense at my plain speech."

Glenna returned his smile.

"Mistress Harriet didn't wish to disturb you, but she bade me give you this." When Glenna held out her palm, Alec placed a metal object into it.

Glenna's eyes widened. It was her father's shawl brooch, round, silver filigree with a double bar across its center, adorned with a small, polished onyx stone. Glenna wondered where Harriet had found it—Glenna had not seen the piece in years and had all but forgotten about it.

Or perhaps, in the back of her mind, she'd thought Iain Douglas had sold it long ago.

"Thank you," she repeated, and then turned away slightly to fasten the brooch at the top of the yoke of her kirtle, near the black embroidery. She turned back to Alec, who nodded.

"Just the thing," he said approvingly.

Glenna inclined her head in thanks and almost laughed as she turned away with a sweep of her old, patched skirts and descended the stairs. This time she did not cower into the stones when another approached her, but looked them in the eye boldly, and it was they who stepped aside for her passing, acknowledging her presence.

"Good evening, mistress."

"Miss."

"Beg pardon, miss."

The roar of conversation and thin strains of music swelled as she neared the great hall, and when she drew close to the doorway, she could feel the heat blasting from it like a forge, carrying the scent of cologne and roasted meat, the hoppy smell of ale. Glenna took another deep breath, lifted her chin and stepped inside the hall.

It was alive with sound and color, so vivid and loud that Glenna was thrown temporarily into a state of wonder—could this lively, bright place be the same haunted, black hall of a month ago, that dripped water onto worn, bare wood, and where the winter winds blasted unchecked through yonder windows, now festooned with billowing draperies and folded-back shutters? The walls rippled with candlelight and colorful woven pictures, the air shimmered with twanging music and the smells of the steaming platters of food coursing along the current of bustling servants.

Glenna's stomach growled, and she had to swallow the saliva that flooded her mouth. She'd not seen this much food in one place her entire life—perhaps she'd not seen this much food in total in her entire life. And now it was overflowing the long trestle, its considerable length augmented by what appeared to be a half dozen more tables and benches.

A kitchen servant Glenna recognized as one of Harriet's favorite pupils approached her side with a tray in hand brimming with metal chalices, and she held it toward Glenna with a smile.

Glenna took one with a murmur of thanks and brought it to her lips. The wine was warm and rich and delicious, and as she drank, she glimpsed Tavish Cameron standing beneath the old portrait before the hearth, talking in earnest with a trio of men that included Captain Muir. She held her head high as she weaved her way through the sea of strangers; no one moved aside for her here, and few paid her any more heed than a passing glance.

She did notice a young, finely dressed man appraising her with a pleased expression, and when his gaze at last met Glenna's she nodded at him.

"Welcome to Tower Roscraig," she said.

The man's eyebrows rose for an instant before closing into an offended frown, and he turned away. Glenna's stomach clenched at the blatant snub, and the tiniest spark of fear began to smolder once more as if to try to warn her.

She ignored it as nothing more than nerves.

At last she came upon the group of men. Tavish Cameron caught her gaze and looked away and then looked back at once, realizing it was her.

But it was Muir who spoke first, and with a short bow. "Good evening, Miss Douglas."

The other two men followed suit, murmuring their greeting and then turning toward each other in a return to conversation and drifting away from the hearth.

"Captain Muir," Glenna said. Then she looked up at Tavish Cameron, who—although he had been staring at her the entire time—had yet to speak a word.

Muir cleared his throat. "If you'll excuse me, I believe I see someone I know."

Glenna didn't watch the captain depart; she couldn't take her eyes from the tall man standing before her with chalice in hand, his hair slicked back from his forehead, his fine, light-colored linen tunic adorned with a dark, silken shawl and wide, embossed belt. She could detect his scent—the same fragrance that had taken over her chamber.

He looked her up and down blatantly, and a slight frown creased his forehead as he gave her a confused look.

Glenna let a small smile play over her lips. He was pleased.

"Good evening, Master Cameron," she said, her confidence letting her grant a bit of leniency to their heretofore tense interactions. She felt good this evening, hoping that perhaps there was yet chance that the misfortune that had haunted not only Glenna but all of Roscraig—crowned by the arrival of the merchant before her—could be concluded happily. "I am ready to play hostess as you requested, although your feast seems to already be a success."

His frown deepened. "What are you wearing?"

She blinked and glanced down at her dress quickly. "I—what?"

"I said," he growled through his teeth, "what are you wearing? I instructed you to dress appropriately."

Glenna swallowed, feeling her cheeks begin to tingle. She opened her mouth—to say what, she didn't know—but was interrupted by a gay hailing from behind.

"There you are, laird," a woman's voice called, and Glenna knew it was Audrey Keane. She reluctantly turned. And gasped under her breath.

The woman was bedecked in such a costume as to seem fantastical. Her gown was purest white, the kirtle so finely woven that it shimmered in the candlelight, the sleeves of her underdress glistened, and Glenna knew in a moment that they must both be silk. Audrey Keane wore two long strands of pearls, one nearly to her waist, and each boasted an oval ruby the size of one of Roscraig's pigeon eggs. Her red hair had been combed out and plaited into what appeared to be a hundred tiny ropes and then gathered into a swag within a white-corded snood, fastened to her crown with a tiny silver-spiked crest. Her pale skin was translucent in the glow, her lips perfectly shaped and darkened with wine. It was like looking at a field of winter snow where an angel had strewn red rose petals.

Audrey Keane was accompanied by two young women wearing glittering brocades and striped silks, their necks and ears dripping with gold and polished gems; their cheeks rouged, their faces powdered white beneath severely plucked eyebrows.

Glenna couldn't help but glance down at her own gown, nearly a score of years old, made for a girl and patched with her own hand. Glenna thought she could feel her careful seams pulling beneath her arms with every strangled breath, as if the kirtle would fall apart at any moment. She may as well have been a peasant woman, just come into the hall from the fields.

"Why, Miss Douglas," Audrey Keane said with a sly smile. "How quaint. The quintessential country lass. If only for want of a crook, one might take you for a shepherdess."

The two companions twittered.

"How rude of me," Audrey continued, when it was clear that Glenna was not going to respond to her comments. "Allow me to introduce my friends. This is Miss Conner and Miss Haversham, from Edinburgh. Girls, this is Miss Douglas. *Her father* claimed to be laird of Roscraig, before

Laird Cameron rightfully inherited the hold from his father. *An English baron*," she emphasized.

Beneath the heat in her face, Glenna felt the rage burning like a hidden oven in her chest.

"What's she still doing here then?" one of the girls asked as she looked Glenna up and down with a smirk.

"My father *is still* the laird of Roscraig, until the king says otherwise," Glenna said, being sure to meet Audrey Keane's gaze. "And unless that day arrives, you will address me as Lady Glenna, if address me you must."

Audrey Keane's two companions gasped and looked to their friend with twin expressions of anticipation, while the pale woman's powdered cheeks bloomed with pink contempt.

"*Her father is still alive?*" one of the women whispered salaciously. It was a glorious playing out of outrageous gossip.

Audrey sniffed. "I expect he'll drop dead of embarrassment as soon as he hears of his daughter's barbaric behavior. What more can be expected of a recluse girl raised by a fraud?"

Glenna stepped toward Audrey Keane, eliciting a trio of shrieks from the women. But she was stopped by a tight hand on her arm, and Tavish Cameron pulled her back to his side, turning her with a jerk to face him.

He glared down at her. "Go to your chamber," he said through his teeth.

"I'll not allow her to slander me or my father." Glenna turned her head to look over her shoulder. "Speaking of fraud as though she wasn't but a festooned tinker's brat."

"And so you will go to your chamber," Tavish repeated, shaking her arm to draw her attention once more.

Glenna's angry trembling increased to accommodate her confusion. "But you wished for me to—"

She was cut off by Tavish Cameron's curt "Excuse us."

He pulled her through the hall, keeping her tight against his side as the crowd parted for him and leaned down to speak near her ear. "I wished for you to entertain the guests, aye. But not by creating gossip and bringing shame to me."

She jerked away from him, and he let her go with a glance around, obviously not wishing to attract more attention than they already had. He herded her through the doorway and into the cooler corridor between the two flights of steps.

Had she shamed him? Her father?

"That is still my hall," she insisted, shocked at feeling tears come into her eyes.

"For all your insistence that you are a lady, princess, your behavior and appearance say otherwise. You're dismissed to the upper floors." He turned and abandoned her there in the corridor, his wide back disappearing into the bright slashes of laughing and talking guests, the servants milling about with their clean, buff-colored skirts and white caps, their sturdy, shining leather boots.

Glenna looked down at her kirtle again and saw it now as compared with the bright silks and embroidery worn by the wealthy merchant class of Edinburgh. She raised her face to regard the hall once more and realized with horror that the kitchen maids Tavish Cameron had hired were dressed far better than she.

Her hand still holding the forgotten chalice of wine dropped to her side; she heard the liquid pouring out, felt the droplets on the tops of her feet, revealed by the skirt that was still too short. Her fingers went limp, and the chalice fell with a clang.

Glenna turned away from the feast and began to climb the steps.

* * * *

It was well past midnight when Tavish ascended the eastern tower, leaving behind the last lingering guests who seemed intent on finding the bottom of each wine cask now housed at Roscraig. Tavish himself had drunk more than his share. He was feeling fine, still enjoying the effects of the boisterous singing and dancing that had taken place in the hall. Audrey had not surprised him very much when she had demonstrated her talents of voice in a duet with the hook-nosed Miss Haversham—even Captain Muir had whistled and stomped his feet after their song. And she and Tavish had been paired more times than not in the dancing—a fact that Tavish knew was not mere coincidence.

Audrey's abilities and popularity among Edinburgh's wealthy merchant class had not surprised Tavish. After all, she'd been stolen away from his and Muir's games in the alleys of Edinburgh years ago to be groomed by the very best in the city. She would bring wealth and connection to whomever her father chose for her, and Master Keane himself had already hinted at the generosity he would bestow upon his new son-in-law.

He arrived at the upper corridor and nodded to Alec, who—while he did answer up a curt "Laird"—did not meet Tavish's eyes.

Tavish opened the door and saw a tumbling pile of rags straighten from the middle of the bed to stand upon the floor. He could feel Glenna's petulant glare on his back as he shut and bolted the door. When he turned he saw the tray of food upon the coverlet, picked at, perhaps, but the sampling of the dishes enjoyed at the feast still largely intact.

"Mam catering to you again?" he asked, the drink making the already snide words uglier than he'd intended.

Glenna immediately reached out and took the tray from the bed, sliding it into the shadows covering his wide table. She kept her back to him while he walked toward the fire, surprised to find his cup still in his hand. It was mostly full, and so he drank from it while he looked into the flames.

"Do you think you might somehow shame me into marrying you?" he demanded.

"What?"

He ignored her feign of ignorance. "Poor Lady Glenna—so hungry and poor and beautiful. You mocked me tonight. Goading Audrey before her friends. Coming to the hall in the garb of a peasant; as if I commanded you to wear such rags. *Triumphant conqueror!*" he bellowed, raising his cup. He chuckled in the back of his throat, shook his head, and then drained his chalice. She had said nothing, and so he turned to look at her.

She was staring at him, the flickering light barely reaching her cheekbones, forehead, the tip of her nose.

Her silence was maddening. He set the empty chalice on a table with more force than was necessary, and then walked to the tall wardrobe and opened it. "What have we here?" he said and reached out to take hold of the long drape of material. He shook it before him and saw that it was nothing more than the old gray shawl she'd worn the day he arrived. He tossed it on the floor and then reached back inside the cabinet.

He pulled out the faded, striped kirtle; it soon joined the shawl. But when he went to retrieve another garment, his hand met bare wood. Tavish stepped back, allowing the firelight to illumine the inside of the empty wardrobe.

"Are you looking for the gray gown?" Glenna asked. "It's across yonder chair near the fire, drying."

"Where are the rest of your gowns?" he demanded, turning to her.

She shook her head. "There are no more."

"I don't believe you."

Glenna shrugged. "Your belief or nae doesn't change the fact that I have three gowns. But it does say much about your pigheadedness that you would think me willing to humiliate myself in front of scores of strangers in my own house in an attempt to prick your puny conscience."

"Where are your clothes?" he demanded, becoming unreasonably angry at her refusal to confess.

"I don't have any more clothes!" she shouted at him at last. "As they wore, they couldn't be replaced." She took several shallow breaths. "I had no…I had no idea that everyone would be dressed so finely."

"I told you it was a feast," Tavish began.

"There's never been a feast like that at Roscraig before!" Glenna shot back. "We've considered ourselves fortunate to have enough food for one full daily meal for years. You think my father would squander what we had to entertain a bunch of greedy merchants?"

"He certainly squandered it on something." Tavish would be damned if he would apologize for his success where Iain Douglas had failed. "The Tower is in a prime location on the firth, with no tolls to pay. The land is rich; there are woodlands and pasture. You'd have to *try* not to prosper."

"What would you know of running an estate?" Glenna challenged in a choked voice. Her face was colorless now, such a change from when she'd arrived in the hall. Her hair was soft and mussed, her pathetic kirtle faded nearly white in the fire glow. The violets in her hair were shriveled, drooping and black now. "The king's taxes—they take all."

Tavish watched her, acknowledging only to himself that, indeed, Roscraig wasn't in arrears in taxes, and never had been. Had this woman been kept in poverty her entire life for the sake of the Tower? So destitute that she couldn't clothe herself properly, couldn't obtain adequate sustenance; had been made to struggle for the basest survival alongside the likes of Frang Roy while repeated sickness swept the village?

He briefly recalled his mother's warning, her mad idea that Iain Douglas had been poisoned; the possessive way of Frang Roy, and his expertise with the land and its plants. He'd been the last villager to see Iain Douglas well.

Had it not been for Tavish's arrival, Glenna Douglas would have likely been claimed by the brutish peasant, an idea with which Tavish found himself very uneasy. He also recognized that at least part of his irritation with the woman this night was that her inappropriate attire had stolen away the opportunity for Tavish to observe her in the hall.

"You'll not shame me before my guests again," he said at last. "Keep to this chamber or your father's."

"I'd not dare offend them further with my hideous appearance." Her cheeks flushed, and Tavish knew he had succeeded in chastening her. "I assume Miss Keane will be more than eager to step into my role."

"Audrey will remain here until the king comes."

"She must ensure you aren't stolen away by your shepherdess in the meantime."

Tavish felt his lips quirk, and whether it was the drink or his victory, he liked the soft look of her just then, appreciated it over the cologned and powdered women who had made eyes at him and not so veiled overtures. Glenna Douglas did not pretend to be enamored of him; but neither did she begrudge him an honest word of praise.

Or an impassioned response to his body.

"Perhaps she has reason to worry," he said.

Glenna met his eyes, and her chin lifted a fraction. Honest.

The idea that she had been naught but truthful in all their interactions suddenly troubled him in a mysterious way.

Tavish turned away and began to unbuckle his belt. "Get in bed, princess," he said. "Perhaps you will yet prove yourself useful this night." He laid his shawl and tunic over the back of the chair near the fire, covering up the old gray gown. He caught sight of a slickstone on the hearth and a small basket containing thread and tiny scraps of fabric the same color as the kirtle Glenna had worn tonight. He paused in his movements, realizing that she'd genuinely done everything she could to look her best. Tavish turned around to face the bed.

Glenna was beneath the covers, but turned on her side toward him, one arm outside the coverlet dragged beneath her chin. She was watching him unabashedly, and he liked the way her eyes lingered on the bare skin of his chest. Besides her face, Tavish could only see the yellowed sleeve of her underdress.

"I'm nae accustomed to sharing a bed with a woman fully clothed," he said, hoping his gruffness concealed the foreign wave of regret that wanted to rise up in him.

Her green eyes met his. "Would you have me remove my gown?"

He knelt on the bed and crawled toward her until he loomed over her and she rolled onto her back. "Would you remove it if I said aye?"

Tavish saw her throat convulse in the fire glow before she spoke. "You wounded me unnecessarily tonight," she whispered. "But I will keep my word to you." The very ends of her hair trailing out from her coif trembled.

Tavish slid his palm behind her slender neck, lowered his head, and pressed his mouth to hers, kissing her slowly and deeply until he felt his desire grow to the very edge of his restraint. *I'm sorry,* he tried to convey. And yet this time Glenna did not respond. He drew back at last and looked into her cat eyes once more, and he saw fear there and sadness and still a good deal of resentment.

"Go to sleep, princess," he said to her. "I'll not hurt you twice in one night."

She rolled over to face the wall and squeezed her eyes shut while still within the cage of his arms. The faint perfume of violets wafted up from her. Tavish looked at the fringe of her pale lashes against her cheek for a moment, took his time in examining the texture of her skin in shadow before he finally pulled away and lay on his back beside her. He sighed silently and then stilled.

He must speak with Muir at once.

Tavish rose from the bed once more and slipped into his tunic and boots before departing the room and making his way down the dark corridor to the stairs. He was nearing the bottom when he saw the man he sought outside the hall, speaking with none other than Audrey Keane. Tavish's boots scuffed against the stair, and when Audrey looked over her shoulder at the intruder, Tavish could see that her eyes were teary.

Audrey turned back to Muir, saying something too low for Tavish to hear before pressing the man's arm briefly and fleeing away down the other stairwell.

The captain followed Tavish's approach with a guarded expression. "Laird," he said. "I thought you had retired for the evening."

"So thought I," Tavish said ruefully. He glanced down the stairs. "Is aught awry with Audrey?"

Muir's gray eyebrows rose. "Is the lady Glenna not in your chamber?"

"What? Aye, of course she is. What sort of answer is that?"

"Audrey is troubled by the fact that her husband-to-be would take on a mistress even before he is wed. I don't know who would blame her—you look as though you just left the woman."

"I did just leave her. Audrey and I aren't wed yet, Muir."

"True. So you plan to loose the Douglas woman after you take Audrey as your wife?"

Tavish felt his irritation returning. "Would you of all men lecture me on morality? Many lairds keep mistresses; it has naught to do with their marriage. I've not agreed to a betrothal with Master Keane, and even if I do, 'tis best Audrey understand now that she'll not rule over me—Roscraig isn't Edinburgh. I'll do as I please. And I'll bed whom I please. Now and in the future."

The corners of Muir's mouth turned down. "I see."

"I sought you because I have several items I wish brought back from Edinburgh, in addition to what we spoke of before. They may be difficult to obtain on such short notice."

The captain's demeanor changed almost at once from that of a disapproving if concerned friend to a businessman about his task. "That sounds like a challenge; I accept."

It was only several moments later that Tavish was climbing back into the warm bed at Glenna Douglas's side. She had not appeared to move in his absence, and he wondered if she was already asleep.

"Good night, princess," he said in a low voice, and then turned over to face the fire before closing his eyes, the wine he'd drunk making the bed undulate comfortingly, like a ship at sea.

"I thought you'd gone to seek another woman" came the whisper from behind him.

Tavish's opened his eyes to the flickering tableau once more. "Nay. Only a forgotten order for my captain."

The silence was complete for several moments, and Tavish thought that she had gone to sleep. He closed his eyes again.

"I was heartened by your efficiency."

Tavish's lips quirked. "Sorry to disappoint you, but my romantic attentions take far longer than a handful of moments."

Glenna sighed. "I guessed as much."

Tavish drifted off to sleep with her quiet lamentation in his ears and an amused smile on his lips.

Chapter 10

Glenna swiped the damp rag across Iain Douglas's face, and his faded blue eyes rolled up in their cavernous-looking sockets, following her every move, studying her.

"You're looking much better, Da," she said softly, hesitant to disturb the peace of the chamber, bathed in bright sunlight, the tiny motes of dust sparkling as if exhaled on a magical breath. "You'll be well soon enough."

Glenna turned to the basin to rinse and wring the rag, the strong smell of Harriet Cameron's herbs tingling the insides of her nose. When she turned back, her father was still looking at her intently, as if he actually saw her and recognized her.

His lips parted, stretching and pulling away from each other slowly. She heard a whisper and leaned closer.

"Who?" The question was little more than a sigh.

Glenna's heart fell and she straightened enough to look into his face. "'Tis I, Da—Glenna. Your daughter."

Iain's head twitched as if refuting her answer. "Who s'ere?"

"Who...who's here?" she repeated.

Her father gave a long blink.

"You mean..." Glenna broke off and felt at a loss as to how to answer his question. In his mind, were there other people in the chamber with them?

Or could he have realized that Roscraig had been seized by strangers?

As if to answer her questions, Ian's mouth moved again.

"'Arr'et."

"Harriet?" Glenna repeated, surprise making her words bright. "Nay, I've nae seen her today." She swallowed. Her father continued to stare at her, as if waiting for her to expound. But Glenna didn't know what to say as her heart thudded in her chest.

She'd never thought to hear her father's voice again, never thought that he would regain enough awareness to question the hostile takeover of his home and his title—and perhaps his only child. He was a proud and quiet man, a private man, and fiercely protective of what was his—especially Glenna. If she told him now that Tavish Cameron had not only challenged his place as laird but had already overthrown his rule and turned Roscraig upside down—even for the better—the shock alone might kill him just when it looked as though he could live.

She pulled the coverlet higher and tucked it around his thin shoulders, avoiding his gaze now. "Are you hungry? Aye, you must be. I'll just pop down to the kitchen for some broth." She straightened with a smile and chanced a glance at his face, but he was still staring at her.

"Sen...t'er?"

Glenna frowned. "Center?"

His head twitched again. "Who...sen...ter?"

Who sent her?

Iain seemed to want to gasp for air, but the best he could manage was a reedy inhalation. "Har...cave?"

"I'm sorry, Da," Glenna said with a feeling of relief. He wasn't making sense at all, which meant that he still didn't realize what had happened. "I don't ken your meaning. Perhaps the words will come easier after a nice bowl of broth. I'll fetch it now."

She leaned down to kiss his thin, cool cheek.

"Har...cave," he whispered, so faint the words were little more than breaths bookended by the clicking of his throat.

"I'll be right back," she reiterated quietly, cupping his face in her hands. Then she stood and fled the chamber as quickly as she could without running.

Once she was on the stairs, however, she slowed her pace, relishing the cool breeze wafting up the dim spiral, the fresh scent of spring from the greening land beyond the walls, and letting it calm her mind. At a narrow window on the level of her own chamber, Glenna paused and looked out at the fields beyond the moat to the left of the village. The tall tangle of feral plants was gone, revealing long, low swaths of rich brown dotted with the bowing shapes of workers already well set to their tasks.

There would be food growing in Roscraig's fields this season. But it would belong to Tavish Cameron.

When she had thought Iain Douglas to die, her bargain with the Edinburgh merchant mattered little. But if her father lived, neither man would accept the other. And where would that leave her? Presuming she had a choice, which would she choose—staying in the only home she'd ever known as Tavish Cameron's mistress or being forced out to a destitute and uncertain future with the only family she possessed and the only person who loved her? Her father had spoken of the remote Highland town of his ancestors once long ago, lamenting it as a place of constant war. Would they be welcomed there after so many years?

And if their ancestry was of a Highland town, what lineage had brought them to Roscraig?

Glenna pulled herself away from the window and started down the stairs again, intent on putting the matter out of her mind for the time being. She ducked into the kitchen only moments later, finding the now familiar form of Harriet Cameron before an enormous iron cauldron on the hearth, a servant girl at her side. The maid was listening intently to the instruction by the older woman, who gave the contents a final stir and then turned over the long-handled ladle with a smile and an encouraging nod.

Harriet noticed Glenna right away. "Good day, milady!" At her greeting, the other servants busied about the benches and shelves of the kitchen gave short curtsies or nods in Glenna's direction. Harriet stepped to the doorway and grasped Glenna's elbows briefly. "How fares the laird this morn?"

"He is…improved," Glenna said, and then added quietly, "He spoke to me as if he knew who I was. Although his questions made no sense."

Harriet nodded. "It was the same last night," she confided and then glanced over her shoulder before hooking her arm through Glenna's and stepping back out into the busy sunshine of the courtyard where the women could speak with some privacy. "I wasna sure what to make of it myself. At first I thought it only ramblings. It's when he gave me the brooch—I assumed I was to give it to you, as I had been going on about the feast."

"I've no idea where he could have been keeping it so close during his illness," Glenna said. "But it was you he was asking after just now, Harriet."

Tavish's mother's eyes widened. "Me, milady?"

"By name. Also something about a cave. The cave on the cliff, it must be."

"Och, *cave*," Harriet said. "I thought perhaps something else."

"I suppose he could have meant anything. Or nothing." Glenna sighed. "Any matter, I don't mind telling you alone that I fear what will happen if he continues to recover. God forgive me even speaking aloud any negative should he live, but when he discovers what has happened at Roscraig during his illness…"

"And the situation his daughter now finds herself in?" Harriet suggested gently. "I wish there were something more I could do to help, milady."

"Oh, Harriet, I already don't know what I would do without you," Glenna said. "Da would have likely died had you not come. But he's asked me who sent you; he'll likely pose the same question to you."

"Why, nae one sent me, milady," Harriet said with a wide-eyed blink. "I came to Roscraig with my son from Edinburgh, where we worked in a shop." Harriet Cameron gave Glenna's arm a squeeze and then led her back toward the kitchen doorway, confiding, "'Tis why I prefer to stay in the kitchens, you see—I canna tell what I doona know."

* * * *

Tavish pushed at the heavy trunk until it thudded against the solid rock at the rear of the small alcove and then quickly ducked away as grit and pebbles rained down on him. Dubhán stepped back in the same instant, sputtering and swiping at his face. Tavish joined the monk and peered through the flickering candlelight to regard the hiding place.

From where Tavish stood in the narrow, steeply domed cave, the alcove where the chest rested appeared to be nothing more than another cleft in rock, or perhaps only a streak of the black and green mosses that grew along the fissures in natural striations. Although Dubhán said that few pilgrims came the way of the cave now, the cavern could be full of people and Tavish doubted any of them would notice the secret niche.

Still, he felt he must ask. "Nae one else knows, Dubhán, you're certain?"

"Those remaining in the village know of the cave, of course, laird," the dark monk replied in his usual calm tone, although his words were deeper and eerie here in this subterranean hole, supposedly once a refuge for an ancient mystic. "The few who knew aught of its alcoves are dead now. All save Frang Roy and Laird Douglas, that is."

"Frang Roy has been exiled," Tavish reminded the monk. "And Iain Douglas…poses little threat to me."

"You seem very confident that the laird will die," Dubhán mused. "His passing would certainly remove many objections the king might have to you holding Roscraig."

Tavish wondered if the monk was investigating his conscience with such leading remarks. "By the time Iain Douglas would ever discover I've made use of the cave, either I will be laird in the king's eyes or I will have left Roscraig."

"I see." The robed man took hold of the stubby, mottled candle and held it up, looking around the walls and ceiling of the cave, and the shadows fled behind some stones, rose up tall from others, and seemed to chase each other malevolently. "You take a risk yourself, though; what if something should happen to *you* and *you* should die? An accident? Sickness, like that which befell Roscraig? You have made a firm enemy of Frang Roy."

Tavish looked Dubhán in the eyes. "I've had worse enemies. Captain Muir knows of my plans. He would come for the trunk if I could not."

"I see. What of Lady Glenna?"

"What of her? Naught I do is any concern of Miss Douglas's." But the mention of the woman pricked again at Tavish's conscience, and so he sought to turn the conversation away from her. "But you understand that I am placing a great deal of trust in you, Dubhán."

Now it was the monk's turn to meet Tavish's gaze squarely. "Come now, laird. I am a man of the lord above all else. I shall speak of it to no one save him."

Tavish held out his hand. Dubhán looked down at it for a moment, a slight crease in his usually smooth forehead, as if he was temporarily perplexed at the offer of cooperation being extended to him. Then he moved the candle to his left hand and grasped Tavish's hand firmly, the monk's grip a strange combination of smooth skin and strong, sinewy grasp.

After the agreement was sealed, Dubhán blew out the flame and replaced the candle on the makeshift shelf, and Tavish stooped to followed Dubhán into the narrowing throat that led from the cave. The two men paused a moment on the stone ledge that fronted the small opening, taking grateful breaths of fresh air. From this vantage point, Tavish could see naught but the sparkling waters of the firth until he looked down at the sheer cliff beneath the overhang and the boulders submerged in the shallows of the Forth. And although Tavish Cameron had taken his own turns climbing the *Stygian*'s mast, he did not care for the way his body felt as though it were tipping forward against his will when he looked over the edge.

Dubhán's sandals scraping on stone drew Tavish's attention back to the firm land beneath his feet, and he set his mind to the task of not slipping to his death along the sheer precipice as he followed the monk up the treacherous path.

Tavish continued to follow Dubhán through the moss-covered monuments toward the small cottage crouched at the edge of the wood, the stone structure nearly overtaken with ropy, arm-like vines. Some of the markers in the clearing were in the shape of crosses; some small, square slabs; others tapering fingers. Many were inscribed with words in the old tongue, but most only bore a symbol or two meant to identify the departed.

Now, Tavish wondered that anyone at all knew the names of all the dead that populated this quiet cliffside burial ground. Some were his ancestors, no doubt, and the idea of it brought a pleasant wash of gooseflesh to his arms. He belonged to this land, just as surely as Roscraig belonged to him.

The tallest monument seemed youngest, a large cross standing crisp and straight and strong behind a wide mound of new grass. Dubhán stopped and turned back as Tavish paused there. A smaller obelisk was to the right, older than the cross monument, and with an English engraving: *Margaret Douglas.*

Glenna's mother, Iain Douglas's wife.

"What killed Margaret Douglas?" Tavish asked suddenly. He looked up in time to catch the surprised expression on Dubhán's normally placid face.

"'Twas thirty years ago, laird. Lady Glenna was only a few days old."

Tavish huffed a breath through his nose, wondering why he cared. He looked back at the stone. Thirty years ago—he and Glenna were nearly the same age, then. "Childbed fever, likely."

"It takes many a young mother." Dubhán glanced at the sky. "If you will excuse me, laird; it is nearly midday." He paused, and his expression brightened as he gestured with his palm to the quietly decomposing cottage behind him. "You are welcome to join me."

"I must decline, Dubhán. It seems the Tower is to play host to a growing tide of visitors leading up to the king's arrival, and there is yet much to be done."

Dubhán gave a gracious nod and then turned toward the cottage. A moment later he had disappeared inside the heap of timber and stone and ivy.

Tavish looked back to the small obelisk. *Thirty years ago...*

Thomas Annesley had definitely been in Scotland at that time, having left a young Harriet Payne with a bastard son. Margaret Douglas had died at Tower Roscraig, leaving an infant daughter and husband behind in the home rightfully entitled to Tavish's father but that he had never claimed.

Could Margaret Douglas and Thomas Annesley somehow be connected? It seemed impossible.

And yet, here were both Tavish and Glenna, in situations both would have at one time described as incredible.

Tavish shook his head, treating the disturbing thoughts as little more than accidental annoyances. The past didn't matter now—there was nothing about it he could change. He was laird of Roscraig, and the future was his for the building. He walked out of the graveyard and down the woodland path toward the village.

He could almost feel eyes on him, though, watching his passing. The cry of a dove diving swiftly into the doocot below had the brief, eerie similarity of a quiet sob, and for one fantastic moment, Tavish had the morbid fancy that it was the ghost of Margaret Douglas, perhaps weeping for the babe she had left behind.

Chapter 11

The tower was alive with music and laughter again, the great hall full to bursting with a crowd of revelers as it had been for the past week. And yet this night the multitude was made up not only of Edinburgh's wealthy merchant class, but the nobility within closest proximity to Roscraig lands. Lairds and their ladies, at least two of them barons, adorned the feast and lent it an air of refinement that perhaps was lacking even at the great gatherings on previous nights. The music went on and on, as did the stream of well-dressed servants flowing up and down the stairs from the entry hall below, in and out of the doorway bearing endless trays and baskets and platters of food; pitchers by the score.

Glenna sat on the stone steps in the shadows above, leaned close into the curving wall so as not to be seen. She watched those invited, those in service, come and go as they pleased, enjoying a freedom in her home that she herself did not possess. Lovers sneaked out singly to rendezvous with giggles or more boldly in pairs as the night grew long, and their fine, glittering dress—each one more enviable that the last—caused Glenna to tuck her old gray skirts more tightly around her calves.

Tavish Cameron had continued to forbid outright her attendance. And while under other circumstances she would have ignored his wishes and done as she pleased, she had no desire to be humiliated again, her poverty paraded before all the land, including the noble neighbors of Roscraig that she knew by name but had never met.

The cowards.

Audrey Keane, too, came and went as she pleased, and in her bright yellow gown Glenna thought she looked like a daffodil turned on its top. The image would have brought her more pleasure had it not been for the fact that Miss Keane's gown was—like all the gowns Glenna had seen belonging to the woman—truly, achingly beautiful. The only thing that helped soothe the sting was that Audrey Keane was now being forced to show her mettle.

Many noble young ladies—perhaps the daughters of Roscraig's neighbors—were in attendance, and it was clear that their attentions were meant for the handsome man who had claimed the Tower. The stress of competition could be seen clearly on the redhead's face when Tavish Cameron had left her what must have been a half hour ago and headed down the stairs toward the entry corridor. The woman's obvious distress had brought a small measure of satisfaction to Glenna even if she had been curious as to why Tavish Cameron would suddenly abandon the feast.

Even so, Glenna propped her chin on her fist and leaned her temple against the stones and wondered what it would be like to be in her own hall, enjoying such a marvelous event.

Audrey Keane reappeared through the doorway of the hall just then, glancing over her shoulder at the revelry she left behind. But she remained on the landing between the flights of stairs, peering into the shadows seemingly right at Glenna so that when the redhead turned to look the other way, Glenna crept upward several treads without making a sound. She would not be found lurking in her own corridor and made a fool.

A bulky shadow seemed to shudder free from the darkness of the descending flight, and Glenna thought Tavish Cameron had at last returned. But it was Captain John Muir who appeared in the light spilling from the hall, his arms full of a fine leather trunk. The two people stood on the landing, seemingly at odds at having discovered each other.

"Captain Muir," Miss Keane said, surprise clear in her voice. "I didn't expect you back at Roscraig so soon."

"Good evening, Miss Keane. The laird wished my immediate return with the items he needed."

"I see. That must be why he so suddenly disappeared."

"He'll be along in a moment, I reckon." The older man paused looked down at the trunk and lifted it slightly. "This is for you, actually."

"For me?" Audrey repeated.

"You didna think I'd return from Edinburgh empty-handed, did you? When he worries so for your happiness here at Roscraig?"

Glenna's stomach clenched.

Captain Muir continued quickly. "I didna wish to intrude upon your private chambers without your...I intended to hail a servant..." he stammered, obviously ill at ease in the woman's presence.

"Nay, nay—I can't wait," Audrey said, backing into the shadows at the foot of the stairs below where Glenna sat and motioning for Muir to follow her. Glenna froze and held her breath, afraid to even blink lest she give away her location. There was no escape now. "Do you mind very much, Captain? 'Tis childish, I know."

"Nay," Muir said mildly as he set the trunk on the bottom step. "I thought you'd be too busied at the feast to—"

"But here I am, at just the right moment, anticipating the laird's return," Audrey rushed on.

Muir did not reply, but only disengaged the clasps and then stepped back from the trunk, giving Audrey Keane room to move forward and lift the domed lid. The redhead gasped and reached in with both hands, and Glenna had to restrain herself from leaning forward in an effort to see what Tavish had bought for the woman.

Miss Keane raised her arms, a sparkling, layered fabric creation draping from the ends of her hands. "Oh, Captain Muir—'tis the most beautiful gown I've ever seen."

"He had it commissioned some time ago," the man said, rather gruffly. "It was ready only yester morn." Captain Muir paused as if considering his next words carefully. "He was sure to tell me that he hopes you will wear it as your wedding costume."

Audrey Keane's motions in admiring the fine dress stilled and she half glanced over her shoulder at the captain. Then she carefully let the gown fold on itself inside the trunk and closed the lid, letting her fingertips rest atop it for a moment while her red head was bowed.

"It would make a fine wedding costume, indeed," she murmured, almost sadly.

"What is it, Audrey?" Captain Muir asked. "You put on as though you're not happy at Roscraig. I ken that you and Tav are both above my station now, but am I nae longer a friend to be confided in?"

Audrey turned to face him, and Glenna slowly let out a silent breath through her lips, relieved that the woman was no longer turned in her direction.

"These people—these neighbors of Roscraig," Audrey began in a whisper. "They hate me, John. They're…they're so cold."

"Give it time. They will soon be as fond of you as Tav and I."

"It's not like Edinburgh," she protested. "I feel as though I've been banished to the very ends of the earth! We're awaiting the king's arrival. *The king*, John! And these people—these country lords…they don't think I'm worthy of him. Me, not worthy of Tavish, whom I've known since I couldn't so much as see over the shop bench! And I'm the one who invited them!"

Glenna frowned in the shadows.

"And it's only promising to get worse by the end of the month," Audrey continued. "Some of the most powerful and influential nobles in all of Scotland will have arrived to hear the king's decision and see the curious new laird of Roscraig. What if—"

Footsteps echoed on the stairs, drawing both Captain Muir's and Miss Keane's attention, and as Tavish Cameron's head came into the light followed by at least two servants, Glenna took the opportunity to back up the stairs farther. Once she was completely hidden by the curvature of the wall, she gained her feet and fled silently to the uppermost level and slipped into her father's chamber, closing the door carefully with a sigh of relief at her escape.

"Good evenin', Lady Glenna," a deep voice rumbled.

Glenna turned as the large figure stepped out from behind her father's tall armoire.

"I told you I wasna goin' anywhere," Frang Roy said.

* * * *

Tavish wasn't surprised to find Muir and Audrey Keane on the landing outside the great hall; Tavish knew the captain still doted on Audrey, so of course he would want to present the gift from her father personally.

He turned to the pair of hands waiting behind him and motioned to the trunk similar in appearance to Audrey's they carried between them. "Take it to my chamber and leave it." Then he turned back to the man and woman who had stepped away from each other to include Tavish on the landing. He looked at Audrey, who was frowning prettily. "Not enjoying tonight's feast, Audrey? A shame, since you arranged it."

"You'd think I was naught more than a servant to these people, Tavish," she retorted, lifting her rounded chin slightly. "My father likely could buy any man in this Godforsaken wilderness several times over."

Tavish had to nod in agreement. "The nobility care more for their pedigree than they do for their coffers, ofttimes. Only consider Roscraig as an example."

"You would make things easier on me by far were you to announce your intentions," Audrey said pointedly. "Or perhaps you are enjoying the care of the eligible ladies who've come to fight over you?"

Tavish ignored the jab. "What of the Misses Haversham and Conner? Certainly the presence of your friends is entertainment for you."

"They are busied with the attentions of the younger sons of a lesser baron," she said with bitterness clear in her voice. "It seems everyone here is looking to make a profitable match."

"Audrey," Tavish said mildly, "you are my guest and my friend. I would not begrudge you doing the same. My position here is not yet guaranteed, and neither is any agreement between us."

"Hoping a better match comes along, are you?" Audrey said, her lips thinning. "Someone noble, perhaps? I hear there is a cave at Roscraig, for pilgrims seeking favor. Isn't that what nobles do? Go on pilgrimages? I shall have to begin at once."

"That's not what I mean," Tavish began.

"You could never hold hope of winning my hand in Edinburgh, Tavish Cameron, and you certainly are not my only option now, no matter what my father thinks." She turned away from him to face Muir. "Thank you, John, for troubling yourself so for me. I—I would like very much to know that you are to stay on at Roscraig for a while—a loyal friend close at hand means so much."

Muir gave the woman a short bow. "As always, Miss Keane."

Audrey's skirts swept across the landing as she reentered the hall.

Tavish huffed a laugh. "Well, I reckon she told me." He looked to Muir for commiseration, but the older man was looking through the doorway with an expression of chagrin.

He did not lose it as he faced Tavish. "I'm speaking to you as a friend and not as your captain, Tav, when I say that perhaps it's best not to string Audrey along."

Now Tavish did chuckle outright. "What are you going on about, John?"

"Like she said, if you intend to wed her, the honorable thing would be to make your intentions clear. I have thought much of taking a wife of my own, of late. Waited too long to properly go about it, I reckon. You have the opportunity beneath your very nose."

"I've never proposed to Audrey Keane," Tavish protested.

"You invited her to Roscraig straightaway."

"I invited her father."

"You accepted a gift of lands from Master Keane."

"Lands he won while gambling and that are useless to him without a title. He is hoping to use my recent elevation to his own business advantage."

"Audrey is no business advantage."

"I never said she was; I wouldn't marry her only for her connections through her father."

"Perhaps you wouldn't now, as laird of Tower Roscraig; but you would have broken both your own legs to get to the chapel to wed her when you were only Tav Cameron of Market Street."

Tavish looked at his friend for a moment, taken aback at the sudden chastisement. "Are you in need of a drink, Muir? Or a woman? I'm certain I can find—"

"Nay," Muir cut in. "I don't need a woman guaranteed in my bed and a score more following me around like heated sows to feel I've succeeded."

Now Tavish felt the first stirrings of anger. "I take offense to that, Muir."

"Good," the captain said with a single nod, meeting Tavish's gaze steadily. "Perhaps it will aid you in pulling that thick head out of your own arse before the king arrives and you make an even bigger idiot of yourself."

"I'm surprised you wish to captain the *Stygian* for such a man."

"I already said I was speaking as your friend and not your captain. But perhaps I will find another ship sooner than later," the man retorted, but his words were calm and thoughtful, as if the idea was one he had already long considered. "Will there be anything else? *Laird Cameron*?"

Tavish shook his head. "Nay, Captain." His stinging pride couldn't help but add, "You're dismissed."

Muir stepped around Tavish and left the landing with his graceful, rolling gait.

"What the bloody hell?" Tavish murmured to himself, shaking his head and already feeling remorse at the words the two had exchanged. Muir was only looking out for him, and he was likely right.

Tavish looked into the hall at the revelry continuing without him and then glanced up the stairs. He'd not caught sight of Glenna Douglas since this afternoon, when he'd reiterated her banishment from the feast. He knew his decision had hurt and angered her, but he'd wager that she would soon forgive him. She wondered if she would be bold enough to look inside the trunk in his absence…

Another glance into the hall showed that everyone in attendance seemed to be enjoying themselves immensely—even Audrey had found a clutch of people to join, and one young fop in particular seemed to be paying her appropriate attention. She even peeked over her shoulder and smirked, having caught Tavish watching her.

He smiled to himself. She'd be fine for a few more moments.

Tavish took the steps two at a time to gain the upper landing, but once outside the door, he paused, suddenly a bit unsure. He raised his hand to rap upon the wood but hesitated.

Whether Muir—or Audrey or Glenna Douglas—liked it or nay, Tavish was laird here. This was his chamber. His door. He could enter it anytime he liked without announcing his intention to anyone. Tavish seized the handle and pushed inside.

The chamber glowed with the soft light of the hearth flames; the furs on the bed were smooth and neat. A tray of foodstuffs and a pitcher rested on Tavish's table. The trunk sat in the middle of the floor, undisturbed.

Glenna wasn't here.

Tavish frowned; she was likely sitting with the old man, in the chamber above. Tavish put his hands on his hips and looked around the room with a frustrated sigh, as if he expected her to suddenly materialize at his wish.

He would not chase the girl. Tavish had a feast and guests to attend to, and the trunk could wait.

He turned and left his chamber, walking back down the stairs toward the great hall and his guests, and telling himself that feeling at the base of his skull was not shadowy uncertainty. He was just off center from his friend's odd behavior toward him, nothing more. He certainly had no cause to be worried for Glenna Douglas while she sat with her invalid father, in the home she'd known all her life.

In fact, he thought to himself as he took a chalice offered to him by a passing servant, he had no cause to be worried for Glenna Douglas, ever. She meant nothing to him.

He raised his cup in salute to the portrait above the blazing hearth and then crossed the floor to join the group of richly dressed nobles who were hailing him.

* * * *

"I wouldna do that, were I you," Frang warned Glenna as her palm skimmed downward over the wood. "The idea that you didna stand up for me to your lover has put me in a mite of a foul humor."

"I could scream," Glenna said, pressing her back against the door now, praying silently for someone—anyone—to interrupt them.

"Not long enough to be heard over that din," he said with a jerk of his head toward the shuttered window, where the noise of the feast rose on the thin night air. "I'd reach you first."

Glenna swallowed.

"But I didna come here to harm you, even after your poor treatment of me," Frang said pointedly. "I only want you to hear the whole of what I've to say; what I've tried to tell you for a fortnight. I've come once again to offer my help to you, Lady Glenna. Though you've shown me naught but contempt each time before."

"Tavish Cameron has banished you from Roscraig," Glenna said, pausing to press her lips together and take slow breaths through her nose, although Frang Roy's odor was nearly overwhelming. It smelled as though he had spent the days since his exile out of doors. "If he finds you here, he'll kill you."

Frang gave her his crooked, grotesque grin. "Nae if I kill him first." He began walking toward her. "You see, Lady Glenna, I've come to tell you some things about yer da. Yer mam, as well. Things the old man hoped none would ever know."

Glenna lifted her chin. "What things?"

His grin grew sly, sliding across his flat, wide lips and stretching them smooth. "He's nae paid Roscraig's debts."

"That's no secret," Glenna scoffed, although her knees were watery with the man's continued approach. "There's not been enough crops, and…and we've no help. Then the sickness…"

Frang Roy shook his head. "He's never paid the debts. Because he's nae laird."

"What? That's ridiculous, Frang. Don't come any closer," Glenna warned. "You assume too much."

"Once the king arrives, it'll be too late," Frang continued as if she hadn't spoken. "Tavish Cameron is entitled to the Tower—aye, I believe 'tis true. And he will soon have the king's blessing to toss you out on your skinny arse. If yer da yet lives, he'll be thrown into prison." He stood right before her now and leaned down slightly to speak into her face. "As a traitor to the crown."

"That's…that's simply not true," Glenna whispered, though she trembled through the soles of her slippers. "My father grew up at Roscraig, just as I have done. He is a loyal servant to James. He—"

Frang Roy shook his head and placed his wide, crusty finger over her lips, cutting off her argument. The smell of the digit caused Glenna's stomach to rise into her throat.

"You think spreading your legs for Cameron will save you, make 'im marry you. But he willna."

Against her will, Captain Muir's words bloomed in Glenna's memory: *He had it commissioned some time ago...he hopes you will wear it as your wedding costume.*

"You're poorer than a vicarage mouse, and your da's a fraud."

Glenna shook her head free of his touch. "He's not."

"And a murderer," Frang whispered.

"Nay," Glenna rasped. "You lie."

His face was so close to hers now that Glenna could see the fissures of broken capillaries across his nose, in the yellow of his eyes.

"He killed your mother."

She raised her hands into fists then, flailing at his hateful face, but Frang Roy quickly overpowered her, grasping her wrists in one huge hand and then pinning her to the door.

"If you will only think upon what I tell ye, you'll understand 'tis true," he said mildly, as if he had no concern for her abhorrence of him. "Once the king arrives with his court, your time at Roscraig is over. None will help you. You might be sold to the highest bidder, eh? I know of one who intends to visit Roscraig who will give a handsome coin for you. You wouldna care for his attentions."

"Dubhán will speak for me," Glenna rasped. "And for Da."

Frang Roy kept his simple smile. "The only thing Dubhán's word would do for you is bring your fall harder and faster. Nay, nay—we must be rid of Tavish Cameron and prevent the king from coming. Rid ourselves of Dubhán, as well, for good measure; warrant both our hides."

Glenna said nothing, and so Frang continued. "Your lover has a cache on the cliff—I saw him take it there with my own eyes." He raised his hand to stroke her cheek. "Tonight, I fetch it. *For us*," he emphasized. His breaths were coming heavy now, and he leaned closer toward her face...

The insistent rap at the door vibrated into Glenna's rib cage, and she gasped before Frang's palm covered her mouth.

"Shh," he warned, his sparse, coarse eyebrows drawing together. He whispered his hot breath into her ear. "Answer easy, ken?"

Glenna nodded, and Frang slowly removed his hand from her mouth just as another insistent knock sounded. Glenna couldn't help the whimper that squeaked out of her.

"Miss Douglas?" a servant girl queried from beyond the door.

Glenna tried to answer but had to clear her throat before any sound would come. "What is it?"

"Laird Cameron wishes to inquire of you. Are you well, miss?"

Frang Roy sent her a meaningful look.

"My father is resting. I don't wish to be disturbed."

"Beggin' your pardon, miss, but he wants you right away. In his chambers, miss."

She met Frang Roy's gaze as he nodded.

"I'll be along when I've finished here."

"Aye, miss."

The echo of footsteps retreated in the corridor.

"I am nae the only one who knows the truth," Frang warned her quietly. "And once it has been brought out into the open, I canna help you."

"Frang, this is madness," she choked. "Am I to believe such horrid accusations about my own father on naught but your word?"

"That brooch of your da's," he said. "Look closely at the portrait in the hall and you'll see it. You've been lied to all your life." His callused thumb stroked her jaw for one gruesome moment, and then he released her and stepped back, his wide grin revealing the decaying gaps in his teeth as he reached inside the neck of his filthy shirt, withdrawing a small leather pouch on a thong around his neck.

"Look here what I've managed to lay hand to. Steep half o' this in a drink before your lover comes to you tonight, and give it to him." He ducked his head and then pressed the pouch into her chest, where Glenna raised her hands to take it, if only to keep his fingers from brushing against her skin. He continued. "After all in the hold are abed, unbar the door for me. I'll cut his throat while he sleeps. We have nae need to worry anymore about him after that."

Time seemed to stop then, and Glenna felt an icy chill race up her spine. In that moment, she saw Tavish Cameron's blue eyes in her mind, heard the rich timbre of his voice echoing in her memory. Harriet's son, the man who had brought Roscraig back to life...

Glenna shook her head. "Nay. Nay, you can't do that. I...I will be suspect. Of course. After all, it is my home he thinks to steal. And...and my bed he sleeps in. There are guards..."

"Then give him all of it," Frang said pointedly. "It'll take longer that way, mayhap a pair of days. I'll wait nae longer than that for a sign that I have your cooperation, you ken?"

Glenna shook her head slightly, the roar in her head making his words and their meaning foreign.

"I'll already have all the coin I could ever want. If you refuse my help, you're free to stay behind and fend off the king," he said. "I'll find another woman, aye. Mayhap even the mouthy Miss Keane might be persuaded to comfort me in my new wealth." He raised his hand and cupped her breast.

"Although 'twill be your face I see with each stroke." Glenna's nostrils burned as he stepped away. "Go, lest he send another maid after you and discover me here."

She turned and grasped the door handle and then looked back over her shoulder at her father. She glanced up at Frang Roy but could not bring herself to hold his gaze.

"You swear you won't harm him after I am gone?"

"Aye, I swear it," he answered. "He's the only one who'll be able to convince you what I say is true."

It took every ounce of strength in her arms to open the door and step into the corridor, leaving her father with that beast of a man.

But Frang Roy had opened another door in Glenna's mind that night. And she was infinitely more fearful of walking through that figurative portal than the one she exited now.

She closed the door behind her.

Chapter 12

It seemed to Tavish that the maid had been gone for more than an hour, and it became increasingly difficult to concentrate on the conversation with the two barons before him. He felt more than a pinch of chagrin that he'd allowed himself to send the maid to locate Miss Douglas in the first place, but now that he was waiting for an answer, he could barely pay heed to the old noblemen who were quite openly curious about his plans for Roscraig.

"—waste of such a fine location," one was harrumphing. "James has been too accommodating, I say."

The other nodded. "Aye, but why should the king care what is on such cursed lands when he is profiting twice its worth in fees?"

Now Tavish's attention was caught. "Profiting twice from Douglas, you mean?"

The two old men exchanged guarded glances, but before either could answer, Tavish saw in his peripheral vision the maid he'd sent to find Glenna inching through the crowd.

"Excuse me, gentlemen," Tavish said, then turned to meet the maid halfway. "Did you find her?" he asked straight away.

"Aye, laird," the woman squeaked. "She was in the old man's chamber, as you thought." Something inside Tavish relaxed, and the maid continued with her report. "Miss said she didna wish to be disturbed but that she'd be along."

Tavish cocked an eyebrow. "Did she, now?"

"Aye, laird."

"Very well." Tavish turned from the timid woman even as she was curtseying and felt his ears heat a bit. Whatever tingle of concern for

Glenna Douglas's welfare had seized him dissipated behind a shimmer of stinging pride.

The princess didn't wish to be disturbed, did she? Very well. She could sit in the chamber and wait for *him*. And Tavish would not give her another thought.

Although he had planned on cutting his evening with the boring barons short so that he could watch the woman open the trunk Muir had brought from Edinburgh, now he thought he'd stay on a bit. Get to know his neighbors, dismal as they were, and perhaps continue the conversation about the Tower's supposedly substantial fees.

"I beg your pardon," he said to the two frowning gentlemen, obviously put out with Tavish's earlier dismissal. He exchanged his empty chalice for a full one from a servant's tray. "Roscraig is experiencing a bit of an adjustment with the staff."

The baron with the hairy ears harrumphed and met Tavish's gaze squarely. "You'd be wise to correct with an iron fist at the verra start, Cameron. Left unchecked, those devil's maids will believe 'tis they who rule the hold rather than you."

Tavish saluted the man with a dark chuckle and then drained his cup.

* * * *

Glenna would have perhaps been furious to have returned to her chamber at being summoned by Tavish Cameron only to find him absent, if not for the fact that she couldn't get the damned leather pouch out of her grasp quickly enough. She shoved it between the wall and the back of the wardrobe as deeply as her fingers could wedge it, then dashed to the bowl and washed her hands with the strong soap while her heart pounded, her legs trembled.

She paced the chamber in a wide arc from wall to hearth, letting the enormous leather trunk that was now in the middle of her floor squash the ludicrous idea that she anticipated Tavish Cameron's return. Why must Miss Keane's wedding costume be stored in her own chamber? Was it so that Glenna might look inside curiously and be beset with a case of outrageous envy? Glenna would not satisfy such delighted imaginings by opening the trunk.

After all, unbeknownst to Audrey Keane, Glenna had already seen more of the gown than she wished, and was sufficiently bitter.

No, now the larger source of Glenna's torment lay in the dilemma presented to her by Frang Roy's words. She must find a way to examine the portrait hanging over the hearth. If the painting showed the unique barred brooch...

She heard the scrape of the door and turned quickly to face the man as he entered. Tavish Cameron stood in the doorway for a moment, his gaze finding her immediately. Glenna stared back, a traitorous relief in her heart; almost a sigh of her beleaguered emotions that he was here at last.

The spell was broken as Tavish Cameron stepped into the room and closed the door behind him. "Did you open it?" he asked as he slid the bolt closed.

Glenna frowned and glanced at the large object sitting conspicuously in the floor. "The trunk? Nay. It doesn't belong to me."

When he turned, his handsome mouth was curved in a knowing smirk, but he said no more about the trunk. "How is your father tonight?"

Glenna swallowed. Iain Douglas had slept through her encounter with Frang Roy. "He seemed very tired."

"Is he waking more?"

"He has been." Glenna's frown increased. Tavish Cameron had never seemed so interested in her father before. "Why do you ask? Hoping that he died and no one wished to disturb you from your elegant feast?"

"Do you truly think me such a villain to bar you from attending when you had nothing appropriate to wear? If anything, you should thank me."

"Aye, I'm so grateful for your disdain. Perhaps with all the visitors to Roscraig, you might inquire as to whether there is one willing to take the burden of an unwanted lady from you. No one notices my absence, any matter; your servants, your rich guests, my own father—certainly not you."

He sighed, his hands on his hips. "You're being childish. I'm sure I would notice your absence—the silence alone would be deafening."

They stared at each other again, and Glenna felt a sudden, odd swelling of painful tears behind her eyes. She was a fool for ever trusting him. He couldn't care less what happened to her. She was nothing more than a temporary amusement.

His smirk fell from his face when she didn't rise to his hurtful bait, and his expression became enigmatic. "It actually does belong to you."

Glenna blinked, and her eyes ached at the motion. She turned to follow him with her gaze as he passed her. "What?"

"The trunk." He poured a chalice of wine from the decanter and replaced the stopper with a scrape of rough glass.

Glenna's mind instantly went to the leather pouch hidden behind the wardrobe, filled with an unknown poison. *Steep half o' this in a drink and give it to him...*

Then Tavish faced her, his cup in hand. His eyes flicked to the large case. "It's yours."

"Nay, it's not," she said, wondering what game he was playing now. Why would he be so intentionally cruel? "I've not seen it before tonight."

Tavish shrugged. "It's yours all the same. Open it."

She shook her head. "Nay."

"Why?" he said with a bemused smile.

Because I know what's inside; I know it's the wedding gown you had made for Audrey Keane. I know it is just the beginning thread to the end of my time here at Roscraig; perhaps the end of everything I've ever thought I was. And I do not want to see.

But outwardly she only continued to stare at him.

Tavish Cameron took a long drink and then set his cup down on the table before crossing the floor once more. This time he stopped before Glenna so that her straightforward gaze was on the hollow of his collarbone, visible through the V-notch in his high tunic. The smell of him was warm and tangy and made Glenna's jaw prickle, causing her to swallow.

"You *are* still angry with me, aren't you?"

Glenna shook her head. She didn't know what she was with him any longer, but angry wasn't an accurate description of her feelings.

His hand came under her chin and tilted her face up so that she was made to look into his eyes. "I want you to open the trunk," he said. "Obey me, princess."

She pulled her face from his touch, wounded that he had revealed himself to be as cruel as she originally thought. It should have eased the troubled knowledge of Frang Roy's intentions for him, but it did not. She turned to the trunk without a word and sank to her knees before it, steeling herself to show no reaction whatever to the sight she knew would be revealed. She would not give him the satisfaction of feigned surprise, nor would she humiliate herself by confessing how she already knew what the trunk contained.

Glenna turned the two thumb latches and then lifted the hasps. She drew a deep, bracing breath and raised the lid.

There was indeed a folded width of shimmering cloth inside, and yet it was a deep violet hue rather than the light-colored gown that Audrey Keane had held in the torchlight of the corridor. Glenn turned her head to find Tavish sitting on the edge of the bed, watching her.

"What is it?" she asked.

A faint smile played at his mouth again. "I don't know. Take it out."

Glenna turned back and hesitantly took hold of the topmost corners of the fabric, raising it from its resting place. It was in fact a gown, the color of the dark violets on the forest floor, the skirt—most of its length still folding in on itself in the trunk—covered with tiny embroidered green vines climbing the peaks and valleys of lavish fabric. It was heavy and luxurious and felt like a physical manifestation of royalty in her hands.

"It's beautiful," she whispered.

"It's yours," Tavish said from behind her.

Glenna stood slowly, drawing the gown up out of the trunk and then stepping backward to pull it free. She held it against her chest and turned to face him.

"The color suits you," he said with a smile, his eyes traveling the length of her body. "Fortunate that the young lady whose trousseau this was to be was of similar size. I could only guess."

"I don't understand," Glenna whispered.

"I sent Muir around to a tailor I knew on Market Street to see what could be done about your lack of wardrobe. Luckily enough, he didn't just have one or two gowns nearly finished for another patron, but was ahead of schedule on an entire trousseau for a wealthy young lady. I paid him double what he was owed for it, and now,"—his lips quirked again—"the princess shall be obligated once more to fulfill her royal duty to me and to Roscraig."

"There's more?" Glenna said even as she turned back to the trunk. She sank to her knees again and laid the heavy gown across the crook of her arm while she hesitantly peeked inside, using her thumb and forefinger to gingerly explore the puddles and tunnels of cloth—silks and linens; corded beltings; gossamer pieces so fine and delicate that Glenna dared not slide them free.

This was not the same trunk Captain Muir had given to Audrey Keane—it was filled with an entire wardrobe of wildly expensive items, all purchased for Glenna by Tavish Cameron. He'd clearly spent a small fortune on her. But why?

Before she could begin to puzzle what the clothing meant, Tavish Cameron was pulling her to her feet.

"You can't look at everything properly while it's in the trunk," he chastised.

"I'm afraid I'll tear them," she said lamely, and her heart began to pound. "Tread on them or…ruin them somehow."

But he was already reaching into the container, pulling out rivers of rose, snowy white, indigo, saffron, crimson, and tossing them into Glenna's arms until she staggered and laughed despite herself.

Tavish Cameron laughed too as he stepped to her side and steadied her with his hands on her waist. Glenna smiled up into his face, and although she felt the merriment leaving her expression, she let the bemused curve of her lips stay.

"Why?" she asked quietly.

Tavish Cameron's eyes sparkled. "Because you're beautiful. I like beautiful things. And I want to see you in my hall, in beautiful clothing. I want others to see you."

"Am I no more than a thing to you, then?" she asked, waiting for that spark of fury to ignite the blazing hatred she felt for him. But the warmth spreading through her body was not hateful, and she leaned into him, grateful for his strength. "Something to be purchased? Or strategically moved aside in order for you to get what you want?"

"I couldn't find you earlier," he said, his face drawing closer to hers, but it was no answer to her question. "I *did* notice your absence. And I didn't like it."

"You don't own me, Tavish Cameron," she whispered against his mouth, but she felt the tension drain from her then; he had come for her. He had thought of her. Perhaps...

"And yet you belong to me," he replied and the vibration of the words and their meaning traveled from Glenna's lips to the soles of her cold feet. "My own princess. Do not vex me so by hiding yourself away from me again when I am in want of you. I canna conduct my business, I canna think; I—"

It was she who rose up on her toes to fit her mouth to his. Her arms went around his neck, the fine, expensive gowns sliding to the floor, and his hands found her waist through the thin, gray wool. She felt his fingers rove up her back to the bare skin at her nape, then slide into her hair, pulling it free of its simple twist. Her curls fell around her shoulders as Tavish pulled her closer, deepening their kiss.

It was madness, the way she responded to him, the way she let herself go in his arms; as if Tavish Cameron wasn't the reason her life was falling apart, would be the man who wanted to see her ruined, wanted to ruin her. And yet she clung to him as if he was the mast on the ice-slicked deck of a ship at sea. Her only hope of survival, and still the thing that could send her down to the very depths. She hated him, was terrified of him, but she could not tear herself away.

And she would not step aside and leave him vulnerable to Frang Roy's fatal plan.

It was Tavish who pulled his mouth from hers then, his warm breath smelling of spirits fanning her cheek. "Take off that rag you wear," he whispered. "I don't want to see you in it again."

Glenna stilled in his arms. It was to be tonight then—the night he collected the spoils from their agreement. Glenna thought of the ocean of expensive clothing around them, and realized that—like the time she was borrowing at Roscraig—the gowns were simply another form of payment. Payment for a whore. And Tavish Cameron wanted what he had paid for.

Glenna dropped her eyes as her trembling fingers went to the time-suppled leather laces at her bodice, holding the thin wool closed over her old underdress. She told herself that her hands shook with fear and humiliation; hatred for the man still standing with his hands at her waist. But her heart pounded, pounded in her chest in that now-familiar way when he was near.

"I like it when you are obedient, princess," he said, and the smile in his words stirred something of her pride.

She slapped him without thinking, and Tavish caught her wrist and swatted her other arm away before she could make a second attempt. In the blink of an eye he seized both sides of the laces and ripped the gray wool kirtle down its front. Glenna staggered backward out of his reach, the coolness of the chamber causing her skin to prickle beneath the dingy underdress.

"Take it off," he repeated, a devilish sparkle in his eyes that had deepened to indigo in the shadows.

Glenna didn't know why she suddenly wished to provoke his anger when only a moment ago she had been willing to meekly do as he commanded, but she now she only lifted her chin.

He took a measured step toward her. "Is it your wish that I do it for you?" he asked, the smile back in his voice again and even lifting one side of his mouth.

Her stomach clenched, and she shrugged out of the ruined kirtle, dropping it to the floor. His blue eyes held her captive, acknowledging her game.

"Give it to me," he said, and then pulled it from her hand when she offered it. He strode to the hearth, balling the old cloth between his fists. In a moment, it blazed against the stones.

Tavish turned and strode back toward her, glancing pointedly at her old underdress. "That, as well."

Glenna shook her head. "I needn't remove it for you to have me."

"True," he conceded, stepping even closer. "But what I want right now is to see your naked body. So…" He stopped. "Take it off."

Glenna's knees felt watery, her breaths came like ragged bellows. Tavish Cameron's blue eyes held her just as surely as his strong hands had a moment ago, and she felt powerless against the sorcery of his words.

"Does it make you feel more of a laird to wield your power over me?" she asked in a breathy taunt.

To her dread and her delight, he began stepping toward her once more, and this time he did not pause. "I am laird here. And what I demand is only what you freely promised me." He reached out and slid a warm, callused palm along her jawline, into her hair once more, and it took all of Glenna's strength of will not to turn her face into that palm, press her lips to his skin. But she could not stifle her jagged inhalation.

Tavish pulled her gently but steadily toward him, and as she came up against his chest, his left hand slid over her breast through the thin underdress, cupping it, molding its roundness with his fingers. He leaned his head down but rather than kiss her again, his mouth went to her collarbone, and Glenna closed her eyes as the warm scent of his hair filled her nose and the hot, wet sensation of his tongue traced a fiery trail to the center of her chest.

Both Tavish's hands went to her rib cage now, pressing in and up, causing her décolletage to swell above the thin linen. He caught the frayed edge of underdress puckered between her breasts in his teeth and then smoothed both palms forward to press her hardened nipples into her flesh before raking his fingertips together in a plucking motion, taking great fistfuls of the material.

He rent it with his teeth, pulling it apart with his hands as he sank lower, between her breasts, over her abdomen, the ripping linen preceding his hot breath. He dropped to his knees and licked the skin around her navel in a quick circuit while his hands finished ruining the underdress and then jerked it downward from her shoulders.

Glenna heard the startled gasp coming from her as if from another person. She swayed on her feet as Tavish Cameron's hands slid up the backs of her calves, then her thighs, then gripped her bare cheeks. He looked up at her then, his eyes ablaze in the shadows set dancing by the fire and without breaking gaze with her he nuzzled his mouth into her most sensitive flesh.

Glenna cried out, and her stiff posture at last broke, but rather than retreat from her in a show of mercy, Tavish Cameron merely turned her toward the bed, urging her into a seat with his hands and his mouth. She braced her hands behind her and Tavish took hold of her right ankle, forcing her foot upward and her bent knee out. He delved fully into her then, and Glenna went back on her elbows, unable to control her passion as she watched him taste her over and over, and she felt her pleasure coming to its peak.

He pushed her other foot onto the bed and her legs fell open, her back bowed. Her eyes finally closed as she cried out at the powerful vortex that seized her, deafened her, blinded her, and she wanted to bring her knees together but Tavish held them back, pressing her until she writhed to escape him. He crawled up her body then, latching on to her nipple and pressing his swollen breeches between her legs, and Glenna felt her body continue to pulse against his hardened length while he suckled her and she raked her fingers through his hair.

He released her nipple and crawled farther up her naked body, kissing her neck and her lips, and Glenna tasted her own essence.

"I didn't intend for this tonight," he rasped in her ear and rocked against her. "But each time I see you, I desire you more. I want you more. I canna stop myself."

Glenna held his head and kissed him deeply, letting herself go in his embrace, wrapping her legs around his hips. She could not pretend in this moment that she did not desire him, desire the feelings he provoked in her body. Tavish groaned against her mouth and pressed himself against her pubic bone before pulling away slightly and reaching down with one hand to loosen his ties.

A bit of her recklessness left her then; Tavish Cameron would ruin her in an instant, just as he ruined one of the last articles of clothing that she could call her own. She felt his hot length against her for only a moment, and then he rolled away onto his back and dragged her half onto his chest for another hard kiss before pulling away and urging her down with his hands on her shoulders.

Glenna understood what he wanted then. She backed into the space between his leather-clad legs and lay over his thigh, taking his heavy manhood into her hand, and then the tip into her mouth. It was marvelously smooth, and as her lips closed over him, Tavish cried out. She realized that she now held the same power over him that he had held over her moments ago, and she suckled him gently, instinctively, as he raised his hips. The sounds her mouth made were so arousing that she felt herself heating again, and her rising passion gave an enthusiasm for pleasuring of Tavish Cameron that in only moments had brought him to his own peak. He pulled her roughly up and against his body just as she tasted his fulfillment, and she could feel his ejaculation pulsing hot against her stomach.

They kissed, long and leisurely, as the firelight played over their bodies, and neither spoke. After a bit, Glenna shivered in the cold, and Tavish reached across her to drag the coverlets over their bodies before pulling her close once more and placing a kiss on her forehead.

Glenna laid her head on Tavish Cameron's chest, and her eyes closed in sleep, the tens of lavish gowns still littering the floor like ribbons from a celebration.

Chapter 13

Tavish woke with the dawn and could feel the smile upon his face before he opened his eyes. His body felt alive, refreshed, invigorated—and craving the touch of Glenna Douglas's soft hands around him. Her perfect pink lips and silky tongue…

He rolled over with a groan of anticipation but felt only a hard twist of abandoned coverlet in his hands. He opened his eyes, and the gray light of the room revealed that he was alone in the bed. Tavish pushed up on an elbow to look around the chamber, sending a slithering, hissing wash of heretofore neatly laid-out gowns to the floor.

She had obviously chosen something fine to wear before she left him.

Tavish fell back onto the mattress, his arms spread wide, and stared at the shadows on the ceiling as they slowly retreated into the corners. He felt a tinge of anger at himself for his eagerness to see her, his disappointment at her absence.

I should have taken her fully last night when I had her beneath me. Then perhaps my mind would be free of the torment of her, and I would be free to make the right decisions for Roscraig.

But even as he thought those things, he wondered at their truth. Glenna Douglas had managed to pierce his thick skin, wriggle her way between his muscle and bone and become a constant disturbance to both Tavish's normally cool mind and his well-laid plans. The taste of her he'd had last night, the display of her innocence as she'd fully surrendered to him as a woman even without admitting defeat—it had only made his desire for her grow. She was a mystery to him, not only her presence at Roscraig, but her very heart and mind, and he longed to own her as completely as he boasted.

And so it vexed him why he had not simply taken his full desire of her last night—and every night—until the king's arrival.

Because I am not Thomas Annesley.

Tavish growled and threw back the coverlet, sliding out of the bed and doing his best to ignore his insistent cock, which had obviously not received the message that Glenna Douglas was present only in memory. He retrieved his discarded breeches but donned a plain shirt in place of the fine tunic he had worn to the feast. His old brown leather vest looked too inviting to pass up, and he relished the familiar feel of it as he laced it over the white linen.

Tavish was belting on his sword as he descended the shadowed stairs when he saw Muir walk into the hall below him. Tavish paused while he attended properly to the task of securing his weapon.

Good, he thought. *It is well that Muir and I are reconciled this morn. I have regret for the words passed between us last night, and I would put it behind us before he departs Roscraig.*

But just as Tavish looped the tail of the leather strap of his hilt to his leg, Muir emerged from the hall again and turned toward the Tower's entry, this time with a woman on his arm.

A woman in a rose-colored gown, newly fashioned by one of the finest tailors in Edinburgh, her blond curls twisted atop her head.

Glenna.

Tavish watched from the shadows as the pair turned left into the wide entry passage, toward the courtyard, Muir looking straight ahead but with his ear leaned toward that perfect pink mouth; his large captain's palm covering the small, soft hand that was hooked in his elbow. When they disappeared around the stone corner, Tavish completed the flight of stairs and turned into the hall, passing by the busy servants and heading for the window on the right side of the hearth. He looked out over the newly thatched and shaked roofs of the buildings in the courtyard until he caught sight of the fresh splash of color that was Glenna's skirts. The pair was walking along leisurely in the soft morning light, looking quite natural and at home as the flow of animals and keepers swirled past them. Muir's rolling gait seemed to allow Glenna to float along at his side.

Tavish watched them until they came to the isolated point of the courtyard that jutted over the rocks and the waves below. It was clear they had sought the location for a private conversation—but why? What could Captain John Muir and Glenna Douglas possibly have to discuss? They were little more than tiny shapes now, and had Glenna not been wearing the bright new gown, Tavish might have never noticed them.

It seems no one at all notices my absence; your servants, your rich guests, my own father—certainly not you.

Her words—taken as little more than a taunt before—seemed to carry a much greater significance. Perhaps they had been a warning.

I have thought much of taking a wife of my own, of late. Waited too long to properly go about it, I reckon.

Muir was wealthy in his own right, thanks to his keen sailing abilities and experience, and his trustworthiness to his employers. There would be little shame in an impoverished noblewoman marrying a respected man who could afford to keep a wife anywhere in the world, in a comfort and fashion not far beneath that of nobility—certainly in a better fashion that Glenna Douglas had found herself in the last several years at Roscraig. And a better fashion than what she would encounter should King James formally deny her title.

A better fashion than the terms under which Tavish was keeping her.

What man would not wish to boast of a wife of such beauty? Glenna's passions—whether in anger or desire—were mighty to behold; and Tavish knew himself of their magnetic power. She was no simpering maid, no fortune-seeking shrew the likes of whom had crowded the Tower's hall of late, but a woman full-grown who still retained her innocence and a measure of dignity through her trials.

Some of those trials for which Tavish was to blame.

Tavish left the window and strode through the hall, his boots skipping lightly down the stairs as he swept through the entry hall and beneath the raised portcullis. He told himself he was being ridiculous, paranoid; but something prickled at the back of his neck—pride, perhaps, or fear—that he should not show that he was seeking them out in their meeting. And so he strode behind the row of dwellings on the left—the kitchen, the stables, the lean-to where the smithy's shop was being rebuilt. And there, behind that last building, he stopped.

The southerly spring wind blew warm and fragrant over the firth, carrying John Muir's words to his ears.

"...depart at dawn with the cargo. One needs no permission in that port to marry. Although..." There was a pause, and Tavish knew John Muir was considering his thoughts carefully before he spoke, as was his way. "The king may side with you, milady. I doona dare boast to know his mind."

"He may," Glenna conceded, but her tone was thin and hesitant. "But even if he would affirm that Roscraig belonged to my father, I do not think Laird Douglas to live long. And then I know not what I would do. You saw the state of the Tower when you arrived; to say that I am impoverished is kind."

Another pause. "You have another option, come the morrow. Would that you consider my offer."

A heavy weight settled upon Tavish's chest, like a slab of granite placed ever so carefully.

"Aye, consider it I will. Your suggestion has given me hope, Captain. Hope that I could promise myself to a man who would honor me and value me, and with whom I can perhaps put the nightmare of this life in my past. Should I leave Roscraig, it matters little to me where I call home. Any country, any port that you choose. Perhaps even Edinburgh—none know of me there."

"Nae Edinburgh. I am ashamed to say that I have spoken to some of your beauty. And—God, forgive me—your obligation to Roscraig," John advised gravely. "You would find no peace there."

Tavish's heart began to smolder, twist, with black anger. So this was the reason behind the captain's sudden chastisement for not announcing a betrothal: He wanted Glenna for his own. John Muir had always possessed a keen eye for fine goods to be had at a bargain, and there before him now was a lady abandoned, deserted, desperate—and dressed in the garb of a princess. John Muir had no need of any dowry with a prize such as that.

Tavish might as well have tied a ribbon about her and placed her aboard the *Stygian* himself.

"Perhaps, though, it is best that I take you far from Roscraig. Tavish will be furious with us all when he discovers what we have done," Muir said. "In truth, I didna imagine you to consider my suggestion with any gravity."

"Captain," Glenna said gently and reached out to place her hand on John Muir's forearm and look up into his face. Tavish could see her earnest and tearful expression even from this distance, her skin luminous in the morning light as the wind blew stray ringlets across her forehead and cheeks. "I am honored that you thought to help me. *Honored*," she repeated and Tavish saw her fingers flex around the man's arm. Her voice broke when next she spoke. "I would owe you a debt for the rest of my life."

"Doona cry—we've nae gone yet." The captain covered her hand with his own, and Tavish could not stop the tide of fire-lit memories from flooding his mind of Glenna's naked body, her passionate surrender to him, her easy slumber at his side.

It should have been Tavish who had rescued her. He should have been her champion—Glenna had given him every opportunity, and he had squandered it, playing the gentrified cock.

Tavish thought his teeth might crack. He trembled with the desire to leap from his coward's hiding spot and run at Muir, sending him to the rocks below. And Glenna...

His heart seized in a queer manner so that he winced.

The captain dropped his hand. "I'll not take you without your da's blessing, lass," he said, abandoning the proper address he'd always used. "'Tis not right, for a man to go behind a father's back in such a way with his only child—and a wee daughter, at that. I'll do my best to take him with us, of course, should he wish it."

The betrayal was doubled now, hearing Muir's damnation and feeling the shame it implied. The scene before Tavish vibrated in his vision, his rage building up inside him like the molten scorn of a volcano.

He hated them both in that moment.

Glenna stared into the captain's face, and Tavish could see that she was fighting to contain her emotion. "I'll speak to him this morning," Glenna promised. "I'll make him understand, somehow."

"Well, doona stand there looking all cow-eyed at me then, lass," Muir ordered gruffly and offered his elbow. "I've duties to attend to in readying the *Stygian* to depart—the wool and hides willna load themselves."

"Tell me about the ports. Belgium, perhaps." Glenna slipped her hand around his arm and interlaced her fingers, and they began walking back up the point of the courtyard. Their voices were muffled as they passed in front of the smithy's building, and when they emerged they were both laughing.

Had Tavish ever made Glenna Douglas laugh?

Had he ever heard her laugh before that moment?

Tavish turned his back to the rough wall behind him, his boots feeling mired in the rocky soil among the straggling tufts of weeds. He stared out over the firth.

The breeze had turned cold.

* * * *

Glenna pushed open her father's door and peeked inside. Harriet Cameron was seated in a familiar-looking piece of furniture next to the window, chattering away as she took in the view. The old, ornate chair had still been in her own chamber this morning, as far as she could recall; before that it had lived for years in the old guest chamber, along with the damning portrait now hanging above the hearth.

Apparently the chair had been moved here, to die alongside the other ancient artifacts of Glenna's life after Tavish Cameron's invasion: a small wooden table, a dented metal basin, Iain Douglas. They had all been relegated to this highest tower chamber, imprisoned together for the crime of steadfastness, of daring to remain loyal to Roscraig all these many years. She'd never asked why her father had kept such seemingly arbitrary furnishings when he'd sold most everything else, and now she thought that if she had only guessed at their implications, she would have burned the lot.

Iain Douglas appeared to be staring at the handsome old woman, and Glenna hoped that he was in fact lucid, although his mouth still pulled dumbly to the right and the room smelled of sour sweat.

"Good morning," Glenna said and entered the room fully, leaving the door standing open to encourage the breeze from the window.

"Oh, good morning, milady." Harriet stood with a warm smile. She held a small hoop in her hand, the stitchery obviously forgotten in her cheerful monologue to her captive audience.

Glenna walked to her father's side and smoothed her palm over his forehead. "How are we today, Da?"

His eyes jittered to the left to find her, a good sign of his mental clarity, but the whites were sickly yellow today, and the sight of them shocked her.

"I've likely talked him deaf," Harriet admitted and joined Glenna at the bedside. "But he's taken quite a bit of broth and some mead. What man refuses mead, though, I ask you? The likes of none that I've ever met."

Glenna smiled at her father and turned to Tavish's mother. "Da does fancy a"—her words faltered as she looked into Harriet Cameron's face and saw the deep tears glistening in her eyes above her smile—"he fancies a mug of good mead."

Harriet was nodding enthusiastically. "And he should have all that he wants, I say."

A thorny lump grew in Glenna's throat. What the old woman had feared, what she had warned Glenna of when first taking over Iain's care, was manifesting; had manifested in the night. While Glenna had been sating her erotic curiosity of Tavish Cameron in her bed, her father had begun dying in earnest.

She forced down the lump and gave her own nod, but she had to clear her throat before the words could struggle through that scratchy cocoon. "I will stand at the ready," she said.

"Well, then," Harriet said briskly while gathering up a tray of discarded bowls and linens, "I'll just pop down to the kitchen and see about things. Is there aught I can fetch you, milady?"

"Nay," Glenna said. "I—I haven't any need at all. Thank you, Harriet."

Tavish's mother paused, the tray in her hands, as she looked to Glenna with an expression of pained sympathy. "Very well, milady." Then she whirled and left Glenna alone with her father.

She turned back to the man who still watched her with his yellowed, bloodshot eyes, the flesh of his face sagging on his skull. She opened her mouth to speak some inanity—what, she couldn't say—but then closed it again as her father's eyes beheld her. His gaze was more intense, more purposeful than it had been since he'd fallen ill—almost fever-bright—and yet his forehead had been cool to her touch.

He was listening, she realized. He was listening for what she would tell him. And now she must tell him all.

"I think I'll steal Mistress Harriet's chair," she said to him with a small smile and squeezed his stick-thin forearm gently.

Only it wasn't stick-thin any longer, she realized with a start. She glanced down and saw that her fingertips had left dimples in the smooth, spotted flesh, like footprints in wet sand.

Glenna walked around the end of the bed and dragged the heavy chair away from the window to move it closer to the side of the bed. Iain's eyes followed her as she positioned her seat and sat down on the edge of the threadbare and faded cushion.

"After you woke," Glenna began, "you asked me who was here. I put on as though I misunderstood what you were asking.

"By now, Mistress Harriet might have told you that she has come with her son from Edinburgh, where they tended a shop. As I know it, that is very true. However..." She paused a moment, struggling to order her words as best she could. "That is not all of the truth. When Harriet arrived at Roscraig with her son, Tavish Cameron, they begged shelter from a storm. But Master Cameron also had business to address at the Tower, and he requested audience with...with the keeper of Tower Roscraig."

Iain Douglas's gaze did not waver, nor did it dull. He was still listening.

"I am ashamed to admit that I granted them entry in exchange for the handful of coins he offered in payment. If I had known..." She broke off, swallowed. "Perhaps not. I'm sorry for it though, Da." She reached out then and took hold of his fingers, spindly and yet at the same time seemingly encased in a thin leather glove that had been filled near to bursting with water.

"He carried a document with him. A document that says he has inherited the Tower from his father, the rightful laird of Roscraig. A man called Annesley."

Iain's left eye widened almost imperceptibly, and his lips seemed to flex as his jaw made a series of chewing motions. A strangled hum came from his throat. Glenna waited for him to speak, but his chest only rose and fell rapidly beneath the coverlet.

Glenna went on. "He has taken over the Tower in your illness. Brought in servants and workers. Done wonderful things for the keep, really. I—I wish you could see the hall. There have been feasts for days—grand ones.

"It's all in preparation for the king's arrival," she continued quietly. "Da, Tavish says…he says that you aren't laird of Roscraig. That you never were. And that when the king comes, he will make a decision about us."

Glenna tried to push down the emotion that was rising up within her at speaking all this aloud, at the anticipation of what she was about to say. But she knew her chin trembled, could feel her eyes swelling.

"He's wrong, isn't he, Da? Tell me he's mistaken—you *are* laird of Roscraig, aren't you? Won't the king tell him so when he comes?"

Iain Douglas's eye began to leak a thin thread of tears.

Glenna sniffed. "And then there's this." She fished in her purse for the silver, double-barred brooch and held it out in her palm before his eyes. "It's in that portrait—the one that hung in the west tower. The man in the painting wears it. Is it true? Is it Thomas Annesley's?"

Her father continued to weep silently, and as she looked into his yellowed, dying eyes, the fissured ground that made up the foundation of her life began to tremble and crack. His chin jerked downward.

"Nay," she whispered, the image of him growing watery through the thick wall of tears in her eyes. She sniffed and blinked, setting the sadness free to run courses down her cheeks while she took up his hand once more and turned it over, pressing the brooch into it and curling his thick, rubbery fingers around it. "Roscraig is ours. You are the laird here—you always have been," she whispered quickly, like an incantation, hurrying to speak the words aloud so that they might be made true.

She doubled over in the chair and laid her forehead against her father's hand, still clasped tightly in both her own. She squeezed her eyes shut, and her breaths were hard-won.

"Am I even your daughter?" she rasped.

The weak hand encased in her own flexed, and Glenna raised her face to look at her father. Even in his illness, she saw the fire of his answer there. He struggled to open his fingers against hers and then grasped for her hand. The brooch slid free and fell to the floor with a tumbling clink.

Glenna felt the weak tug, and she rose, bending Iain's forearm up until their clasped hands were between their chests and Glenna's face was only inches from her father's.

His lips pulled apart slowly and with much effort. "*My,*" he exhaled, and his breath was hot and tinged with the smell of wet vegetation.

She wanted to reassure him with a smile, but it felt as though the corners of her mouth were hung with weights. "If the king grants Tavish Cameron Roscraig, we've nowhere to go, Da. Tavish—he seeks to wed another and doesn't want me here. The king might see me cloistered, or wed to someone of his court. But you..." She broke off, unable to speak aloud the possibility that James could have her father charged with some crime.

"I've a friend, though—John Muir. He is captain of a merchant ship and, with your blessing, has offered to take us both from Roscraig. I trust Captain Muir; he feels for our situation and—"

"Go," her father interrupted in a whisper. His head twitched in a weak nod. "Go."

"He said he will take you, too. We only—"

Iain Douglas jerked his head to the side.

Glenna stared into his eyes for several moments, and the silent communication between her and her father was more painful than any words either could have spoken aloud.

I will not live long enough for the journey.

I can't go without you.

I want to die at Roscraig.

But you're all I have left.

"Da," Glenna pleaded on a quiet sob.

His jaws made the chewing motion several more time, in fits and starts, before his lips peeled apart once more.

"Ann'sley," he slurred. "Good."

Glenna stilled. "You knew him?"

His head twitched in another nod, and this time his yellow eyes held a glint of the man Glenna remembered from her youth. "Good." His jaws worked futilely for a moment and his next words were like a creaking wind. "You...go. Sssoon," he slurred.

Iain Douglas was clearly not afraid of the judgment of the king, but he seemed to want Glenna away from Roscraig before the monarch's arrival. Which led to another question burning a hole in Glenna's brain.

"Da," she began softly. "What happened to Mother?"

"Harr'et," he replied.

"You want Harriet?"

Iain shifted his gaze away from her to the window.

"Please tell me," Glenna pressed. "It wasn't fever, was it?"

He wouldn't look at her again.

Glenna stepped back from the bed, and a beam of sunlight glinted off the silver brooch lying on the floor just beneath the edge of the bed. She stooped and picked it up, looking at it as perhaps a stranger might, as if she had never seen the thing before.

In truth, perhaps she hadn't.

"You're tired, I understand. There is another feast tonight, and I have been ordered to attend. Perhaps after you have rested…"

Iain didn't blink, didn't nod. He seemed to have retreated back into his catatonic state, perhaps in exhaustion, perhaps in defense against Glenna's questions. Either way was acceptable for what Glenna felt she had to say next.

"I think I love him, Da. I think I'm in love with Tavish Cameron. In the beginning, I thought to marry him to save Roscraig—I thought I could convince him." She looked down at her hands, polished the silver of the brooch with one thumb. "But he still doesn't love me. And now he never will." She looked up.

Her father made no indication he'd heard anything she said.

"I'll fetch Harriet." She leaned over and pressed a kiss to his forehead while she curled Iain's fingers around the brooch. "I love you, Da. No matter what." And then she straightened and left the room quickly, eager for the fresh air of the stairwell.

On her way down the steps she spied a servant girl descending before her and called out. "Maid?"

The girl stopped and turned, looking up with a patient expression. "Aye, milady?"

"Please tell Mistress Cameron that the la—" She broke off. "That Iain Douglas wishes to see her."

"Aye, milady." She bobbed her head and was gone.

Then Glenna stood before her closed chamber door, a flutter of dread in her stomach. She hadn't spoken to Tavish since leaving the bed they'd shared the night before, and although she doubted he yet slumbered, her heart raced at the idea that he could be just beyond this barrier.

She hated him, hated what he was doing to her father, her life, her dignity.

She longed for his comfort in her distress, for him to love her again, and set aside his prejudices and consider that they were well matched, that she could be his companion—to choose her, please choose her.

She took a deep breath and opened the door.

Her deep breath turned into a relieved sigh at the empty chamber. Glenna closed and bolted the door. The conversation she'd had with her father had shattered her, but she could not yet let the pieces fall. Her mind whirled with the choices before her and their myriad consequences, but she could not order them. And so she threw herself into preparing as best she could for an unknown future, not thinking of the why or the how of the task.

She chose for the feast the shimmering violet with slit sleeves that allowed the embroidered emerald underdress to flow through. A white veil paired with a tall birdcage headpiece; silken stockings and new leather slippers completed the fine ensemble.

Then Glenna searched through Tavish's large table, her eyes going over the surface quickly, spying the inkpot and quill in its stand. She rifled through cubbies until she discovered a stack of small pieces of paper and carefully removed the top leaf. She paused with the quill raised over the pot.

What had she planned on writing? There were so many things she wanted the courage for speaking aloud to Tavish Cameron; but perhaps there was not enough ink in all the oceans to express the regret and heartbreak she felt if this letter was to be her goodbye, not only to him, but to all of Roscraig, to the life she'd known up to that very morning.

When Glenna at last began to write, she was finished in only a moment—the truth she now knew was concise, after all. Once the ink had dried, she folded the note and placed it in the center of one of the fine linen handkerchiefs, where it could be refolded without suspicion. After replacing it in the trunk, she quit the room to see about having water sent up for a bath.

She must look her very best upon playing the lady of Roscraig at her first—and last—feast.

* * * *

Harriet came into Iain's chamber once more, her arm pressing oddly against the front of her apron. She closed the door and bolted it, then went around the end of the bed, fishing in her bodice as she approached.

"Is this what you wanted, milord?" she asked, holding up the stolen vellum and writing utensils.

Iain grunted in assent and struggled against the ticking.

"Just a moment; just a moment." She placed the items on the stone sill and then rushed to his side, helping him to curl against the rough headboard. Then she turned back to the window and retrieved the vellum. "I canna write, milord; just my name, I'm afraid. Neither can I read."

Iain's head twitched, and his left fingers swung inward in a "come" gesture where they lay on his hip.

Harriet laid the vellum atop the blanket and uncorked the inkpot, nearly overturning it. "Oh! Mercy! All right, then. Here we are." She picked up the quill and dipped it, tapped it as she'd seen Tav do a thousand times, then placed the quill in Iain's limp grip. She slid a sheet of thick vellum from the roll and then fed it awkwardly between Iain's wrist and the coverlet, until the ink-darkened tip of the quill shuddered over the top of the page. She was shocked when the words began to sound out on the paper; skittering, quick, shaking. The swift writing was juxtaposed to the man's blank face, his slowly heaving chest.

Iain's good eye was rolled down toward the vellum, watching his efforts, although it couldn't be said whether or not he actually saw the script. It didn't matter—the story he wrote was vivid in the part of his mind that wasn't damaged, and he had no doubt that he would remember it all exactly as it happened.

Unlike his daughter's swiftly composed farewell, Iain Douglas's note would take a very long time.

Chapter 14

The already long trestle table had been further augmented by the addition of several quickly hewn extensions, and the finely carved chairs were now interspersed with both short and long backless benches to accommodate the scores of guests that had come to Roscraig in anticipation of the royal visit. Sixty-seven, at Tavish's last count; which brought the number of invitees now seating themselves at his feasting table to sixty-nine, counting himself and his mother.

Only one seat at the table, six places down on the right from where Tavish was seated at the head, remained conspicuously empty. The idea that she would deliberately disobey him by refusing to attend had not entered his mind before that moment. But then he remembered that Glenna was planning to leave him at first light, with the man now seated two down on his left—Captain John Muir.

If she thought so little of him as to leave him completely, surely she would think nothing of failing to appear at the feast. She could be hiding aboard the *Stygian* at this moment, seeking to evade him altogether before her escape.

The idea of it maddened him so that Tavish pushed back his chair and stood, even as the first in a line of servants bearing laden trays appeared in the hall doorway. Dinner be damned—he would find her, and he would bring her to the hall, bodily if need be.

But then the first maid jostled around and slipped sideways back into the darkness of the corridor, and an iridescent wash of violet and green swept through the doorway and came to a swinging halt as Glenna Douglas stared at the scores of people within the hall.

And they all stared at her. Tavish's breath caught in his throat as her eyes met his.

He'd always thought her beautiful, from the first moment he'd seen her pale countenance and cat eyes within the blackness of the entry corridor in the storm. And it was true that she had grown even more beautiful to Tavish in the interim. But tonight she was exquisite—slender and sparkling like a dark scepter in the gown Tavish had bought for her, the stone doorway around her like a royal fist.

The Lady Glenna, of Roscraig.

She broke gaze with him and gave an elegant curtsey to the room before sweeping across the boards toward the empty seat, her chin lifted. One by one, the male guests pushed back from their chairs or stood from their benches until Glenna had sat.

Only Tavish remained standing now, and he knew that his blatant attention for the woman whose own eyes seemed fixed on the candelabra in the center of the table was drawing awkward glances, but Tavish didn't care the least.

This was his hold, his hall, his table, his woman. And he would look at her whenever, and for as long as, he liked.

Glenna finally turned toward him, and the way her eyes glittered in the candlelight, holding the memories the two of them had made the night before, nearly caused Tavish to lose his composure and drag her from the feast.

Dinner *and* guests be damned.

"Forgive me, laird," she said. And Tavish wondered if she was speaking for her tardiness or her plot to escape him.

But he was saved from his impetuous urges by the entrance of the servants, and so he finally sat and, as he did so, relieved chatter burst forth along the table in an accompanying clatter of knives.

The meal seemed to last hours. Thankfully, Tavish was kept in distracted conversation by the guests to either side of him, participating when he could tear his attention from the blond woman farther down the table. Glenna herself seemed to be in high demand of the male guests particularly, and once again he heard her laugh rise above the crude clatter, like the tinkling of crystal. When Tavish determined the last course had been partaken of sufficiently, he rose with his chalice, signaling to the guests and the servants that the meal had ended.

The musicians who had been playing quietly in the front of the hall struck up a lively melody to lure the guests away from the clearing efforts, and several couples formed up immediately for a dance, while others milled to greet those whom they hadn't been seated near. Tavish himself struck out through the crush toward the sparkling gem that was Glenna, but before he could reach her, Audrey Keane had taken her arm and was pulling her toward the dancers, bringing Tavish to a rocking halt on his feet.

The two seemed to have come to some understanding. And he realized that it was perhaps that Glenna was leaving Roscraig—and Tavish—to Audrey.

Tavish watched Glenna swirl into formation, bobbing, kicking out a delicate ankle, clasping hands with Audrey and circling another couple. She was of course graceful on her feet, a talented dancer. And it was clear by her easy smile that she was enjoying herself and filled the role she played perfectly.

Of course she would fill the role perfectly, he said crossly to himself. *This is her home. It is I who am standing in the center of the floor like a simpleton.*

He felt like a fool, in so many ways. He exchanged his empty chalice for a full one and made his way to stand at the hearth and compose himself. It did not help his sour mood that Captain John Muir chose that moment to join him.

"More people here than I reckoned," the captain said mildly.

Tavish stared out over the crowd, trying not to strain too obviously for a glimpse of Glenna. "Aye."

"Glad I'll be to take up less crowded quarters. This noble life holds little appeal for a seaman."

"Does it not?" Tavish goaded. "Certainly, not now that you think you've secured what you wanted."

An awkward silence fell between them for a moment, and then Muir asked, "Is aught amiss, Tav? I ken we've had words, but—"

"After you take the hides to market," Tavish interrupted, "it is my wish that you turn the *Stygian* over to your first mate. I shall pay you your contracted wage, plus a generous separation fee. Perhaps if I had known of your plan in the beginning, I might have called it a wedding gift, I suppose."

Muir went still, but there was no alarm or dismay in his matter of fact demeanor. "You seem sure I will wed."

"I know you've schemed a way to lure her from Roscraig. Played on her doubts about me."

"I played on naught, Tav," Muir said with a sigh, clearly not so dishonorable that he would deny it. He turned his mild gaze back to the room of swirling guests. "Any doubts she had about you are your own doing. You were clear enough that you don't wish to marry her. What is she to do? Stay here at Roscraig forever, humiliated? You care not even for her father's reputation."

"You betray me. Both of you."

John turned to him then, and quickly. "No one's betrayed you. 'Tis your own disloyalty at fault here. You've railed against the nobility and their egos, their greed, for years. But learn you your blood is a wee bit violet, and you become Count Cockhead."

"You're only jealous I'm something you'll never be."

"A fool?" Muir laughed his salty laugh, hearty and genuine. "Nay." He drained his chalice and placed it on the tray of a passing servant. "Seems I truly doona belong here. So I bid you farewell, Tav. Farewell, and good fortune."

"She'll not go with you," Tavish warned, somewhat surprised that the end of such a long friendship had come so swiftly and with so few words.

"Send my wages to the *Stygian*. We'll be casting off at first light. *Laird*." John Muir walked away.

Tavish watched him weave through the guests, nearly bowling over the thin crier who had just stepped into the doorway of the hall. The young man stumbled aright and smoothed down his tunic while clearing his throat and tossing a cross look over his shoulder at the vanished Muir before projecting over the crowd.

"Lord Vaughn Hargrave, Baron Annesley."

The crier stepped aside, and a tall, thickly built older man stood in the doorway, surveying the hall with a sweeping, arrogant gaze. His hair was the color of the loch when it was whipped into a storm frenzy: dark gray with a crest of white along the beach of his forehead. His hat was wide and plush, hanging fashionably alongside his head and punctuated with a tall, white plume. His tunic was adorned with loops of hammered chains, their links glinting in the candlelight. A discernible murmur rippled through the crowd.

Vaughn Hargrave? Tavish frowned. That was the name of the man living in the estate that was Thomas Annesley's childhood home—but why was he using Darlyrede's title? Had there been a judgment handed down from the English king?

Regardless of the title he used, Tavish certainly hadn't invited the Englishman. Alarm rose in the deep recesses of Tavish's mind.

Then he saw Audrey Keane approach Hargrave and give a graceful curtsey. The lord bent low over Audrey's hand with a smile and a kiss for her knuckles, and then Audrey turned and gestured to the beautiful woman in violet at her side. Glenna did not curtsey, but did nod and offer her hand, upon which Hargrave bestowed the same affected show of homage.

Tavish had had quite enough of being thwarted in his own home. He struck out through the crowd, pushing between those who leaned their heads together and murmured as they covertly watched the elegant Englishman interacting with the enigmatic blonde. Tavish was surprised and rather cross that his mother was not at Glenna's side; he looked around the crowd briefly for her, but she seemed to have disappeared from the festivities.

It was Glenna who noticed Tavish's approach; she turned her head, and her gaze seemed to ignite at the sight of him. There was such a different guise about her tonight, not only her costume, but her demeanor. One of challenge and boldness that he had not seen before, and he wondered if thoughts of her escape heartened her.

The very sight of her made Tavish's knees weak. But before he could reach the group, Glenna turned away to disappear into the crowd.

Hargrave be damned—Tavish would deal with him later.

"Laird Cameron," Audrey called out with a smile and forcefully grabbed Tavish's arm to draw him into the group with a laugh. She snaked her arm fully through his. "You'll not escape before greeting Lord Hargrave—he's only just arrived. I must tell you how wonderful it is to encounter an old friend of my father's here at Roscraig."

So the man's presence was Audrey's doing.

"Old?" Hargrave mimicked, a palm to his chest and his eyes wide. "Miss Keane, you dash all hope."

Audrey's laughter tinkled. "Perhaps I should have said longtime friend and business partner. No one could possibly deny your youthful vigor, my lord."

"You are too kind, my dear," Hargrave said with a grotesque moue of sincerity.

"My lord, this is Laird Tavish Cameron of Roscraig," Audrey continued. "Of course, you are already well familiar."

Tavish frowned but said nothing, but he'd no need, for the older man spoke right away with a bow.

"I thank you for your gracious hospitality, Laird Cameron," Hargrave said, and Tavish wondered that Audrey could not see through the man's blatant dramatics. "It is no small feat for a lesser lord to engage the interest of a monarch. Especially a lord whose lineage is perhaps in question. Quite an honor, indeed, for the king of Scotland to deign to visit your wee demesne on the firth. You must have God's own ear. I should do well to watch the laird of Roscraig closely."

It was all said with a broad smile and even a chuckle, but Tavish felt as though the man had spat on him with the veiled insults.

"Lord Hargrave, I was not aware of your intent to attend our hosting of the king. It's no matter, though—many elderly lords and ladies were invited to Roscraig by Miss Keane as a courtesy. There was little necessity in me learning all their names."

Tavish actually felt Audrey's surprise ripple up his arm. "I didn't—I beg your pardon, laird. I thought it was you who had invited Lord Hargrave. That is why I was so surprised at his arrival, and pleased that you and my father share such an esteemed friend."

Tavish held the man's glittering gray gaze, and in that moment, a battle line was formed.

"I must apologize to you both," Hargrave said with an exaggerated hangdog expression. "I was invited by neither of you; I'm here at the behest of King James himself."

The awkward silence exploded as the musicians again picked up their instruments and a lively dance began. Audrey was pressed to join by one of the young lords mooning over her the past week, and so she whirled away with a somewhat relieved smile for Tavish, leaving him alone in the crowded hall with Vaughn Hargrave.

Tavish wasted no time and trifled with no false courtesy—at heart, he was still an Edinburgh merchant, and he knew when he was being sold a load of ballast.

"Why are you really here, Hargrave?" he challenged. "We both know James didn't invite you—you're not important enough to Scotland."

"No?" the man dared with a superficially surprised expression. He helped himself to a chalice from a passing tray. "I dare say I am. For not only am I the man whose daughter was killed by your murdering, bastard father, I'm also the man who's been paying Roscraig's taxes for thirty years." He gestured toward Tavish with the cup in a mock salute and then drank.

Tavish felt the bottom drop out of his stomach. "It was you? Why?"

Hargrave chuckled. "Ah. For a supposed man of business, you have little head for protecting your future interests, do you, boy? Ah, well—as the father is, so the son."

"You have no claim to Roscraig," Tavish argued. "It was left to Thomas Annesley when he was yet a boy."

"Think you that will matter now that he is hanged as a murderer?" Hargrave asked in mock curiosity. "I have filled the Scottish kings' coffers with Roscraig's worth many times over. That is not something James is likely to overlook. Especially as my power grows in the south."

"Roscraig isn't for sale," Tavish said. "And I'll not allow you to remain in my hold so that you might petition against me."

"Nay?" Hargrave repeated and then nodded with a sigh. "Very well. I shall depart with the dawn and leave you to your rightful home."

Tavish's eyes narrowed.

Hargrave let a sly smile slip at the corner of his mouth. "After you have reimbursed me the taxes I've paid on Roscraig, of course."

"What?"

"That's right," Hargrave said quietly. "Thirty years of taxes. In silver and gold. Every penny accounted for by morning. After all, it is I who's kept your hold from reverting to the Crown." Then he looked across the room and gestured with his chin. When Tavish turned to where he indicated, there was Glenna.

"Of course," he went on, sadly, "perhaps I was only paying the taxes to protect poor Iain Douglas, who was taken for everything he had by your father in exchange for this falling-down pile of rocks. *Perhaps*...I am the only one who knows that Thomas Annesley made an earlier transfer of the property to a man called Douglas, who aided his escape from the soldiers who would have dragged him back to England to meet the judgment due him."

Tavish's blood ran cold. Whether it was true or not, Hargrave's word that Iain Douglas was rightful laird of Roscraig could hold weight with the king—especially if Hargrave had been paying Roscraig's debts all these years. His story was plausible.

"Is it truly Roscraig you want?" Tavish asked.

"Me, want this gull shit–covered rock? Oh, please Lord, nay." Hargrave clapped Tavish's upper arm with a hearty laugh that drew indulgent smiles from those closest to them. The man was still chuckling as he leaned closer to speak in a low voice, his eyes still squinted with false mirth.

"I want revenge. Revenge for so many wrongs done to me. I want to destroy every hint that Thomas Annesley ever lived on this earth. I have waited a very long time, and spent large sums of money preparing for the time that I could bring down his filthy legacy, and I shall begin my recompense now with you—his mongrel pup. You will never speak his name aloud again, unless it is in a curse."

Tavish's jaw clenched. "I don't have the fortune you require for repayment," he said, nearly choking on the words. "A debt of that amount would destroy me—and well you know it."

"What I well know is that you do indeed have quite a tidy sum tucked away in private. Don't you? Your own worth and a large portion generously given you by Master Keane." Hargrave winked and nodded.

The trunk in the cave.

Muir.

Muir had to have told Audrey's father on his last trip to Edinburgh, who had likely relayed the information to his old colleague. Perhaps Muir had known all along Hargrave's plan.

"It's not enough," Tavish repeated. "Thirty years'…"

"You're likely right," Hargrave admitted. "And so, because I am a reasonable man who understands that your father's sins are not of your doing, instead of the whole of such an admittedly outrageous sum, what coin you have hidden away along with the surrender of your whore to me shall satisfy the debt in full."

Now Tavish's heart ceased beating in his chest for a moment. "I don't know what you're talking about."

"Don't feign innocence with me, boy. Everyone in Edinburgh is aware of the painful situation in which you've placed the lovely Miss Keane—especially her father. I know Glenna Douglas warms your bed. I even know that just last night you ripped off her clothes before savaging her. Not that I blame you one whit—she is exquisite, and I want her for myself. Already, I imagine what I will do to—"

Tavish's anger was white-hot. "How did you get into the Tower last night?"

"Why, I only just arrived here an hour ago. I'm offended you would think me worthy of such a petty crime. But it should teach you that I know absolutely everything that has gone on at Roscraig since your arrival, and even everything that's happened before. I'm quite good at finding things out. You have no secrets from me."

Hargrave leaned in even closer. "For instance, I know that you beat your own stepfather to death with a poker. Eh?" Hargrave leaned away with a nod and a chuckle. "No secrets. No shame. I'm certain he deserved it. It felt good, didn't it, lad? Beating that old bastard like he'd beat your poor, peasant mother. Beating him until his brai—"

Tavish lunged forward and seized Hargrave by his gilded tunic. But the man unexpectedly moved toward him and threw his arm around Tavish in a hearty embrace with a roar of laughter and lifted his chalice high even as Tavish struggled away.

"To Tavish Cameron, laird of Roscraig!" Hargrave announced, and the hall answered him with a chorus of "Huzzah!"

Tavish stood in the center of the floor as the guests drank to his name, his chest heaving, his mind whirling. Hargrave winked at him and then raised his cup again.

"Welcome to the nobility, Tavish Cameron." He drank, and his smile was still visible in his flat, gray eyes over the rim of his cup.

Chapter 15

Glenna was surprised when her next revolution in the dance brought her around face-to-face with the imposing Lord Vaughn Hargrave. He took her outstretched hand without hesitation, pulling Glenna along in the steps so that they missed not even a quarter beat. They stepped toward each other, twisting their torsos in opposing directions for a count of three.

"We meet again, Lady Glenna," Lord Hargrave said with a confident smile.

"Lord Hargrave, you surprise me," she said.

They stepped away from each other, bowed, and then turned to the partner behind. The steps were repeated before Glenna was in his grasp again, this time for a slow, skipping circuit around a new set of paired dancers. His ability exceeded that of a man half his age.

"I am surprised at your surprise," he said, continuing their conversation. "Of course I would seek to gobble up any crumbs of time with the lady of Roscraig. Your beauty and grace restore my weary soul."

Glenna felt her cheeks heat at the flattery, but there was an uneasy sensation in her stomach. "You are too kind."

"Not kind at all, my dear. Only selfish. You would be a sensation at the balls in Northumberland. Have you ever been to England?" They filed into the center of the circuit as the other dancers began to skip about the perimeter. Hargrave bowed.

Glenna curtsied. "I have not."

They stepped toward each other and joined right hands again before turning away from each other and walking as if around a maypole.

"You absolutely must come to Darlyrede. As my very special guest."

Glenna had to force herself to swallow as they changed both hands and directions. It didn't matter what she told him—she still had the option of escape on the *Stygian* with the dawn—and yet his boldness made her uncomfortable. "I am an unmarried woman, Lord Hargrave, and my father is quite ill. It would be unseemly of me to depart Roscraig without his permission."

"Unattached, are you?" Hargrave pressed, the words spoken in such a way that Glenna looked into his eyes. "I am loath to admit that there have been rumors about your...*arrangement* with the Laird Cameron. I would not mention it, save that I am concerned for your future, my dear."

"My future is none of your affair," Glenna said stiffly, her face flaming once more. "We are strangers."

"Be not shamed in my presence," Hargrave insisted in a low, earnest voice as they came together once more. "My own daughter would be only a handful of years older than you had she lived, so you must understand my motive at seeing so fine and beautiful a young noblewoman so sorely used. None in Northumberland know of this tempest brought on by Tavish Cameron's arrival. My wife and I would be pleased to host you in the search for a suitable match should King James's decision not favor you."

Glenna looked up again. "Your wife?"

Hargrave's eyes widened, and then he threw his head back and laughed his hearty, amused laugh. "Oh, my dear, you are precious. Forgive me for not being more clear. I knew your father very briefly when he was a young man. I have kept Roscraig—and you—in my thoughts these thirty years. And it seems I have arrived in just the nick of time. Lady Caris would be so relieved at your arrival."

"I don't understand," Glenna said warily.

They began their skipping circuit again. "My wife has suffered much loss during the course of our marriage. Our daughter—our only child—was killed on the eve of her wedding. Lady Caris never recovered from the blow, but her broken heart was pieced into use when we took in our orphaned niece to raise as our own. The girl disappeared in the night some years ago. We've never stopped searching for her."

"Disappeared? She ran away or was abducted, you mean?" Glenna couldn't help asking.

Lord Hargrave wore a pained expression. "God knows." He paused while they circled each other, and Glenna thought she saw him catch his lower lip between his teeth, as if bracing himself against an onslaught of emotion. They met again.

"Any matter, my wife has suffered the loss of essentially two daughters. Lady Caris would welcome the opportunity to nurture a beautiful and deserving young woman such as yourself into a profitable match. That is, unless you have determined to remain at Roscraig and fight for your father's legacy, of course."

"I really don't see the wisdom in that," Glenna admitted stiffly. "I seem to be without claim, or funds to support the towers."

"Oh, no, my dear. No, no, no. Not without claim," Lord Hargrave said with widened eyes. "Roscraig's care was given over to your father before you were even born. I have no proof beyond my word, of course, but perhaps it might be of some assistance with the king were you of a mind to challenge the commoner upstart seeking to oust you from your home."

Glenna felt her feet slowing to a stop, knew the other dancers were flowing around her and the intimidating old lord, but she didn't care.

"Roscraig was given to my father?" she asked. "By whom?"

Lord Hargrave took her hand again and dragged her back into the formation. They changed direction at once, and the Englishman looked pointedly to the large portrait over the blazing hearth. "By the man who was once that boy." He looked into her eyes, and Glenna saw a black fire there. "Thomas Annesley, of course."

The music ended, and the other dancers clapped as they moved away from the center of the floor. Glenna stared up at the composed gentleman, unable to command her feet to carry her from the spot.

"You're certain of this?" she asked. "My father has a legitimate claim to Roscraig?"

"Unfortunately, quite certain." Lord Hargrave nodded solemnly. "There is none other than Thomas Annesley to blame for the death of my daughter, Cordelia. He escaped into Scotland after her murder, knowing all his holdings would become forfeit. And so to prevent their total loss, he gave over Roscraig to his friend. I have heard that your father is not expected to live, and that burden must weigh heavily on a lady without family. I will do everything in my power to prevent Thomas Annesley—or his son—from profiting further from my daughter's murder."

"I don't see how I could succeed," Glenna said through numb lips. "What is there to prove?"

"You need only leave that to me, Lady Glenna. It would be my honor—no, my privilege—were you to place yourself under my guardianship. Considering the precarious state of your father's health, I would have a document drawn up so that your protection is utterly binding, and there would be naught Tavish Cameron could do about it. Then, should you decide to quit Scotland and put this whole ugliness behind you, we will depart for Darlyrede without another word of it, and you shall live there as our own family. Or, conversely, I shall gird my loins against Tavish Cameron's threats and wait in the rain if

I must for King James's arrival. Whence forth I shall stand before his court and testify on your father's behalf."

"Tavish has threatened you?" Glenna asked.

"Of course he has, my dear," Lord Hargrave said quietly and with a small smile. "He knows that I have the power to return him to his common shop and restore *you* to your rightful station as lady of Roscraig." His smile grew infinitesimally larger. "He wasn't expecting me, you see. I am his worst nightmare."

Lord Hargrave reached out and touched her cheek. "But I am afraid of no man, be he merchant or king. No—for you, my dear, I will scrape Tavish Cameron from my heel like the dung from which he was spawned."

A young man approached them before Glenna could formulate any sort of response. He bowed and held out his hand, and Glenna realized that the music had begun once more.

"My lady?" he queried with a charming smile.

Movement over Lord Hargrave's shoulder drew Glenna's attention to the doorway of the hall, and she saw Tavish Cameron striding toward her with a quartet of rough-looking men.

"You may take her with my compliments, lad," Lord Hargrave said to the young lord, apparently giving the man permission to dance with Glenna—an idea that briefly stuck in a tender part of her mind before it was lost in the whirlwind of emotion churned by Tavish's approach.

"But only temporarily." Lord Hargrave gave a bow and a wry grin. "Never fear, beautiful Glenna—I shan't be far away from you all the night, and I shall be present for king's arrival, come what may. I swear it."

The young noble swept Glenna into the formation just as Tavish came upon Lord Hargrave. The older man spun on his heel at once, walking far in advance of the four sailors who rolled in his wake toward the door. But rather than make a meek exit, Vaughn Hargrave called out hearty farewells to the guests, even pausing twice to shake hands as if it were his own feast. Glenna's head whipped around to keep sight of the man until he had disappeared into the corridor.

"He's quite admirable, is he not?" the young lord asked in an amused tone.

Glenna had all but forgotten the presence of her partner. "What?"

"Lord Hargrave," the man clarified. "I hope to be half as accomplished when I am his age."

"Oh. He does seem shrewd."

Her thoughts were further interrupted by the firm gripping of her upper arm. Glenna looked up to find the face of Tavish Cameron glaring down at her.

He glanced at the young lord. "You'll forgive me the intrusion," he said.

"Well, I—" the man blustered.

"My thanks." Tavish placed his right hand on the lord's chest and pushed. Then he swung Glenna into the formation, backward and going the wrong direction.

"What are you doing?" Glenna stammered.

"What did Hargrave say to you?" he demanded.

"Ow, Tavish—stop."

"I'm dancing with you—if we stop, it will seem suspect."

"You're stepping on my feet, and we've just run over the marquis!"

"Fine." He whirled her out of the circle to the shadows of the far wall. "What did Hargrave say to you?" he repeated.

Glenna looked up at Tavish towering over her, his expression full of barely restrained fury. She'd hoped to impress him, make him realize how good she would be for him; how, together, they could conquer any problem created by their less than conventional lives.

She wanted him to love her, not Audrey Keane, who had suddenly that night seemed to want to make friends with Glenna.

But the first words he'd said to her were an interrogation pertaining to an old man who perhaps had the power to threaten Tavish's claim on Glenna's home. And the repercussions of that were very clear now. A chill twisted up her spine, freezing any heated emotions that wanted release, but also helping her to stand taller and stirring her anger into a manageable simmer.

"Very well. He told me that Iain Douglas is Roscraig's rightful laird."

She saw Tavish's thick, whisker-shadowed throat convulse as he swallowed, and his fingers around her arms gentled. "It's a lie, Glenna."

"You'd like me to believe that," she said as she jerked away from him. "I knew when you first came here that my father would have never claimed something that didn't belong to him. But I listened to you—you, who has everything in the world to gain by making me think my life was a lie, that my father was a liar. *I believed you.*"

"Glenna, Hargrave is only telling you what you wish to hear so that he can gain control over you."

She leaned closer to him, trying to ignore the now familiar scent of him that wanted to soften her with whispered memories of how he had held her in his arms.

"Is he now?" she challenged. "That rather sounds like something you would do."

"What are you talking about?"

"You know exactly what I'm talking about," she said between her teeth. "You made your intentions for the hold and me clear straightaway, and you have not deviated from your plan. The only reason you've shown me any care or attention was to keep me enamored of you until after the king handed down his decision. You manipulated me."

"I've never manipulated you, Glenna. Vaughn Hargrave has ill intent toward you."

She stared in disbelief at him, huffed a mirthless laugh. "And what exactly have your intentions toward me been, Tavish? Honorable?" She waited a scant moment for a reply that she knew wouldn't come. "Lord Hargrave recognizes me as the lady of Roscraig. Now, I think I have performed enough for one evening; I must look in on my father."

She made to move past him, but Tavish grabbed her arm again. "You will return directly to the hall afterward. Go nowhere else, and do not leave this hold."

Glenna wheeled around and struck him soundly across the cheek, the blow echoing over even the music in the hall and drawing shocked glances from the guests.

"You are neither my husband nor my father," Glenna said in a loud, clear voice, uncaring who watched, who heard. Let them witness it, these strangers, these people who had been neighbors to Roscraig for years and turned their backs on her father. She hoped they enjoyed every salacious moment.

"And until the king has given his word, *you are not* the laird of Roscraig. Dare you to lay your common hand upon me again, *Master Cameron*, and I shall see you arrested upon the king's arrival."

His eyes hardened. "A lady now that you're no longer in rags, are you? I bought the dress you're wearing."

"And I kept Frang Roy from slitting your throat in your sleep," she parried. "We all make mistakes."

Glenna turned and took the arm of the marquis who had unabashedly approached to listen to the altercation. The nobleman gallantly escorted her from the hall and even waved to the musicians to once more strike up their lively tune. Once in the dark, cool corridor, Glenna calmly thanked the marquis for his accompaniment and held her head high as she mounted the stairs, as slowly and with as much dignity as possible.

It was only once she rounded the shielding curve of the landing that she allowed herself to pause against the stones with a gasp, the shock of her heartbreak so severe and final that it left her eyes dry; her chest cold and dark and hollow.

Chapter 16

Tavish felt the surreptitious stares burning through his tunic in the wake of Glenna's bold rejection and departure from the hall, but he didn't care. Let them look—none of them meant anything to him. There was not one person in the hall now he could call his friend—even Audrey had vanished sometime in the past hour. And so now he was surrounded by vicious strangers, bloodthirsty cannibals, these noblemen and rich merchants.

Welcome to the nobility, Tavish Cameron. Hargrave's words haunted him, and Tavish felt like a fool.

Hargrave. Tavish had made the wrong choice in rounding up hands to remove the English lord from the feast before seeing that Glenna was out of harm's way, thinking that Hargrave would surely raise objection. By the time Tavish had returned to the hall, Hargrave had her firmly ensnared in his web, filling her head with the lies that Tavish had hoped were naught but grandiose threats meant to bully Tavish into giving the man what he wanted. He had then departed easily, having already set in motion his dastardly plan for achieving his goal.

Of which Tavish was as of yet unsure. Hargrave didn't want Roscraig, and he'd been willing to forgive the bulk of the debt of the Tower's taxes. He'd said he wanted revenge for the wrongs done to him, but how could that be achieved by stealing away with Glenna? She had no connection to Thomas Annesley—had never so much as heard the name when Tavish had arrived at Roscraig.

How had Hargrave known such intimate details of the goings-on in the keep, and of Tavish's younger years? Had Vaughn Hargrave been spying on him all this time, knowing who Tavish's father was?

But why? And how?

He didn't know the answers, but he did know that, no matter Glenna's anger with him in the moment, and no matter the king's decision in the days to come, Vaughn Hargrave was a danger to the beautiful woman whom Tavish had so taken for granted since he first stepped foot inside the Tower.

And it was his duty to protect her, whether she wanted his protection or nae.

Tavish strode through the crowd toward the doorway, feeling the inquisitive stares all but pushing him into the corridor. He bounded up the stone steps two at a time until he came to the uppermost level of the east tower. He paused before Iain Douglas's door.

My door.

He wrapped his fingers around the handle, but then paused.

No. Not his door. Iain Douglas's door. The door behind which Glenna's beloved father lay dying.

Tavish released the handle and raised his fist, rapping swiftly. There was no sound from within, and Tavish's concern rose.

Hargrave could have lain in wait for her. Glenna could already be gone from Roscraig…

Tavish pounded on the door in earnest now, shaking the very planks against the stone walls.

"Glenna!" he barked.

"Tav?" a voice called out hesitantly from the other side of the door.

"Mam?" Tavish asked. "Is Glenna with you?"

"Are you alone?" Harriet asked.

"Aye, 'tis only me."

Tavish heard the scrape of the bolt and then the door creaked open a hand's breadth. A slice of his mother's face appeared in the opening, and she seemed to be wielding the same old sword that Glenna Douglas had threatened him with on the night of his arrival at Roscraig. The eye visible to him looked pointedly around the corridor before Harriet opened the door completely.

"Aye, Lady Glenna's within. What do you want with her?"

Tavish tried to look around his mother. "I've come to escort her back to the hall, Mam."

"Ah-ah!" she said in warning and raised the tip of the sword. "Nae ye don't. She'll nae be coming back to your grand feast, Tavish Cameron."

"Mam, you don't understand," Tavish said, fighting to reign in his temper. "Glenna isn't safe without me."

"Oh, I think I understand a mite more than you do, ye wee kipping brat," Harriet said with a stern expression. "Ain't none of us safe with the likes of Vaughn Hargrave about the Tower."

Tavish froze. "You know Vaughn Hargrave was here?"

"I'm nae deaf, Tavish. As soon as I heard him announced in the hall, I came straight to the laird's side." Harriet at last lowered the sword that, until that moment, Tavish had been unconvinced she wouldn't use on him.

"Why would you come here?" Tavish asked, feeling reality growing stranger and stranger with each passing moment.

Harriet Cameron opened the door even wider, and Tavish's eyes searched the room. Glenna stood before her father's bed, and her eyes were cold as they met his.

Mam sighed and stepped away from the door. "You may as well come in then. It will save me breath not having to say it all twice."

Tavish walked past his mother, his eyes only for the beautiful woman who didn't give him a chance to speak to her.

"I'm not going anywhere with you," she said. "This is my home, and I'll do as I please."

"I have a hold full of guests, princess," Tavish said. "I can't be wandering the corridors after you all the night."

"Go back to them," Glenna said, flinging her hand toward the door. "Lot of two-faced, greedy hypocrites. You deserve each other."

"Children," Mam interrupted sharply. "That's quite enough—you'll disturb the laird with your bickering."

The scolding caused Tavish's gaze to skitter reluctantly to the still figure on the bed. Iain Douglas appeared as though nothing could disturb him—his mouth gaped, the bony prominences of his throat reached for the ceiling. He was clearly dying.

"Forgive me," Tavish said in a low voice.

Harriet arched a sparse brow. "That's better. Now." She turned to walk toward the window and indicated the armchair with a flick of her hand as she passed it. "Milady, if you'll make yourself comfortable, Tav will mind the door for us." She reached the stone sill and leaned against it, taking an obvious look at the ground far below. Apparently satisfied with what she saw, she turned to face the room once more, settling her back against the wall along the window, closest to Iain Douglas's side. She looked at both Tavish and Glenna in turn before speaking again.

"I saved Tommy Annesley's life. Saint Brigid herself delivered him to me on her own feast night, and 'twas she who gave me the knowledge to heal him and the courage to keep him hidden in me da's barn all those weeks without being caught." She looked at Glenna, and her expression softened somewhat. "I know what Hargrave must have said to you, milady; that was Tommy killed his daughter. Cordelia, her name was. But he didna. *He didna.* He wouldna tell me exactly what happened—if even he knew, but he did tell me that Hargrave had a hand in it."

"Lord Hargrave killed his own daughter?" Glenna asked. "Did Thomas Annesley say how? Did he have proof?"

Mam dropped her eyes to the floorboards for a moment. "He was just a boy," she said softly, wistfully. "A beautiful boy—ten and eight. And I,"—she chuckled here—"I was even younger. He cried himself to sleep in my arms for his sweet Cordelia, and then would wake in a terror, screaming her name, sobbing 'the blood, the blood.'" She covered her mouth with her hand for a moment, then looked up again, this time at Tavish. "He was scared. Scared that Vaughn Hargrave would somehow find him, even in the hinterland Scots haymow he was hiding in. I've never seen a person so afraid in all my days since."

"Perhaps he feared justice," Tavish couldn't help himself from positing.

"His fear was that there would be nae justice," Mam snapped. "Someone did come to the farm for him. A band of ruffians led by a woman, of all things." She looked back to Glenna now. "A woman with blond hair and green eyes. I remember hearing them arrive at the cottage, and I crept to the top of the stairs to listen. They'd been to the village asking about Tommy and the horses, and someone told them my father had recently acquired such a pair as was runnin' wild in our wood. When she mentioned the name Hargrave, I knew Tommy was in great danger."

"Why?" Glenna asked, her expression almost painfully intense; it seemed to Tavish that her features were carved from the finest alabaster.

"The woman never said Tommy was wanted as a criminal. She referred to him as Hargrave's own beloved son, whose return was sorely desired after a horrible row. A family spat, said she.

"Well, I knew right away that if they found Tommy, if he was made to return to England with that woman, he was as good as dead. I heard the woman offer Da coin to let her see the horses and search the barns, so I crept back upstairs and went out the window. It was raining, and my hands slipped from the sill and I landed badly on my leg."

Tavish was taken aback. "The one you limp on?"

"Aye, me bad leg. It wasna broken, though, thank the lord."

Tavish found himself frowning at the imagining of his mother as a young girl, injured so, yet desperate to warn Thomas Annesley.

She continued. "I told Tommy about the woman and the men, and he whispered one word. 'Meg,' says he."

Tavish's gaze went to Glenna again as he recalled the intricate grave marker on the cliff overlooking the firth. *Margaret Douglas.* But Glenna said nothing, her expression stony.

"Tommy left out the back of the barn with the black horse, just as Da opened the front doors. There was no way out for me, so I hid down in the hay, way in the back, praying they wouldna search there, but they did. They overturned what seemed to be every piece of hay. It was clear someone had been living up in the mow, and Da saw that one of his fine new horses was missing."

Harriet paused, and the intervening years seemed to accumulate on her ashen face all at once, so that she aged before Tavish's eyes. "I doona think Da would have beaten me so if they had left that horse. But he took a flail to me. Threatened to kill me if I didn't tell him where to find Tommy so he could claim the reward. I fell down the slot trying to get away from him, and that's how my bad leg got bad. I wasna allowed in the house again from that night forward. Within a fortnight, I was wed to Dolan Cameron and moved to Edinburgh, and I never saw me da again. Never wished to, either."

Glenna at last spoke. "Did Dolan Cameron know that Tavish was not his son?"

"He was a sharp man," Mam conceded, and although the stony look had fallen from her face, it had left behind a sagging expression of exhaustion. "He could not have succeeded so well with the shop were he nae. So, aye, he figured it out soon enough. It would have been in his rights to turn me out or have me da jailed, but he was cruel enough; telling me that if the bairn was a girl, he would throw her from the highest building on Market Street and dash her brains against the stones." She looked up at Tavish. "But it was Tav, of course. A good strong lad that Dolan was happy to claim as his own."

"He *was* cruel," Tavish corroborated. "And I thought that monster was my father until I was sixteen."

Mam dropped her eyes to the floor for a moment. "I thought that was best for your future. I daren't so much as breathe the word 'Roscraig' lest it somehow lead back to Tommy."

"What made you decide to tell him about his true father when he was sixteen?" Glenna asked.

"To warn me," Tavish said, cutting off his mother's reply. "What has your tale to do with the issue at hand, Mam?"

"To show Lady Glenna—to show you both—that Vaughn Hargrave has been out for Tommy's blood for more than thirty years. He has waited all this time in the hope that someone connected with Tommy would surface, and it seems that 'twas Tommy himself who alerted Hargrave by turning himself in. He didn't come here to wish either of you well."

Tavish looked away from both women toward the darkened window, not wishing to repeat the vulgar and lascivious comments Hargrave had made about Glenna.

"Perhaps," Glenna said in a thoughtful tone, "he is nothing more than a father who was devastated by the murder of his daughter."

Tavish looked back at her quickly as she rose from the chair.

She looked to Mam now. "Tavish is your only child. If someone killed him and then fled the land to escape their deserved punishment, would you not exhaust every coin, every resource, for the rest of your life hunting that person down to see that they paid for what they did?"

Mam's face was pained. "Tommy didna—"

"You don't know that, Harriet," Glenna interrupted, her words nearly a shout. "You weren't there when Cordelia Hargrave died—none of us were. You want to believe that the man whose child you bore was good. That he was not capable of the heinous crime of which he is accused. But what if Thomas Annesley did kill Hargrave's daughter? What if it was even an accident? What if Vaughn Hargrave only wishes to accomplish what he told me—which is to stop Thomas Annesley from hurting anyone else, even beyond the grave." She paused. "Harriet, he says Thomas gave Roscraig to my father. Before I was born." Now she turned to look at Tavish. "And if he testifies to that before the king, your inheritance is worthless."

Tavish stepped forward. "Did he also tell you that it is he who has been paying the taxes on Roscraig all these years? If he testifies before the king, aye, it could temporarily save your place at the Tower—until he demands repayment." He made sure to meet her gaze.

"You're absurd," Glenna scoffed. "You really would do anything to keep Roscraig, wouldn't you? The more I learn about you, Tavish Cameron, the more I am certain you favor your sire. You would use me, just as Thomas Annesley used your mother. The only difference between Harriet and me is that I am not so foolish as to have fallen in love with you."

Mam bowed her head for a moment, and then she looked up, her chin lifted, her face proud. "I'm sorry if I am foolish, milady. If loving a person makes me a fool, then so be it. I could do little to save Tommy from Vaughn Hargrave thirty years ago, but I wanted to do all I could to protect you now. Please excuse me." She crossed the floor between them and struggled with the bolt only a moment before escaping the room.

Tavish felt his anger flare and was glad for the burn that cauterized the wound he felt.

"I've never used you, Glenna. Had I wished to truly ruin you, had I not cared a whit for you, I would have taken you fully a score of times already," he accused. "It's not as if you didn't want me to."

Glenna shrugged. "That has little to do with love. Fortunate for me you were too much of a coward to go through with it. Learned at least one lesson from your old da, did you? Careful you don't leave a bastard behind?"

"Aye, I did learn that lesson from Thomas Annesley," Tavish shot back. "I can only imagine the hell Mam went through for my sake. My earliest memories are of Dolan Cameron beating her until she couldn't walk, couldn't see. But she had nowhere to go with me, and so she stayed and took the beatings. She took them until I killed Dolan Cameron."

She was staring at him, and he let her, unable to snatch the confession back. He hadn't wanted her to know the violence he was capable of, lest she compare it to the crimes of which Thomas Annesley was accused. Somewhere in the back of Tavish's mind, he thought much the same as Glenna—perhaps Thomas Annesley *had* killed the girl. Perhaps he *had* double-crossed Iain Douglas. But even if those things were true, Tavish knew beyond any shadow of doubt that Vaughn Hargrave was a liar, and a very real danger to the people most important to him at Roscraig.

"When you were sixteen," Glenna guessed.

"Aye," he said, knowing she was putting together the clues. The rest didn't matter now. "I came upon him in a temper, flogging Mother with a baton. I think he would have finally killed her that day. At least, I feared he would. I was sick of it. And I was bigger than him by then; stronger. I took the baton from him; hit him but once. I was so horrified at what I'd done—patricide—I'd decided to turn myself in. But Mam...Mam told me he wasn't my real father. And, just like that"—he snapped his fingers—"Dolan Cameron became nothing more than a stranger who had been allowed to abuse my mother for my own sake."

Her expression had softened somewhat, but her cat eyes were still glittering. "How did you explain his death?"

"I explained nothing. His body was found at the docks with his purse strings cut."

She nodded vaguely as if agreeing with the course of action, and Tavish wished in that moment that he had taken Glenna, planted his seed in her. The very imagining of it caused his heart to beat in a funny rhythm, for he knew there would be no running for Tavish. The idea that he could leave Glenna and their child, no matter if it meant that his life was threatened...

The regular paths Tavish's mind took when working a problem suddenly vanished, and a new, barely discernible trail through deep woodland was the only track available as a new idea pressed him toward the unknown territory.

If Hargrave had now decided to transfer the guilt of his daughter's death from Thomas Annesley's to Tavish's own head, did that mean Glenna would be in danger as long as she was connected to him?

Perhaps Thomas Annesley had not only been preserving his own life in leaving Mam the way he had—perhaps he had been protecting her. It hadn't been some band of anonymous swords come to find him—Thomas had known the woman by name.

Meg.

And he'd told Mam about Roscraig. That didn't sound like a man whose only goal was saving his own skin.

If Tavish stood aside and let Glenna's plan to leave at dawn on the *Stygian* play out without protest, he knew that Muir would keep her safe. Hargrave could never know where she had gone and would never think to look for her as the wife of a sea captain. Glenna would be beyond the king's scrutiny and judgment, and away from the rumored talk their cohabitation at Roscraig had generated. In another country, she could get what few people were granted: a new life.

"Will you come back to the hall?" he asked, hoping that she didn't hear the insecurity behind the query. There was no way she could know the weight her answer held or the unspoken questions it would answer.

"Nay," she said, her gaze meeting his across the breadth of the room. She stood up and went to the bedside, fussing with the furs that covered the old man, and did not turn to face him when she continued. "I don't know how long my father has left, and shame on me should I choose such pompous, heartless parasites over him. If it means that you cry foul on our bargain, so be it. You may add it to the long list of grievances you have against me to air before the king when he arrives. I'm certain the court will be thrilled to hear the details of it."

Tavish felt his jaw clench and a wave of foreign emotion wash over him. He couldn't identify it beyond the similarity it bore to the many moments in Edinburgh when he had been made to feel less than the burgess and his cronies; when he had been forced to tolerate the thinly veiled allusions to his class status, and when the burgess himself suggested how odd it was that Tavish did not resemble Dolan Cameron in the least.

But Glenna Douglas was not shaming him for what he was not; she was merely holding up a mirror so that for the first time since his arrival at the Tower, Tavish could see himself as the laird of Roscraig he had become.

"Don't go...don't go outside the hold without alerting me," he said quietly, and then added, "Please."

Her motions stilled, but she did not turn around. "I'll be in this chamber until dawn."

Tavish swallowed. *Dawn.* He should let her go. Just let her go with Muir and let him keep her safe.

"I hope that what you said to Mam was untrue. I hope that you do care for me." He turned to the door, but paused with his fingers gripping the handle, gathering his courage, his pride about him. "God dammit—I'll not marry Audrey, Glenna."

"You've told me that what you choose to do at Roscraig is none of my affair," Glenna said. "I don't see why I should bother with thinking on it now."

"Perhaps you might search your heart for a reason to think on it tonight," Tavish suggested. "And if you perchance find even the smallest interest as to why I would refuse her, we might discuss it on the morn."

She turned her head then to look at him, and it pained him to see her green eyes so full of hurt and resentment. "I don't trust you. You've done naught but play games with me since the day you arrived."

"No games. I am not Thomas Annesley, and I will keep you safe, Glenna. From Hargrave, from the king. I swear it now, before your father." He glanced pointedly toward the still form on the bed. "You look very beautiful tonight," he said. "You..." He struggled for the right words, and in the pause, Glenna turned her face away from him toward the window, and the candlelight illuminated her skin as if it were made of porcelain.

"You lit up the entire hall. Iain would be proud," he finished quickly. Then he opened the door and stepped through it, leaving Glenna and his heart in the laird's chamber.

Chapter 17

Glenna sat by her father's bed the whole of the night, watching the shallow rise and fall of his abdomen, pacing to the window to look out at the black water of the firth, the full moon trailing a flowing ribbon to the horizon like a road paved with crushed pearls. Glenna couldn't help but imagine that, were she able to set her feet to that fantastic path, her wildest dreams would be waiting at the end. And while the scene should have been soothing and peaceful, inside the dark, quiet tower chamber, her heart waged a vicious battle with her head.

If she left on the *Stygian*, she could have a new life, in a new country. She would be safe. But she would never see her father again; she would miss his last breaths. And Roscraig and Tavish Cameron would become nothing more than painful memories.

If she aligned with Vaughn Hargrave, perhaps there was a chance that she could retain her place at Roscraig, save her father's legacy, and deal back the blow delivered to her on that fateful day when Tavish had arrived bearing that damned decree. Or, conversely, she could accept his invitation to Darlyrede, his offer to play matchmaker. But with either of those choices, Roscraig and Tavish Cameron would be forever lost to her.

She could not help recalling the knotted feeling in her stomach when the old lord had held her; her uneasiness at his enthusiasm to help; the way he had granted permission for her to dance in her own hall as if she were already his possession. He was wealthy, powerful, and determined to have his revenge on Thomas Annesley. Iain Douglas had not raised his only child to be a fool, and Glenna knew instinctively that—no matter his complicity in the death of his daughter—she would be placing herself in peril should she surrender her autonomy to Vaughn Hargrave.

Her only other option was to trust that Tavish would protect her as he has sworn to do.

Glenna had no inkling of the outcome in that scenario. Had he meant the vow as a declaration of love? As a promise of a life with him? Or was it only yet another ploy to keep her docile until he had won the ultimate prize—the hold and title he had hungered for for so many years? This choice was the biggest gamble, at the risk of losing her home, her reputation, her future. And yet it was the only chance she had—however slight—for her wildest dreams to come true.

Could Tavish love her for who she was?

The sky began to lighten from black to steel, then glowing gray traced the creeping clouds. If she was going to leave, it must be now. She might still have time to reach the dock before the *Stygian* cast off…

Glenna turned from the window with tears in her eyes to look at her father, and her breath caught in her throat when she saw that he was looking at her with bright eyes.

"Da?" She stepped to the bedside and leaned over him, placing her palms along his face. One side of his mouth hitched slightly, perhaps an attempt at a smile, and he nodded once.

His skin was warm, flushed; his eyes were still yellow, but they contained more life in them than she had seen in weeks.

"Good morn, Da," Glenna said gently, as tears spilled over onto her cheeks. She'd never thought to say those words to him again. "I love you."

Iain nodded again, and in her mind Glenna heard his voice repeating all the wisdom he had given her over her life: *Always keep your word, Glenna. Do what you know is right in your heart, and the devil with the rest of it.*

"I'm not leaving, Da. I'm staying here at Roscraig with you—at our home—for as long as we are able. I don't know what will happen when the king arrives, but I'm going to trust Tavish Cameron. Because I trust you. You told me Thomas Annesley was good, and you are no fool. Harriet Cameron said as much, and she has cared for the both of us like no other ever has in the whole of my memory. I am going to trust him, Da. And the devil with the rest of it."

Iain Douglas nodded again, and his gaping smile grew a bit wider before he pressed his lips together with some difficulty. "Mmm. Mmm-ead." His head bobbed. "Mead."

Glenna laughed. "You wish for mead?" At his jerking reply, Glenna kissed his forehead then straightened. "I'll run and fetch it now. As much as you want. A hogshead if we have it." She looked out the window again, and now bright rays of yellow streamed over the frolicking waves. If she leaned out, she might catch sight of the *Stygian*'s mast as it sailed away without her.

But she didn't care to watch it go; her decision had been made, and she hadn't known she could be so happy to be gambling her future in order to fetch a cup of mead.

"I'll only be gone a moment." Her slippers flew over the boards, her stiff, wrinkled silk skirts rustling like thunder as they swayed to a stop at the door. She swung it open and would have fallen over Tavish Cameron as he was rising from the floor had he not reached out and caught her.

"Glenna," he said in an alarmed voice, gripping her arms so tightly that she could feel the bruises that would come. "No."

She pulled away. "Let me go, Tavish."

"It's too late—he's gone." His hair was untidy, his eyes shadowed and, like Glenna, he still wore the same costume that he had at the feast.

Her heart pounded in her chest. "Have you spent the night in the corridor?"

His throat convulsed as he swallowed. "I meant to keep you from leaving. From leaving…me. I knew Muir asked you to go with him."

"How did you…?" she began, but he cut her off.

"I found the good-bye letter you had hidden in our chamber. Even if now I am your second choice—nay, even as a last resort—I pray that you will still consider me. You must see now that you were meant to stay with me—it can be the only explanation as to why you slept through the dawn."

"I haven't closed my eyes the whole of the night, Tavish Cameron," she scolded and gripped the front of his tunic with both fists. "I watched the sun rise. How dare you suggest that I—"

He thwarted her outrage with his kiss, drawing her fully against him, wrapping his strong arms around her shoulders while she pulled him closer and answered his kiss with her own of equal measure.

Tavish pulled away too soon, but he did not release her from his embrace. "You meant to miss the *Stygian*'s departure?"

She looked into his eyes, and for an instant the doubt wanted to creep into her heart. "Aye. I meant to stay…with you. If it is truly me you want, and not only Roscraig."

He drew her against his chest again, this time cradling her head in his palm and laying his cheek against her crown. "My princess," he murmured; then he looked down into her face. "Your father?"

"He is awake, and asking for mead," Glenna said with a smile. "I was going to fetch it when you tried to send me to my death."

"I'll go," he said, releasing her. "I'll find a maid to bring it and some food. Now that I can be sure that you won't run off while I'm not looking, I would speak with Audrey as soon as she has made her way from her covers. There is a discussion we must have that is long overdue. Certainly before her father arrives." He touched her cheek. "You've made me very happy."

She smiled at him as he turned away and stepped quickly and lightly down into the gloom of the corridor, and then she closed the door and rested her back against it for a moment. What lightness she felt now, what hope, in this chamber that had seemed so despairing through the night. Her father was alert, seeming to have regained a portion of his health with the dawn, and while Tavish Cameron had not made a declaration of love to her, he had stood guard outside her door all the night, worried that she would leave him.

Perhaps for him, they were one and the same.

* * * *

Tavish met Mam as he reached the entry corridor, her hands laden with a tray, and he leaned in to peck her cheek and squeeze her elbows in a fond embrace as she greeted him.

"Well, this is quite a change from your foul humor of last night."

"I have fair reason for my lightened mood. I've just left Glenna; Iain Douglas is awake and asking for mead."

His mother's face wore a startled expression. "He's awake? Are you certain?"

"Aye. A good omen, I say. I was just on my way to find a maid."

Harriet lifted the tray in her hands. "No need."

Tavish kissed her cheek again. "You're no maid, but you are a saint, Mam. Glenna will be glad to see you." He began backing away from her. "Audrey's not been about, by chance?"

Mam snorted. "At this early hour? Good heavens, if Miss Keane is out of her bed so soon after dawn, never mind your good omen, for you can be sure the world is nigh to end."

Tavish laughed as he turned and mounted the stairs leading up to the west tower. Not even the prospect of rousing Audrey and confirming what she'd already accused him of could dampen his good mood. He would apologize and take the berating owed him. It was Audrey, after all—they had been friends for a score of years, and she had likely suspected Tavish was in love with Glenna Douglas long before Tavish himself had.

He paused on the steps between floors. He was in love with Glenna Douglas.

The sound of a door opening drew his attention upward, and he saw a young maid backing carefully out of Audrey's room with a covered tray in one hand. The woman closed the door and started down the stairs.

"Is Miss Keane awake?" Tavish asked, resuming his climb.

The maid gave him only the briefest, frowning glance as she passed. "She said she doesn't yet wish to be disturbed, milord."

Tavish chuckled as the girl carried the obviously heavy tray awkwardly down the stairs. Apparently, Audrey had refused such an early breakfast. He came to the door and rapped softly with the backs of his knuckles, hoping not to rouse any of the other guests on the floor.

"Audrey, it's Tavish." She didn't answer, and so he knocked again, a bit louder. "Audrey?" He engaged the handle and pushed the door open a bit. "I'm coming in. Don't throw anything at me."

The drapes at the windows had been opened, allowing the bright glow of morning to creep into even this west-facing room, yet the chamber was cold, the fire having gone out sometime in the night. The maid had likely been miffed at her swift ejection and not deigned to lay the demanding miss a warming blaze to help thaw her icy demeanor. The drapes about the bed were still drawn tight, and that caused Tavish's grin to return. Everything seemed promising this morning, even this task now before him. It was the proper thing to do, and he felt no shame in it.

Tavish cleared his throat. "I'm sorry to disturb you so early in the day, Audrey. But I wished to speak with you privately. With as many suitors as you've had laying siege to Roscraig, I knew this was my best opportunity."

He waited for the curtains to twitch, billow. But the bed behind the heavy drapes remained still.

"Your father sent you here with the intention that the two of us should wed. I think you and I both know that that's not in either of our best interest. You would hate living so far from Edinburgh, and you want a doting husband who will play the role of senator at your social functions. We have been friends long enough that you know I can never be that man. Perhaps it is because we know each other too well that this would never work."

She shouted no denials. He stepped closer, noting the elegant, silk-embroidered chamber slippers on the floor near the bed. One was on its side, revealing its plush, wooly lining. Audrey Keane's slippers to be worn in private were finer than most people's only pair of shoes.

"Muir was right. You were right. Glenna Douglas has taken hold of my heart. I'm not certain when it happened exactly—perhaps you could tell me that, as well," he said ruefully. "I've not done the honorable thing by any of you, and for that I am truly sorry. I hope you will forgive me my foolishness. Muir as well, if he should know me well enough to return and call me out for the arse I've been. You are, of course, welcome to stay on at Roscraig for the king's court and as long after as you can tolerate it, if one of the nobles here has managed to catch your interest. If there is anything I can do to assist, you need only speak it."

He waited a moment in the silence. "Well. That's the whole of it, I reckon. You may shout at me now."

He sighed and placed his hands on his hips, looking about the room awkwardly. He noticed a silken dressing gown tossed over a chair near the wardrobe, of the same light hue as the slippers and with matching embroidery. But the shoes were near the bed, and the gown was across the room.

Now Tavish looked more closely and saw that the wardrobe door was partially open, and a jumble of clothing was spilling out of the bottom; brushes, combs, and colognes had been scattered on the silver tray on the table, and several other items had been knocked to the floor. The small stool that belonged to the table was on its side.

Tavish's gaze went back to the curtained compartment. "Audrey?" He went to the side of the bed and yanked the drapes open.

The coverlets were completely smooth; the numerous tasseled cushions arranged just so. Tavish frowned.

She said she doesn't yet wish to be disturbed, milord.

Immediately, thoughts of all Hargrave had known about the goings-on at Roscraig filled Tavish's head. There were so many strangers about hired on as servants with complete run of the hold, Tavish only knew a handful by name. Whoever that maid was, she had some explaining to do.

He left the room with the door swinging open and started down the stairs. He paused, though, at the window between the landings, where the heavy silver tray had been shoved onto the stone sill—its lid was knocked aside, and whatever had been concealed beneath it was now missing. He continued on down the stairs, bursting into the entry corridor.

"Where did the maid go who just came from the west tower?"

A score of people stopped to turn and stare at him, and to Tavish's dread, all the women servants were dressed exactly alike.

A middle-aged woman stepped forward. "I was in the west tower this morn, laird."

Tavish shook his head. "Nay, it wasn't you. Just now. She only just came down."

The servants' eyes were wide.

"*Where did she go*?!" Tavish demanded.

A man behind a handcart pointed through the open door leading to the bridge. "A gel left that way a moment ago, laird. I didna know her."

Tavish dashed through the door, and the pounding of his boots echoed in the space under the bridge. His eyes scanned the path ahead, the narrow road twisting into the village, but he didn't see her. He looked to the right where the trail wound up toward the cliff, but it was also empty. He stopped, his head turning this way and that, his heart hammering against his ribs.

The maid was gone.

And so was Audrey Keane.

* * * *

Glenna busied herself helping Harriet to care for her father while they waited what seemed hours for Tavish to return. Glenna had worried that there would be some awkwardness between her and Tavish's mother after the tense words they had shared last night, but Harriet behaved as if none of it had ever happened.

If anyone here has reason to hate me, Glenna thought to herself, *it is this woman. And yet she has done little else but exhaust herself caring for people who, in all likelihood, she should have considered enemies.*

Iain was still awake, having taken some mead and even a bit of gruel, and was doing his best to vocalize answers to questions and to join in the conversation the women strove to keep animated and light as they changed bedding and freshened the laird. There was no talk of Vaughn Hargrave.

By midday, Tavish had still not arrived, and Glenna was growing anxious.

"I've a need for a bit of fresh air and to change my gown," Glenna said in as nonchalant a manner as she could. "Do you mind terribly, Harriet?"

"Of course not, milady," Harriet said, tucking the corners of the blankets around the mattress. She glanced up only briefly. "I am wondering myself if Miss Keane hasna run him through."

Glenna felt her cheeks tingle but did not deny the idea. "I'll have a repast sent up for us," she said, walking to her father's bedside and kissing his forehead. "Careful of Mistress Cameron's honor, Da," she warned playfully. "We can only have one scandal at a time in the family."

His stuttering wheeze at her jest was beyond heartening—perhaps Harriet was wrong; perhaps her father would live. Perhaps everything would be better now, even better than she dreamed last night while wishing on that moonlit path across the Forth.

She quit the room for the lower-level chamber and quickly shed the cumbersome formal costume in favor of a slim-sleeved red silk and belted her familiar golden chain about her waist. In moments she was stepping into the wide entry corridor.

Glenna went first to the kitchen and gave instructions for a meal to be sent to her father's room, and during the return trip through the courtyard, she kept watch for Tavish. He was in none of the craft buildings, and so she came back to the hold. The handful of servants she questioned didn't know his whereabouts, although the last—a heavyset washerwoman—said she thought she'd seen the laird heading up the path away from the Tower.

Glenna stood on the threshold of the main door for a pair of moments, her eyes flicking between the eastern tower corridor and the village. She impulsively grabbed a basket from a peg near the door and set off across the bridge.

She took the path through the center of the village, more crowded with folk than Glenna could ever recall, and though everyone seemed to know who she was, not one face was familiar to her. She kept a tight smile on her lips and answered the openly curious greetings, and by the time she found herself on the far side of the settlement at the base of the cliff path, she felt quite uneasy.

Who were all these people? And where was Tavish?

Glenna started up the path to the doocot, glad for the shaded quiet and the familiar rounded roof that came into view around the bend. Her slippers crunched the twigs and leaves from the chestnuts and oaks overhead, each step sending forth the smell of fresh green. She looked down as she neared the stone threshold of the doocot and stopped.

Splotches of dull red marred the verdant forest carpet, in a line leading directly to the aviary. She gathered her skirts in one hand before following the splattered trail farther up the cliff amidst the disturbed detritus of the path, as if something had been dragged. Glenna walked back to the stone dwelling; the splotches started just before the door.

They could only be blood.

She looked up the path once more. Could Dubhán be injured?

She recalled Frang Roy's suggestion that the elimination of the monk could only be to their mutual benefit. Could the rough farmer be even now lurking in the wood, watching her?

Could he be the reason Tavish had not returned?

Glenna left the basket on the stone threshold and then used both hands to hold her hems from the menacing splotches as she hurried up the track. The gravestones rose up from the crest of the clearing like ancient and curious sentries from a long-forgotten dream. She weaved through the plots quickly toward the small, vined hermitage when a flash of swaying color at the cliff edge caught her eye.

She glanced to the right, gasped, then stumbled on her feet and fell behind a wide obelisk whose markings had been scrubbed smooth by the salty air. Glenna crouched there for a moment on her hands and knees, heart pounding, telling herself that what she had seen had been nothing more than a trick of the shadows, a flash of water and tree bark through wind-tossed boughs.

She gathered her feet beneath her and rose up slowly, cold perspiration breaking out at her hairline as she looked across the gravestones toward the firth. It was no trick of the light.

The upper half of Frang Roy's body was visible in the dappled shadows over the edge of the cliff, hanging from a thick, ropy vine around his neck. His face was purple-black.

Glenna screamed.

* * * *

Tavish had just finished searching the last of the cottages when Alec rushed around the corner of the path.

"Have you found her?" Tavish asked in a low voice.

Alec shook his head. "But you'd best come quickly, laird; there's been screams heard from the cliff. A woman's."

Tavish didn't question Alec further but broke into a run toward the snaking path. His boots flew over the gravel and ruts as his strides lengthened to climbing lunges. He heard it then himself, a woman's sobs in the graveyard ahead.

"Audrey!"

He burst into the small clearing and saw her there, standing among the stones. But it wasn't Audrey, it was Glenna—her hands covering her mouth to stifle her cries.

And there was the dark hermit monk, Dubhán, his face pivoting, seeming unsure as to whether he should fly to Glenna's side or to the cliff. But why…?

"Tavish," Glenna gasped, seeing his arrival. She pointed toward the firth, where Frang Roy hung dead from a tree.

Tavish went to her, wrapping his arms about her and turning her away from the corpse. "Glenna, what's happened? What are you doing here?"

"I came to the—I was looking for you and…and I saw blood on the path," she breathed into his shoulder. Her body trembled against his. "I thought Frang had hurt someone. Then I saw…I saw…"

"Shh," Tavish said. "All right. You're safe."

"I thought perhaps he had harmed you, like he said he would. He never left Roscraig. He wanted me to poison you. He said—"

"Poison?" Tavish repeated, but then running footsteps sounded behind him, and Tavish looked over his shoulder at the man at arms.

"Is it her, la—good lord!"

"No, it's not Miss Keane," Tavish said.

Glenna pulled away slightly. "Why would Miss K—"

"Audrey wasn't in her chamber this morning," Tavish explained. "All her things are still there. I've searched the entire village for her. It's as if she's vanished from the earth."

"And now we find Frang Roy dead," Glenna breathed, her green eyes wide.

"Something else you must know, laird," Alec said. "There're trumpets on the road, just now."

"The king," Tavish said grimly, and he felt Glenna's hold on his tunic tighten. "I'll take you back to your father and Mam." He looked to Alec. "Help Dubhán cut this man down, then gather our most trusted and start searching the beaches. Have a dinghy sent 'round to this side of the point to search the rocks below. Send word to me at once if you find anything. I alone," he emphasized. "I'll join you as soon as I am able."

"Aye, laird." The man walked toward the cliff, drawing his sword as he went.

Dubhán's smooth hands were pressed together before his chest, as if he had already begun praying for Frang Roy. "What would you have me do with his body, laird?"

"Put him in the ground," Tavish said. "He was trouble when he lived, and I cannot help but think that word of his strange death upon the king's arrival will taint the court, on the same day Audrey has gone missing. Did you hear nothing in your cottage, Dubhán?"

The black man shook his head, his expression grave. "Nay, laird."

Tavish remembered the feeling of being watched after he'd hidden his coin chest below the cliff. "Think you he was trying for the cave?"

Dubhán's normally generous mouth was pressed into a thin line. "It is possible. With all the rain, the path has been nearly washed away."

"Stupid bastard got caught in the vines," Tavish muttered.

"An accident?" Glenna asked. "But what about Audrey? And the blood I saw at the doocot?"

Before Tavish could answer, the monk thrust a bandaged arm from his voluminous sleeve. "'Twas my accident, Lady Glenna," he said with a serene smile. "I was careless with my own blade in making cuttings of branches for the doves, nothing more. I regret to have caused you distress."

Tavish tucked the pale Glenna beneath his arm and turned her toward the cliff path. "If anyone from the village should come, Dubhán, let's keep this incident quiet lest we cause a panic among the guests."

"Aye, laird," Dubhán called after him. "Not to worry. The lord will keep us all, of that I am certain."

Chapter 18

Glenna followed Tavish down the path away from the cemetery, her hand clasped tightly in his much larger palm. She was grateful for his insistent urging, his deliberate silence; her knees felt too fragile to support her should she come to a halt. Her face tingled with the shock of what she'd seen, her ears buzzed with snippets of conversation from moments ago, days, weeks, even years into the past. The words, the circumstances all whirled together as if in a cyclone until no voice was clear, no meaning evident.

Look closely at the portrait in the hall and you'll see it. You've been lied to you all your life.

Frang Roy was dead. Audrey Keane had vanished. And the king of Scotland was at their very threshold.

The pouch of poison still hidden behind her wardrobe... *It'll take longer that way, mayhap a pair of days.*

Even though the gentle cliff path was just as real and solid beneath her feet as the wide and commanding presence of Tavish Cameron before her eyes, in her mind she still stood in the graveyard staring at the farmer's rough-clothed body, swaying in the brisk wind of the Forth.

I'll already have all the coin I could ever want.

Tavish led her around the village, although if it was an attempt to circumnavigate the residents, his effort was in vain. Glenna heard the loud chatter of the crowd even as they came up the path toward the Tower, and when they at last were in view of the Tower road, Glenna could see that the village side of the moat was lined with onlookers. She kept her head down as Tavish pulled her through the crowd and barely heard Tavish's responses to the calls of those gathered. The abrupt, echoing blare of trumpets seemed to fill the air, causing Glenna to flinch, and in the next moment they were nearly running over the span of the moat.

The darkness of the entry corridor swallowed them up, and Glenna let out a sigh, unaware that she had been holding her breath. Tavish released her and charged toward the courtyard, calling out orders to a handful of men loitering about the portcullis. Glenna herself looked around at the clusters of women servants with their heads ducked together, whispering. Glenna didn't know if their gossip involved her or not, but it didn't matter; they were retainers in her house—while it was still her house—and their king would arrive at any moment.

"You there," she said to the nearest group, marching toward them while she flung out an arm toward another clutch near the east stairwell. "You all, as well. If you wish to remain household servants, you'd do well to act as such. You, straighten your cap; retie that apron—you look as though you've just come from the privy. You—straightaway to the kitchen with the order to prepare refreshments."

"But, miss, I wish to see—"

"Go," Glenna insisted. She felt a lock of her hair being tugged, and she turned with a gasp to see a young maid with a small, plain wooden comb in her hand.

"Beg pardon, miss. Your hair…"

Glenna's hand went immediately to her curls, rioting from her hastily attached veil. "Good lord," she breathed, and her cheeks burned at the idea that she had been chastising the servants when she herself likely looked worse for her trip to the cliff.

The girl smiled and with a quick flick of her wrist had whisked the veil away. Several hard tugs and twists from the maid's deft grip brought tears to Glenna's eyes, but she held perfectly still. The girl shook out the linen, creased the front with a sharp sound between thumb and forefinger nail, and then whipped it back over Glenna's head, reaching up once to tent the peak.

"There you are, miss," the girl said and then gave a quick curtsey before she began to turn away.

"Wait," Glenna said, reaching out and taking hold of the girl's arm. "What is your name?"

"Anne, Miss."

"Thank you, Anne," Glenna said. "Perhaps…perhaps you would consider work as a lady's maid?"

"I've not been a lady's maid, miss."

"And I've not had one. So neither of us shall know when the other has a misstep."

The girl gave a sweet smile before bobbing in a curtsey, and Glenna released her.

Tavish was back at her side in that moment, and Glenna noticed his flushed face, the grim set of his mouth. Even his normally bright eyes were flat and steely. The trumpets blared again, causing Glenna to jump at their nearness. The heavy clomping of horse hooves on the bridge seemed to rap at the door ahead of their riders' arrival. She looked up at Tavish in the same moment that he turned his face toward hers.

"And so the princess meets the king," Tavish said. "Are you ready?"

Glenna straightened her backbone even further and lifted her chin, commanded the trembling of her body to cease even as her heartbeat caused her vision to dance in time to the blood pounding in her ears. "Aye."

Tavish's mouth quirked into a ghost of a smile and then winked. "May the best laird win."

Glenna raised an eyebrow as he reached for the door handle to swing the heavy slab of wood inward. "Forgive me, but I didn't see a laird enter. Is he hiding behind you?"

She saw the edge of his cheek rise in a genuine smile, but then the door was open, and her gaze was only for the somber-looking man commanding the large black horse toward them with apparent ease. The bridge behind James was queued with riders in a line extending onto the road—Glenna guessed at least a score, most of them soldiers by appearance.

Tavish stepped onto the stones just beyond the door and took hold of the reins while the king dismounted. A squire appeared and led the horse through the corridor while Tavish sank to one knee with a bowed head.

"My liege," he said. "Welcome to Tower Roscraig."

"Cameron," James said as Tavish stood. Glenna at last saw the much-rumored red stain covering half the king's face, his long nose and protruding eyes and chin. "'Tis not often I have such leisure to view the Forth from its opposite bank. I've not been to Roscraig since I was very young. I forgot that you were situated on such a promontory—a great military advantage."

"Aye, my liege," Tavish acquiesced. "As well as for commerce. The Forth is deep beyond our dock."

"Is that so?" James said musingly. "I would very much like a tour. Will you accompany me?"

Tavish paused for only half a heartbeat before responding, and Glenna knew he was thinking about the search for Audrey Keane.

"Of course, my liege." Tavish gestured toward the entry.

Glenna had felt her own frustration rising the longer the king ignored her and spoke of Roscraig as if it were already Tavish's. But then James turned his face toward her and stepped through the doorway, and his somber countenance softened as his eyes found Glenna. Behind her, the chamber was filled with the rustling of servants sinking into their bows and curtsies, and Glenna too paid her homage.

"Glenna Douglas," James said. "We are well met. How fares your father?"

"My liege," Glenna replied, startled at his graciousness. "He has improved in great measure only this morn. You honor him with your kindness—I didn't know His Majesty was aware of the laird's illness."

"Cameron informed me of the dire state of your father's health some weeks ago; I've been kept appraised of late by others visiting my court. Roscraig's fate has suddenly become of keen interest to me."

At those words, the line of companions and courtiers traveling with the king began filing through the entry, and a brilliant flash of jewels caught her eye. She glanced up for only an instant to see Vaughn Hargrave leading his horse past, a well-dressed young woman following behind him on her own mount, who looked somehow familiar to Glenna.

Tavish was at her side then, his jaw squared and his eyes hard once more. "I've no wish to offend you, my liege, certainly not when you've just arrived, but I cannot abide the presence of that Englishman at the Tower."

James glanced over his shoulder. "Lord Hargrave, you mean?"

Tavish nodded curtly. "He arrived uninvited in my hall and has made no secret of his intent to cause upset at Roscraig."

"Upset, aye. You would be a fool not to be unsettled by him," the king acknowledged. "I admit the man is more cumbersome to drag along behind me than is his sizeable purse. But as it is he who has lent his support to Roscraig these many years, I cannot discount his testimony, nor will I bar him from the court. Besides, I rather prefer knowing his whereabouts."

"The woman who rides with him," Glenna asked before she could think better of it. "Who is she?"

The king gave her a little smile. "My dear, you would be better content to mind the health of your father this afternoon, and join Cameron and me at supper. I insist that you join us. Aye, that is a more pleasant thought." Glenna's throat tightened as she realized she was being dismissed, both literally and figuratively. The king turned his back to her. "I would see the hall, Cameron."

Tavish looked at Glenna and nodded. His expression asked her to trust him, and although she wished to demand the king's acknowledgment, she sensed that this was neither the time nor the place.

"This way, my liege," Tavish said and walked with the king toward the east tower, leaving Glenna to follow until the men reached the entrance to the hall.

Glenna continued up the stairs to her father's chamber, where Harriet answered her quiet knock at once.

"He's sleeping," she said quietly as she let Glenna pass. "I saw the procession..."

"The king has arrived," Glenna confirmed as she crossed the floor. Upon reaching the bed, she gathered her skirts and climbed upon the mattress and lay down on her side with her head near her father's shoulder. She let her hand rest in the angular hollow of his elbow. "Miss Keane is missing, and Frang Roy has been found dead on the cliff."

Harriet gasped but did not press Glenna for details, and Glenna continued to stare toward the bright square of window without further comment. After several moments, Glenna heard the door close, and the silence in the room swelled around her father's rasping breaths.

"The king is here, Da," she whispered. "And a bad man. And I don't know what will happen to us."

There was no floor now. Glenna was falling, falling, through one disaster after the other, with no way to arrest her descent. The only champion who might have been able to save her lay at her side, now without voice, without strength of body. She didn't think she'd ever felt so tired in all her life. She closed her eyes against the frustrated and fearful tears and escaped into sleep.

* * * *

Tavish walked through the hall at the king's side, discussing with the man the improvements done to Roscraig and the future plans Tavish had for the hold. They spoke of roofs and fortifications and crops; once they arrived at the long windows flanking the hearth, the conversation turned to seafaring industries, ships, and defense of the shores. While the king held forth on the newest advances in artillery fortifications and powdered weaponry, Tavish watched the small, black figures moving up and down the beach in either direction away from the Tower.

The men searching for Audrey.

"—would allow one to fire on an enemy ship from the walls without equipping a ship, and potentially losing the weapon to the depths," the king was saying. He looked left and right out the window. "Aye, the point there would be ideal for artillery fire. I am very much looking forward to viewing it."

"My liege," Tavish began, "the woman with Hargrave, *do* you know her?"

"She is his mistress, I presume," James said, walking to the hearth in order to stare up at the portrait hung on the stones. "At least that is what I've distilled from the wild tales being told at court. Vile stuff, I assure you, although 'tis likely the stories are inflated because he's English. I know of no men who actually crave such blood sport in their bed. This portrait is exquisite." He turned his face toward Tavish. "The infamous Annesley?"

Tavish nodded, unwilling to yet voice his suspicion that the stony-faced young woman riding behind Hargrave as if she were of the nobility had been posing as a servant at the Tower for an unknown length of time.

What if she had been involved in Audrey's disappearance?

I want revenge...and I shall begin my recompense with you.

"Cunning man. I am not of the habit of blaming the son for the crimes of the father," James said carefully. "And I admit that there is a part of me who is secretly hoping you are victorious over the challenges you face. However, I have already collected much information about your past that is forcing me to question the wisdom of allowing you a lairdship, Cameron. Hargrave is not the only man who has spoken out against you."

"My liege?" Tavish asked, startled by both the king's candor and the nature of the warning.

"Master Keane complains that you have yet to formally accept the betrothal agreement put forth after your arrival at Roscraig. He claims his daughter has been humiliated by your relationship with Glenna Douglas." The king cocked his head. "Are you sleeping with her?"

Tavish ground his teeth together. "We have...become close, my liege. But there is no betrothal agreement. Miss Keane and I have been acquainted for some years, and her father sent her in anticipation of my acceptance."

"I see," James said with a knowing nod. "Far be it for me to shame a man for the company he keeps—especially when that company is as beautiful as Glenna Douglas. I couldn't help but notice that Miss Keane was conspicuously absent at my arrival. And now perhaps you can understand why I discouraged Miss Douglas from accompanying us. You already know that Master Keane is held in high regard by the burgess." The king paused. "Who is now prepared to swear an oath that you caused the death of your stepfather. He claims Dolan Cameron discovered you were not his true son, and before he could disavow you, you killed him."

Tavish swallowed. "That's not true."

"And that it was you who caused the fire that took not only the shop on Market Street, but several of the adjoining dwellings, so that the burgess had nothing to assume for the tolls he says you still owe."

"No, my liege. I was already at Roscraig when my captain brought word of the fire. The *Stygian* was current on her tolls when we left the city."

The king sighed. "We will not argue it here, of course. But you should know that the burgess has asked that your license be revoked on suspicion of smuggling. He's requested the *Stygian* in payment for the tolls and as compensation for the buildings consumed in the blaze he claims you set."

Tavish was speechless for several moments. "I can only hope that I will sufficiently disprove those accusations when I am called upon to do so, my liege."

"As do I, Cameron," the king said. "Were I you, I would command your captain to give Leith a wide berth until this is settled."

"I will certainly do that, my liege."

"Good. Now, I think I'll rest a bit before this evening's festivities."

Tavish's head was spinning so that it took all his control to speak calmly, move with steady purpose, as he accompanied the king's leisurely progress down the stairs and to the west tower, while the king admired Roscraig's thick masonry work. By the time they reached the quarters reserved for the monarch, Tavish was ready to jump out of his own skin. Two of the king's soldiers already stood guard, and they straightened to attention at James's approach.

"Roscraig is at your disposal if you should be in want of anything, my liege," Tavish said at last, feeling the relief of his imminent escape.

"My thanks, Cameron." He seized the handle but then paused. "One more thing—perhaps I should not mention it to you now, but I do not think Hargrave is yet aware, and my instincts tell me that you should be first to have this knowledge. It shall likely mean little to you any matter, never having known him. Thomas Annesley was never hanged in London. He somehow managed to escape before the trial, and the only signs found of him indicate that he chose to take his own life rather than be executed." James opened the door. "Until tonight, then."

Tavish bowed woodenly. "My liege."

He turned and walked down the steps, pausing at Audrey's closed door. He leaned his forehead against the wood and knocked softly before engaging the handle and pushing the door open, praying that he would open his eyes and see her sitting on the little stool, reading one of her books of poetry. The door creaked, and Tavish looked inside.

Nothing had changed since that morning; her slippers still languished near the bedside, the curtains hung haphazardly where he'd thrown them open, the stool still surrendered to the rug.

"Audrey, where are you?" he whispered. Then he scrubbed his hands over his face with a sigh and quit the room, closing the door softly behind him.

Tavish went immediately to the switchback stone steps leading from the courtyard to the beach to find Alec. One look at the man's face told Tavish all he needed to know.

He asked anyway. "What have you found?"

Alec rested his hands on his hips, his chausses and tunic damp with sweat and seawater and sparkling with sand. "Nothing, laird. Nary a footprint, nor a single sign that Miss Keane has ever been here."

"What about the cliff?" Tavish asked.

"The dinghy's been around once," Alec answered. "One of the men fished a boot out of the rocks with a pole, but it belonged to Frang Roy. Another pair have gone back, searching the lower rocks now that the tide is going out." He paused, and the air around the men grew heavy. "I pray they find nothing."

"As do I," Tavish said, looking out over the dark gray water. He sighed. "I'll be at the cliff if I'm needed."

"Aye, laird," Alec said. "But there is likely little for you to do there; that monk already had the hole half dug by the time I'd left him."

Tavish left the beach, and when he came into the courtyard at the top of the stone steps, Mam was waiting for him outside the kitchen. She met him in the center of the courtyard, away from the other buildings and prying eyes. She was once again wearing the old crossed-bodice apron, and had Tavish not known she was his mother, he would have mistaken her for one of Roscraig's servants.

"Lady Glenna told me," she said in a low voice, her eyes shifting about the courtyard. "Terrible about that man, dreadful as he was. Have you nae found Miss Keane?"

Tavish shook his head. "Nay, Mam. But why are you about the kitchens with the maids? You should be preparing to meet the king."

Harriet had begun shaking her head before Tavish could finish speaking. "Nay, Tav. Nay. I'm of no sort to be meeting a king—that's for your position. And I hear that Lord Hargrave has returned. I canna bring myself to be in the same room with that man." Her eyes were doleful when she looked up at him, and once again, his mother looked old to him, frail, the overcast gloom setting the lines around her eyes and mouth. "I'm frightened of him, I am."

"I'll not let Vaughn Hargrave harm you, Mother," he said, taking hold of her shoulders and bending down slightly to look in her eyes. "Never."

"You don't know, Tav," she said in a low voice. "Tommy was no coward, and yet he ran. *He ran*," she insisted, and her voice hitched. "I doona think he ever stopped running."

"Listen to me, Mam, and listen well," Tavish said. "I am no lad of ten and eight. And I will not let Hargrave threaten anything you and I—*you and I*—have worked for all our lives. I don't know anything about Thomas Annesley, but I know us. Vaughn Hargrave didna grow up in the alleys behind Market Street or the wharf of Leith. He doesn't ken who he's made enemies of here. And if he should lay hand to anyone in my care, I will kill him. Do you hear me? I will kill him. Whatever grievance he has with the man who sired me matters not. This is my house now, and I will defend it."

Mam's chin flinched, and then she clutched Tavish to her stout frame. "Just be careful, Tav," she whispered. "You're all I have."

Tavish gave her a quick squeeze and then set her from him. "I'm going to talk to Dubhán."

"But the meal, Tav…"

He was already walking away. "I'll be back in time. I want you to dress for the feast, Mam. You need to be there."

"Tav, nay. I—"

"I need you to stay with Glenna," he said pointedly.

Mam pressed her mouth stubbornly but then she nodded. She raised a hand and called after him, "Take care, Tav."

Tavish turned, and in moments he was through the entry corridor and once more on the cliff path. The sky grew darker as he neared the doocot, the occasional crack of a raindrop being flung through the green canopy as he stopped to examine the blood-splotched path. He only paused a moment and then continued on to the small graveyard.

He saw the dark monk standing on the edge of the clearing, looking out over the rippling water, and although Tavish didn't think his footsteps made any sound in the soft grass, Dubhán turned as soon as Tavish breached the first line of graves.

"Has the young woman been found?" he asked in his calm, lyrical voice.

Tavish shook his head. He looked down briefly at the fresh grave, the mounded dirt slightly higher than the riotously green grass around it, then continued toward the edge of the plot where the earth fell away in a ragged chunk; where he'd once followed the path to the cave, and where Frang Roy had succumbed to the afterlife. He looked down at the jagged rocks and wash of mud that had erased nearly all signs of the treacherous ledge that comprised the trail.

It was the only place left on Roscraig lands that hadn't been checked. *Isn't that what nobles do? Go on pilgrimages? I shall have to begin at once.*

"I need rope, Dubhán."

The monk blinked, his eyes wide. "I've no rope, laird."

"What do you lower the coffins with?" Tavish asked.

"There have not been any coffins for some time. The man in the village who made them is dead."

He was running out of time. Perhaps Audrey was, too.

Tavish pulled his sword from its scabbard and reached out to take hold of one of the long vines looped from a high branch. If the thick climbers could hold the bulk of the likes of Frang Roy, they could surely hold him. Tavish hacked it in two high up on one side and then replaced his sword as Dubhán strode toward him.

"Surely you cannot think to descend so dangerous a path in hopes of finding Miss Keane," Dubhán warned soothingly. "Frang Roy could not have taken the lady to the caves without my knowledge."

Tavish glanced over his shoulder at the monk while he took the now long, dangling vine in both hands. "Really, Dubhán? The man died on your doorstep, and yet you heard nothing. What do you know of his actions before he was hanged?" He yanked hard on the vine several times, pulling its length from the host tree until it held firm.

"I can make no defense for my lack of vigilance, laird," he said with a bow of his head. "But Miss Keane would not have gone willingly, you must agree. Even if she was unable to cry out, the path would have been impossible for Frang Roy to navigate while carrying her."

Tavish gave a short sigh, looked out to the Forth for a moment to compose himself. He turned his eyes back to Dubhán. "Maybe Frang Roy had nothing to do with it. Maybe she went on her own. I don't know. But I must look. I can leave no stone unturned, Dubhán. She is my friend."

"Is she, laird?" the monk questioned softly.

The two men stared at each other for a moment, and in the back of Tavish's mind, he recalled Audrey introducing Vaughn Hargrave to him at his own feast.

No. He'd known Audrey since they were both children. She'd come to Roscraig with the intention of wedding him. She cared for him. In this madness, he was beginning to suspect everyone he knew of treachery.

Dubhán folded his hands together inside his sleeves. "I will watch over you, lest you fall."

"If I should fall," Tavish said, looking down as he stepped one foot over the side, "there will be little you can do for me. Watch over Glenna."

The instant his other boot left the damp grass, his foot slid through the earth as if it had no more substance than cream. The vine ripped through his hands like a hot blade and Tavish fell full body against the muddy cliff face, traveling downward at least five feet before the toe of his boot caught on a buried rock. He clung to the vine, the side of his face slick with cold mud, panting as the waves washed over the rocks still far below him.

Dubhán called down, "Shall I pull you back up now, laird?"

"I'm fine, Dubhán." Tavish spat the dirt from his mouth. He looked down and saw the mud-covered rock ledge marking the entrance to the cave some ten feet down; there was perhaps only three feet of vine left in his hands. "This vine won't be long enough; you'll need cut another piece to affix to the end to bring me up."

"Aye, laird."

A ropy root horseshoed from the cliff, and Tavish let himself slide down until his boot caught it like a stirrup. Only a foot of vine left, and the distance to the ledge was more than his height.

"Audrey!" he shouted, and his voice rang flat between the water and the mud. "Audrey, are you down there?"

Only the cry of gulls answered him.

If she were trapped, yet able to walk, she would have been shouting for help. There would be footprints in the mud.

If she was in the cave, she was injured or she was dead. And if she was either of those things, it was Tavish's fault.

He took a deep breath, stretched out one arm and leg and then leaped for the ledge. He landed hard on his left leg and hip and slid across the shelf, scrambling and clawing for purchase with his hands as he came to a stop at the edge. Not daring to stand, Tavish crawled toward the opening of the cave, sinking into the deep mud nearly to his elbows until he slid through the muck and into the darkness.

The smell of seawater and beeswax, old incense and gull shit filled his nose as he gained his feet and blinked, letting his eyes adjust. He crouched and walked deeper into the cave until he came to the grotto, where it was dry and quiet and still.

And empty. Audrey wasn't there.

The shadows were deep, and so Tavish scoured every inch of floor, every low-lying alcove, but there was nothing there to indicate anyone had entered the cave since he and Dubhán had left it weeks ago. A dark thought occurred to him, and so he reached up into the highest niche, but his fingertips felt the end of his money chest just where he'd placed it. Tavish turned and sat down on the edge of the stone altarpiece with a sigh, and cradled his head in his hands. His roar of frustration echoed back against his own ears.

Damn his pride. Damn it! He'd been so sure of himself, so certain of his success as laird. Determined to show everyone who had ever doubted him that he would rise up and rule his own kingdom. But now...

Now, everything was falling apart. Audrey was gone, he'd driven Muir away. The resentments left burning in Edinburgh had crawled across the Forth while he'd been blissfully unaware, too busy playing lord of the manor, so absolutely certain that now—*now*—no one dared cross Tavish Cameron. But here they had all come to roost around him at Roscraig, them and so many more dangers that he could never have predicted. He was Damocles, and the sword was falling.

He swiped at his nose with the back of his hand and then rose and left the cave. He held on to the edges of the stone entrance as he emerged, turning his head upward at a sharp angle to see the edge of the cliff.

"Dubhán!" He waited while the gulls swooped and cried.

"Aye, laird?"

"She's not here. Throw me the vine."

Dubhán paused. "Forgive my distrust, laird, but what of the trunk?"

"It's where we left it," Tavish said. "The vine, Dubhán. I must return to the hall right away."

Chapter 19

Glenna's fingers were clasped so tightly together beneath the table she had lost feeling in them. Her chest rose and fell shallowly beneath the black-and-red brocade of her bodice. In her peripheral vision, her curls shivered despite the tightly woven coif young Anne had created, betraying her nerves. She couldn't force herself to swallow, and she feared that if anyone should touch her, she would shatter.

Hell had broken loose in the Tower.

The hall roared with guests, the number of people packed into the cavernous room seemingly doubled from the last feast, and yet there was no gaiety in the commotion; no music. The food so lavishly provided remained largely untouched. Glenna kept her eyes trained on the table, occasionally glancing furtively to her right to be certain that Harriet was still seated next to her. To her left, King James kept his own counsel, waving away the shouted approaches, the declarations of outrage while his soldiers maintained a perimeter about their liege.

Once, Glenna had glanced across the table and found that Vaughn Hargrave was staring openly at her, a serene smile on his face as if he were an oasis of calm unable to be touched by the discord raging around them. She didn't look up again.

A man's shout rose above the noise and would have remained indiscernible if not for the repetitions of those gathered.

"Here he comes!"

Tavish.

Glenna looked to her left at the king, who gestured to his soldiers with a single nod. Half the company pushed through the crowd, and a moment later the guests parted, revealing the soldiers half dragging a struggling brown mass of man before James. Tavish shook off their restraining grips and stood in the hall, his clothing unrecognizable beneath the mud.

Glenna began to rise, but Harriet's firm hand cautioned her from under the table.

The short, round, well-dressed man with the thin mustache rushed forward, barreling into Tavish before the guards could pull him away.

"Where is she, you animal?" Niall Keane shouted, flinging away the guards. "Where is my daughter? Where is Audrey?"

The hall grew silent, as if everyone held their breath in anticipation of Tavish's answer. Niall Keane's breaths wheezed in his barrel chest.

King James spoke. "It seems you forgot to mention earlier that Miss Keane has come up missing, Cameron."

"I had hopes she would be found this afternoon, my liege," Tavish said. "I only discovered her absence this morning. I have had all of Roscraig searched—it is where I have just come from."

"You lie!" Niall Keane shouted, struggling once more with the guards to reach Tavish. "What have you done to her?"

"I've done nothing, Niall, I swear it," Tavish said to the man. "I saw her last night at the feast—she was well and enjoying herself."

Vaughn Hargrave's voice cut through the tension like shears through fine silk. "Really? How then do you explain her chamber? Forgive my bluntness, Master Keane, but was she enjoying herself when you tore her apart, Cameron?"

Tavish's eyes widened, and he looked to the king. "What do you mean? I went to her chamber this morn—there was naught amiss. Some things were in disarray, but her belongings were—"

"Disarray?" Keane screamed. "Her bed is soaked with blood! The gown she was wearing is shredded as if an animal attacked her! Like you attacked your whore!"

Glenna flinched but did not look up as the crowd gave a collective gasp.

"What?" Tavish's voice was unlike Glenna had ever heard it, unsure and hesitant. "No—her…her bed hadn't even been slept in. I looked again after the king arrived. There was no blood, no—"

The king stood and interrupted with a wave of his hand. "Take him. I wish to see his face myself once the door is opened." To Glenna's dismay, he gestured toward her. "You as well, Miss Douglas. I would know if you are complicit in this diabolical scheme." The king addressed the hall. "The rest of you remain where you are. I am sure there is a sensible explanation for all of this, and one not so dire as to warrant the waste of this good meal."

Glenna rose on trembling legs and followed the party from the hall—
the king and Master Keane leading the way while the soldiers took hold
once more of Tavish's arms. She pulled her arm away with a gasp when
someone grabbed it, but it was Harriet Cameron, and she reached out once
more and took Glenna's hand firmly in her own.

Glenna squeezed the woman's fingers.

In moments they were in the west tower, and a soldier opened the door
to Audrey's chamber, while the other shoved Tavish inside.

"No, no," he protested loudly. "Someone did this; this was not here
before."

Glenna stepped inside the room, feeling the king's watchful gaze on
her. She couldn't help her gasp, though—the tales had not prepared her
for the sight.

The bed curtains hung limp where they had been ripped from their ties,
revealing the jumbled bedclothes that were no longer elegantly striped, but
covered over in large, dark stains that had ran past the edge of the thick
mattress and soaked into its depth. Miss Keane's incredible yellow gown
lay strewn about the floor in long rags, the silk turned ugly brown where
the spray had splattered.

"Miss Douglas?" the king prompted, startling Glenna from the trance
the carnage had inflicted. "What was the state of this chamber prior to
this afternoon?"

"I don't know, my liege," she said in a rasping voice. "I've not been
inside this room since Miss Keane arrived at Roscraig."

"No one has seen the inside of this chamber except Tavish Cameron,"
Niall Keane accused. "And so it is he who knows what transpired here."
Master Keane's chest heaved, his face purpled. "I will kill you!"

"The maid," Tavish shouted, trying to back out of the guards' hold.
"There was a maid in here before me this morning, only I don't think she
was a maid. The woman I told you about, liege, in Hargrave's party. She
is a spy."

"You liar!" Keane shouted. "You have done to my Audrey what your
father did to Cordelia Hargrave!"

"Enough," James said. He turned to the guards. "Escort Master Cameron
to his chamber, and make certain he stays there all the night. Miss Douglas,
I understand that chamber also belongs to you, and so I will grant you
leave between it and your father's floor. But you will be watched. Any
attempts to aid Cameron in escape or further subterfuge will be severely
dealt with. Do you understand?"

"Aye, my liege," Glenna whispered.

"I had intended to take my leisure at Roscraig, but these issues cannot be left unaddressed. Court will convene in the morning in the hall. Your grievances, Keane, shall be first attended. In the meantime, the soldiers not posted as guards shall take torches and continue searching for Audrey Keane. Venture from the trails into the woods. Scour the ravines." He looked to Glenna once more. "What might she be wearing, Miss Douglas?"

"I...I don't know," Glenna said and glanced toward her wardrobe. "She has so many beautiful clothes. I could see if anything is missing."

"Do so. Then you may retire for the evening." The king looked at Harriet pointedly, but said nothing to Tavish's stricken mother. "I shall return to the hall and seek to restore some semblance of order. Until court tomorrow, Roscraig is solely under my command—none shall be permitted to leave." The king swept from the chamber, and the guards dragged Tavish after him.

Glenna saw the grief and fury on his face. What must he have done this evening, in searching for Audrey?

The guard left behind held up the torch and gestured to the closed doors of Audrey's wardrobe. Glenna opened it gingerly, unreasonably afraid that something or someone might jump out at her. Audrey's gowns were in disarray, but Glenna pulled each one out as she remembered it: the gown she'd arrived in, the one from the first feast, the kirtle she was wearing the night Muir brought her the trunk from Edinburgh...

Glenna paused for a moment, and then pawed through the remaining gowns. She swallowed and then turned her head to look about the room; there was the small leather trunk in a corner, but it was open and clearly empty.

Glenna turned her face up to the stern-looking guard. "There is one gown missing, that I can call to mind," Glenna said in a strangled voice.

"Can you describe it, miss?" the man asked politely.

"Aye. It was ivory and blue, with a silk cape." She paused to swallow. "It was to be her wedding gown."

* * * *

The door closed behind Tavish, and he stood alone in the chamber he had shared with Glenna Douglas. He hadn't been inside it for any appreciable length of time in two days, and the room had a dusty, abandoned feel.

He looked down at his mud-encrusted clothing, turned his palms up to see the stained lines, scars, and scratches. Dirty hands. The hands of a peasant. He turned hesitantly to look around the room, seeing evidence of Glenna's presence: the gown she'd worn earlier, her comb; the smell of freshly applied violet water. He'd invaded her home with the arrogant notion that he would simply assume his role as laird here, run things according to his will. And now here he stood, covered in filth, having ruined his life, Mam's, Glenna's…Audrey's.

He would be put to death for Audrey's disappearance. Hanged, like the common thief he was.

A crisp knock sounded at the door before it swung inward and a pair of maids entered, carrying a round copper bathing tub between them. Two more servants followed, bearing buckets in each hand like human scales. The sound of water being poured into the tub was like thunder. They left without comment, and before the door shut completely, Tavish saw the profile of the king's guard in the corridor.

He was already a prisoner.

There was likely hope that he'd drown himself.

He numbly peeled off his clothes, leaving them in a sodden heap on the hearth, and then stepped into the steaming water. He sat, his knees bent up near his chest, and looked at the swirling brown infecting the clear water, the rivulets of dirt running from his skin. In his mind's eye, he saw the blood-soaked mattress of Audrey's chamber.

It couldn't be her blood.

Tavish didn't know for how long he sat in the tub, but when the door opened again and Glenna entered the room, her eyes went wide.

"Tavish," she whispered, closing the door then walking quickly to the side of the tub. "What are you doing?" She knelt and dipped her fingers into the water. "It's ice cold. Here."

She took up the cloth and cake of soap and lathered it, quickly scrubbing his back and arms, chest, and neck. He shook himself from his stupor and took the cloth from her, finishing his body and then bent his neck so that Glenna could pour dippers full of the cold water over his head while he cleaned his hair. She fetched his robe and held it up before her as he stood and then stepped out of the tub.

"I'll get a towel for your hair," she said, turning away.

He sat on the edge of the bed, and she stepped between his knees, draping the toweling over his hair and starting to rub it dry. Tavish reached up and seized one of her wrists with his hands. Glenna stilled and let the towel fall away, sliding her palms around the back of his neck and drawing his face against her abdomen. How he had misjudged this woman upon his arrival.

"How is your father?" His voice creaked.

He heard her intake of breath through her nostrils, felt it against his skin. "He is awake. Your mother is with him now, entertaining him with stories of the guests. I think it is good for both of them."

Tavish rubbed his face against the softness of her gown, closed his eyes and breathed in her scent.

"There was a gown missing from Miss Keane's wardrobe," Glenna said. "The wedding gown sent from Edinburgh."

Tavish pulled away and looked up at her as the meaning of that slowly sank in.

"I know you didn't hurt her," Glenna said.

"If they hang me," Tavish began.

She gripped the sides of his face. "You mustn't say such a thing."

He reached up and took hold of her wrists. "If they hang me," he repeated slowly, "there is a chest in the cave. It contains a significant amount of gold and silver. I want you to have it. To care for yourself and Mam."

"Tavish—"

"Bring several bags with you to the cave," he interrupted firmly. "You shan't be able to carry the chest. It should be enough to sustain you both for a long time."

"We don't know—"

"Promise me," he demanded, looking into her eyes, deeply shadowed by the firelight behind her. "Promise me, Glenna, that you will do this. You must take care of each other."

The silence draped around them like a mourning cloak. "I promise," she whispered.

"I would have married you," he said, releasing one of her wrists to touch her cheek. "I was going to ask the king for permission after he approved my inheritance."

She stiffened slightly. "After you had secured the Tower for yourself?"

"No," he said, pulling her closer to him. "After I claimed a title making me worthy to offer for your hand. After I could give you what you deserve: your home, your father's home. In a way that no one could ever try to take it from you again. When I was finally good enough for you." He stood from the bed, bringing his hands to her face now. "I love you, Glenna. I've loved you almost since the moment I arrived at Roscraig."

She met his kiss equally, smoothing her hands inside his wet, heavy robe to slide over his ribs to his back. She pulled away from his mouth slowly, with little licks of her tongue.

"Then love me as I have wanted you to," she said against his mouth.

His body ached for her, and he groaned deep in his throat. "I cannot. For the sake of your future."

"You are my future," she said, reaching down to take hold of him, and his resolve wobbled.

His raised his face and closed his eyes. "Glenna, you don't know what will happen."

"I know what will happen tonight," she said, releasing him and stepping back. She raised her hand to her opposite shoulder and slid her gown down. Her thin underdress glowed in the light of the fire, the prominences of her breasts showing in dark relief. She came back to him and pushed his robe away, kissing his chest. "Obey your lady, Cameron." She reached down and cupped him, squeezed him.

* * * *

He seized her, pulled her to his naked body, running his hands over her back to grip her buttocks and lift her to him. Glenna clutched Tavish's shoulders as he picked her up against him and turned her toward the bed. He sat her down on the edge, and she scrambled backward as he raised one knee to the mattress, his manhood pointing heavily toward her. Her underdress had bunched beneath her and she let her legs fall open, brazenly revealing her nakedness.

Tavish pursued her, his gaze hungrily taking in what she was showing him. He leaned over her on one arm, his other hand going immediately to her cleft, testing her, teasing her. She hummed with desire.

"Take off the gown," he said.

Glenna fell onto her back and shimmied out of the fine linen underdress, leaving her arms over her head on the mattress as Tavish brought his mouth to her breast and his fingers primed her. She could feel her time coming already, and she lifted her hips in a silent demand for him.

She felt it then, the hot tip of him, and then she reached down to grasp his firm buttocks, urging him closer, pulling him into her body slowly, relishing the slick discomfort as he displaced her flesh with his own. She expected pain, but the sensation was not unpleasant. In fact, the deeper he pressed, the fuller she became, the higher her climax wound deep in her abdomen. It seemed to go on for a wonderful eternity, this initial claiming. And when he was finally seated fully inside her and began to withdraw, she began to pulse with this new level of eroticism between them.

"Do it," she commanded in a whisper. "Tavish, do it." She slowly pumped her hips until he matched her rhythm with a groan.

And then he was thrusting into her with urgency, deep and slow and firm, his breaths rushing over her as she panted. Glenna cried out as her world narrowed to the explosion of their point of connection. She clung to him as her body pulsed, and in a moment, his guttural cry was near her ear and he stilled, throbbing against her own fading vibration, and she knew his seed filled her. She cried out again.

Tavish rolled to his side, pulling her with him, and she offered her mouth to him as tears slid from her eyes.

"I love you," she whispered against his skin. "I love you, Tavish."

"I swear to you," he said, cupping her breast in a caress, moving against her body again, "I will keep you safe. And I will love you for all eternity. That is my vow."

And as he began proving that to her once again, Glenna believed him.

Chapter 20

Tavish watched the sun rise alone. Glenna had left him in the night, with his blessing, to sit with her father. Tavish had attempted to accompany her, hoping to speak to his mother as well as Iain Douglas, but the king's soldiers thwarted him, adhering strictly to the boundaries James had committed him to.

And so he found himself alone at the window, dressed in his sturdy merchant's clothing, watching the hazy sky lighten behind its thick blanket of smothering clouds. There would be no sun today, and that was just as well. The beach below, the courtyard, was empty. The soldiers were finished searching. Only a lone mast on the Forth, so far in the distance as to perhaps be an illusion of waves to the untrained eye, betrayed any sign of human movement.

A tray was delivered to the room, along with a message that the king required his presence in the hall in one hour. Tavish felt little hunger, but he sat at the small table with the smell of Glenna's violets around him and consumed the meal, reading and re-reading the document detailing his inheritance delivered to him by Lucan Montague what seemed years ago now.

When the soldier opened the door and stood there without word, Tavish rose from his chair, folded the proclamation neatly, and tucked it inside his vest. He walked to the bed where his belt and sword lay and carefully donned them. He paused to look at the soldier, whose expression was openly hostile.

"Was any sign of Miss Keane found in the night?"

"Shut up," the soldier sneered. "For a ha'cup o' drink, I'd sliver yer gullet an' spare the overs th' trooble o' ye. Get on," he commanded, gesturing with his head.

Tavish walked from the room and descended the steps flanked by soldiers. He could hear the murmurs in the hall before the doorway came in sight. Apparently everyone else had already been gathered.

Tavish would be walked into their midst as if he were already convicted.

The hall had been transformed in the night. His finely turned trestle was horizontal before the hearth now, and James sat in the center, the portrait of the Annesley family over his head. Several of the dining chairs and benches were arranged before it with a space in the center serving as an aisle of sorts, and the seats were filled by the highest ranking nobles in attendance. Niall Keane had also been granted a seat on the right, next to the smug presence of Vaughn Hargrave. His mistress spy stood behind him, gripping the back of his chair, her face ashen within her full, close snood, her eyes dark hollows.

Seeing her in the full light of day solidified Tavish's belief—it was her Tavish had seen coming from Audrey's room that morning. And he was prepared to swear to it.

Mam and Glenna sat on the left. His ever-composed princess, her back straight, her hair finely coiffed, her black-and-saffron-plaid kirtle simple and elegant amidst the heavy brocades and gaudy silks. She stared toward the window with her chin lifted. She was the most beautiful woman in the room, by far, and pride filled Tavish; that woman—that *lady*—loved him. She had loved him last night, at his lowest, just as he was.

Tavish was determined to make her proud.

The rest of the attendees were left to stand to either side of the hall, and as the guards' tromping footfalls rang out, those seated rose. Tavish was marched before the king, and then the soldiers fell away to flank the sides of the room.

Tavish dropped briefly to one knee. "My liege."

The crier behind the king stepped forward and held a parchment before him. "Hear ye, all present. Our sovereign laird James, Majesty of the realm of all Scotland and her holdings, does so order and commence his court to hear the challenges both for and again' Tavish Cameron, merchant of Edinburgh, and Iain Douglas of Tower Roscraig and his daughter; as well as the grievance of Master Niall Keane. All without claim shall hold their peace until such time as their testimony is requested." The crier retreated behind the king, his hands behind his back.

James leaned forward, one forearm braced against the table, his other hand gripping the arm of his chair. "Master Cameron, I initially made this journey to judge the veracity of your claim upon Tower Roscraig against that held for the past thirty years by Iain Douglas. To be precise, a claim of inheritance, word of which was delivered to you—so you assert—in Edinburgh by one Sir Lucan Montague, knight of the English crown."

Tavish nodded. "Aye, my liege."

"While I was prepared to see evidence of your claim, recent events have reordered the purpose of this court. A charge has been brought against you that, if should be found true, would render your claim on Roscraig moot. And so I shall hear testimony to that allegation at the first." James turned the ruddy side of his face away from Tavish's view to look at Niall Keane. "Master Keane, say your peace."

The rotund merchant rose, his hands visibly shaking, his normally florid face gray and paunchy. His eyes were swollen and red, his lips devoid of color. Tavish's heart pained for the man.

"My liege," Niall Keane began. "I have done business alongside Master Cameron since the death of his—well, what he would have all believe now was his stepfather. He and my...my beautiful daughter, Audrey, were childhood companions. When he received word of his inheritance, a betrothal between them was discussed, and I sent—" He broke off for a moment, appeared to struggle with the words. "I sent my beloved only child to be in his care at Roscraig until the arrangement was settled.

"But he never honored it," Niall rasped, glaring venom at Tavish. "Instead he took a lover to sate his wicked appetites right under Audrey's very nose—that woman there," he said, pointing an accusing finger at Glenna. "And when my daughter demanded he hold to his word, he *murdered her!*"

The crowd gasped, and low chatter broke out in the echoing hall.

"Silence," the crier demanded.

"Where is she, you bastard?" Niall Keane shouted through the commotion.

"Silence!" the crier barked.

As the noise dwindled, James looked to Tavish. "Do you take exception to this charge, Master Cameron?"

"Indeed, I do, my liege," Tavish said. "The first of what Master Keane has spoken is true: Miss Keane and I have long been friends, and the idea of a betrothal was alluded to. But she arrived at Roscraig without my summons, and although I was without formal obligation to her, it was assumed that we would announce our agreement upon your arrival."

"You changed your mind, did you?" the king asked bluntly.

"Miss Keane and I both became less enthused at the prospect of a union between us," Tavish admitted. "Audrey does not care for the Tower's remoteness. She misses the city, and her father." Tavish looked at the merchant with all the sympathy and sorrow he felt. "She doesn't love me, Niall—not as a woman loves a husband. But she wanted to make you happy."

Master Keane's eyes narrowed to slits. "Wasn't it enough that you humiliated her with that…that guttersnipe imposter?"

The crowd gasped, prompting the crier to call for order once again.

"That's right," Niall Keane declared. "That *lady* was born of servants. Her father is no better than a squatter at Roscraig, who was run out of his own clan."

"Guard your tongue against such slander, Master Keane," the king warned in a low voice. "Lest you have your own charges brought against you."

"What do I care for that now?" Niall demanded, turning fully to the king. "What do I care for anything now if my beloved Audrey is gone? Everything I've ever done…" His words deteriorated into sobs, and he collapsed on his chair.

The king looked to his sergeant at arms. "What of the search last night?" he said. Tavish knew the king had already been appraised, but the facts must be presented before all parties.

"Nothing out of the ordinary was discovered, my liege," the man said, as he stepped forward and placed on the king's table a torn, dingy square of cloth that had at one time perhaps been white. "Only this kerchief, caught on a branch. By the looks of it, it is quite old and has been out of doors for some time."

"It's mine." Glenna's shaking voice rang out in the hall. "The veil, it's…I lost it several weeks ago."

The king looked to Master Keane. "Do you recognize the thing as belonging to your daughter?"

Niall's glance at the kerchief was full of disdain. "Audrey would never wear such a rag."

The sergeant at arms finished his testimony. "There was no other evidence found that Master Cameron had taken Miss Keane somewhere on the grounds, my liege."

Tavish spoke. "There was no evidence of it because I didn't take Audrey anywhere. I was in the east tower all the night."

Niall Keane took a ragged breath and stood once more. "There was no evidence of you taking her because you killed her and then had your servant dispose of her!" He looked to the king. "Frang Roy, a farmer of Roscraig, was found hanging dead near the cliff, my liege; blood on the path leading to him. Cameron had him buried and never told you. He drove the poor man to suicide for what he'd taken part in!"

This time James let the commotion in the hall go unchecked while he motioned for his sergeant to come near. The two conversed, and then the crier called the hall to order.

Vaughn Hargrave smiled at Tavish openly.

"Do you deny this claim, as well, Cameron?" the king asked. "It seems to me that you should be running out of excuses by now."

Tavish could feel the noose tightening around his own neck. "Frang Roy was found dead yesterday before your arrival, my liege. I do not know the circumstances of his death. He was the source of much discord about Roscraig."

"You took care of that inconvenience as well, did you not?" Niall Keane shouted.

Vaughn Hargrave leisurely rose to his feet. "If His Majesty will allow it, I feel I might shed some light on this sorrowful and dark scenario."

James stared at Hargrave for a long moment, and Tavish thought there was a chance he would deny the man his say.

"If it is relevant, Lord Hargrave, proceed."

"It pains me to hear Miss Douglas at all associated with the diabolical goings-on at Roscraig. I am sure she had no knowledge at all of Master Cameron's plot. It was she who assisted in the search by discovering the one gown missing in Miss Keane's wardrobe."

James raised an eyebrow. "How is this relevant to Master Cameron's guilt, Hargrave?"

"Because the gown missing was a special costume meant to be worn by Miss Keane at her wedding, Your Majesty. And it is common knowledge that Master Cameron's true sire, Thomas Annesley, whom the court may see as a young boy in the portrait above you, murdered my daughter, Cordelia, on the eve of what would have been their wedding day."

Rather than erupt in chaos, the crowd in the hall was horrified into silence.

"He did not kill Audrey," Glenna's voice rang out. Tavish turned to see her standing, her fists clenched at her side. "Tavish Cameron was outside my dying father's door all the night, guarding us from the likes of your villainy."

"Sit down, Miss Douglas. Your testimony has no weight in this matter." James leaned both arms onto the table. "Are you suggesting, Hargrave, that Master Cameron has murdered that poor young woman in the same fashion in which you accuse his father?"

"I am, Your Majesty," Hargrave said with a bow. "I beg your pardon for Miss Douglas's sake—Cameron has filled her head with promises in light of her father's illness, and has played to her gentle emotions. She knows not what she says." Then he sat down once more.

The king looked into Tavish's eyes, and Tavish could see the coldness there, the decision already made. He could hear quiet sobs in the hall, and he knew they belonged to Mam.

He was a dead man.

"Have you any rebuttal for this accusation, Cameron?"

Tavish swallowed. "I did not know Thomas Annesley," he began. "I know nothing of his crimes or his guilt. I did not harm Audrey Keane. I never would. And, God help me, I don't know where she is."

The king leaned back with a sigh. "It pains me. A great deal, in fact," he began, "to see such potential—"

The king was interrupted by a commotion in the back of the hall. He leaned his head slightly to the side to see past Tavish.

Tavish turned, and his knees nearly buckled at the sight of Captain John Muir in the doorway.

Audrey Keane stood at his side.

* * * *

Glenna's hands flew to cover her cry of exclamation in the same moment that Niall Keane's strangled shout pierced the air of the hall.

"Audrey!" The portly man ran toward his daughter and enveloped her in his sobbing embrace.

A shriek of dismay went up, and Glenna's head turned to see a clutch of people bending over the collapsed form of Lord Hargrave's mistress.

The court was in chaos.

"She's only fainted," Hargrave was assuring those nearest, irritation high in his voice.

"Call for my physician," the king commanded.

"It happens often, my liege. Weak constitution. The excitement of court. Take her to my room; she'll be fine."

The king looked at his sergeant. "I'd have her seen," he said pointedly. "The woman has appeared to be on death's door the entire time we've been gathered."

The soldiers carried the limp form of the woman from the hall, but Hargrave did not follow, returning to his chair and sitting, crossing his legs in an irritated fashion.

"Would you be excused, Lord Hargrave?" the crier asked solicitously.
Hargrave waved a hand. "I've said she'll be fine."

Glenna looked at Tavish, who had turned to stand in the middle of the
aisle, facing Audrey Keane in her fine ivory-and-blue gown. She was
smiling sheepishly as she walked forward on her father's arm, looking
around hesitantly at the crowd gathered. Muir followed behind them, and
Glenna's mouth fell open as she realized the truth before anyone spoke
a word.

Tavish stepped toward her and embraced her, causing Audrey's trilling
laugh to ring out.

"I must say, I did not expect so warm a welcome." She laughed. She
pulled away from Tavish, and she and Muir stepped forward, sinking low
before the king.

James sat up straight in his chair. "Are you Audrey Keane?"

"I am, Your Majesty," Audrey said in her curtsey, her eyes wide.

"Where the bloody hell have you been, gel?" Niall Keane bellowed.
"And you, Muir; what's your part in it?"

Audrey turned her eyes to Tavish. "I...you don't know? But...I left a
note for you in my chamber. So no one would worry in case we weren't
back before my father arrived. And Muir said you—"

"*Audrey!*" Niall demanded.

"Papa, Muir and I are wed."

"What?" her father shouted.

Tavish drew his head back. "What?"

John Muir spoke then, his slow, careful manner of speech commanding
the hall. "It is no secret to Master Keane that I have loved his daughter
since I first came to sail for him as a boy. I asked for her hand long ago,
and he refused me—saying he wished a noble match for her. I honored his
wishes, wanting the best for Audrey, as well. It's why I left his employ to
captain the *Stygian* for my best mate, Tavish Cameron."

"And I loved Muir, too, Papa," she said. "You thought it would fade,
and I tried to obey you. But...I don't wish to be stuck away in a tower in
the sticks of the Forth. So far from the city, and you, and...and life itself.
Muir is a successful man—I shall have everything I could ever want as
his wife. And so much more."

"No," Niall Keane commanded, shaking his head. "No, I refuse to
allow it."

"It's already done, Papa," Audrey said with a sad smile. "I am his wife,
in word and in deed."

Niall turned to the king. "My liege? Can you not do something?"

"I cannot refuse them, Master Keane," he said. "Especially with all that has transpired here, I would think you eager to discover that your only child is not only alive and well, but happy." He paused. "As much as you have hoped for her elevation, she and Captain Muir are of the same class, and of age." He looked to Audrey. "Miss Keane, do you swear that you have been neither abducted nor murdered by Tavish Cameron?"

Audrey's eyes went wide. "Papa, you didn't think—" She broke off and looked earnestly at the king. "My liege, Master Cameron would never do anything to harm me. I trust him with my life, and that of my husband."

The king then looked to Niall. "I assume you now wish to withdraw your accusations."

Niall turned to Tavish, his face ruddy, and extended his hand. "My apologies, Cameron. I hope someday you can forgive me for ever thinking…"

Glenna was filled with pride, and Tavish quickly took Master Keane's hand.

"It is a happy day for you, Niall," Tavish said.

Niall nodded and looked away, Audrey walking him to his chair and helping him to sit.

Tavish looked up at Muir. "You son of a bitch," he muttered under his breath. "It was Audrey the whole time."

"Who else would it be, Tav?" he asked with a confused frown. Then he cocked a brow and looked over his shoulder. "You thought I was in love with Miss Douglas?" He left Tavish with a shake of his head.

"Now that we have come to a happy resolution in the mystery of Miss Keane's whereabouts," the king announced, calling the court to order once more, "let us continue on with the matter for which I have traveled to Roscraig in the first place." He looked to Glenna. "Miss Douglas, please stand."

* * * *

Glenna's knees were shaking as she took her place at Tavish's side before the king.

"How long have you lived at Tower Roscraig?" the king asked.

"I was born here, my liege." She was determined to keep her voice calm, her answers brief.

"And your father? How long has he been in charge of the Tower?"

Glenna swallowed. "I don't know."

The king folded his hands over his stomach. "Who is his family?"

"Douglas is the only family name I have known. From the Carson Town."

"And you've never met them."

"No, Your Majesty. My father said they were a feuding lot."

James nodded thoughtfully. "I have heard much the same. Your mother?"

"She died," Glenna said. "Shortly after I was born."

"What was the cause?"

"I don't know. I was yet an infant, my liege." The crowd tittered, and Glenna's cheeks heated at the king's unimpressed frown.

"Why has the village of Roscraig been so decimated?" James pressed. "What of the crops?"

"We have been beset by sickness for years, my liege," Glenna said. "The last wave is what has touched my father. He was bedridden after a fit took his speech and his legs."

"And he has always told you that he was laird of Roscraig?"

Glenna lifted her chin. "He never told me; he simply was."

"Hmm." James nodded thoughtfully and then looked to Tavish. "I assume you can produce the decree?"

Tavish reached inside his tunic and withdrew the packet Glenna remembered him showing her so long ago. He stepped forward and handed it to the crier, who opened the page and set it before the king.

James's eyes were fixed on the timbers of the hall ceiling, however. "Read it," he said in a bored voice.

The crier retrieved the page and cleared his throat before reciting the words scrawled across the page. Each syllable was like a damnation against Glenna's testimony. Halfway through, Tavish turned his hand to take hold of her fingers. She glanced at him, and it gave her courage.

When the man had finished the page, he returned it to the tabletop, where James picked it up and casually perused it for a moment. He set it away from him with a flick and leaned his temple against his fingers as his eyes looked past Tavish's shoulder.

"Aye, Lord Hargrave."

"I must take exception to Master Cameron's inheritance decree, Your Majesty—Roscraig is not his to receive, for Thomas Annesley long ago gave it over to the man who helped him evade justice. If the Tower should be granted to anyone upon Iain Douglas's death, it's Glenna Douglas."

The king looked intrigued. "Go on."

"After Thomas Annesley murdered my daughter, he escaped into Scotland. I sent soldiers and a trusted servant to chase him down and bring him to justice. They followed him to Roscraig, his mother's childhood home…"

Vaughn Hargrave was making good on his threat.

This time, it was Glenna who squeezed Tavish's hand.

* * * *

Anne was concentrating on the stitching in her lap and singing a tune under her breath to the ill old laird sleeping in the bed next to her chair when the door to the chamber opened. She looked up, expecting to see the miss's solemn, lovely face.

Instead it was a skinny old man, with long, gray, wavy hair and the weathered skin of the sort that came from a life spent working in the fields or on the water. The sun-stained shade of his face made his blue eyes seem all the lighter.

"Beg yer pardon, lass," he said in a thick brogue as he gripped his cap in his hands. He walked toward the bed, stuffing his cap into his rough belt next to a sheathed blade. "Not meaning to disturb your lovely song, but I've come to fetch the laird."

Anne's eyes widened. "The laird is dreadful ill, you. Surely Miss Glenna—"

He laid his callused hand on her arm, and his smile was kind. "I ken he's ill. Lass, I ken. It's his own gel that wants him."

"I'm supposed to watch over the laird," Anne said. "Mistress Harriet bade me. She…she would whip me."

The old man shook his head. "She wouldna. Nae Harriet. Nay. She wouldna've left you here with him did she nae think you'd do right by him." He patted her hand. "You come along, as well. So you can see that I only do what I must. If the laird could speak, he would tell you. If he could walk, why, there'd be nae need for me now, would there be?"

Anne frowned. Harriet had said nothing of this possibility. But the man was so gentle, and he made Anne feel special. And he seemed to know Harriet.

"All right," Anne said, standing and laying her stitching on the chair. "I'll go with you."

The old man went to the bedside and leaned over the unconscious laird, whose breaths rattled in his throat like a winter wind through dead, dried leaves. His smile deepened, and Anne could see the pained compassion, the bittersweet fondness in the servant's eyes.

"Iain," he said softly, close to the man's ear, and his smooth Gaelic was like a balm to Anne's longing, highland heart. "Iain, *tha mi air tighinn dhachaigh.*"

I have come home…

* * * *

"Therefore," Hargrave said with a slight bow in Glenna's direction, "Tower Roscraig has truly been in the rightful hands all these years. Tavish Cameron has made it very clear that he will do whatever he must in order to oust Miss Douglas and steal her home; he clearly cannot be trusted. And so, considering both the dire state of Laird Douglas's health as well as the years of fees paid on her behalf by myself, I ask the court that Glenna Douglas's guardianship fall to me."

"I am beginning to think you have a grudge against Master Cameron, Hargrave," the king said.

Hargrave gave a smug chuckle and began to speak.

But the king cut him off. "You've said just enough, I think. Let me be clear. Tavish Cameron is not responsible for your daughter's death. He did not kill Audrey Keane. He has done all in his power to provide for the occupants of this hold, including making vast improvements to the Tower than can only benefit the entire kingdom. He is a tradesman of means, which pleases me greatly. And he also—whether it pleases you or nae—carries noble blood in his veins."

Glenna let go of Tavish's hand and took one step toward the king so that he would at last acknowledge her.

"Aye, Miss Douglas?" he said with raised brows.

"If I may, my liege," she said in a shaking voice. "I would pose a question to Lord Hargrave before you make your judgment."

James nodded once. "Go on."

Glenna turned to Vaughn Hargrave. "My mother's name was Margaret Douglas, called Meg by my father. I have reason to believe that…that you knew her. Did you kill her?"

"Did I…?" Hargrave laughed and looked around him. "Did I kill your *mother*?! My dear girl, what would ever make you think such a terrible thing about me? Of course I didn't kill your mother."

"She was the one you sent after Thomas Annesley, wasn't she?" Glenna pressed, not allowing his theatrics to shake her.

"What? No, of course not," Hargrave scoffed. "Who in their right mind would send a woman into the wilds of Scotland after a brutal killer?"

"You're a liar." Harriet's voice rang out in the hall.

The crier turned a frown to her. "You will not speak out of turn, mistress."

"You did send a woman, though," Harriet insisted, her soft jowls quivering, bright patches of color on her otherwise pale face. Tavish's mother was near to collapsing with fright; her words warbled as she spoke. "You sent Meg. I saw her. I thought when I first saw Lady Glenna that I knew her. And that's why—'twas her own mother that I saw that night when she come for Tommy."

The king glared at Tavish. "Cameron. There is no one here to corroborate these wild allegations, and I'll not have hearsay from a commoner spoken against a noble."

Tavish took a step toward Harriet. "Mam, please. Wait until you're called upon."

"It's nae hearsay! I was there—"

Harriet's words were cut off by a loud pounding on the hall doors, and then a woman's voice was heard crying out for assistance.

The king stood and motioned the soldiers to the doors. When they opened them, Anne fell through into a guard's arms.

"Mistress, mistress!" she gasped. "Miss Glenna! Quickly, the laird!"

The other soldiers had dashed into the corridor, and there was a shuffling commotion. Tavish was already striding up the aisle, pushing people aside. Anne broke free and ran to Glenna, falling to her knees at her feet.

"Forgive me, forgive me," she sobbed. "He said you wanted him. He said he was needed. He was so kind. But then he just left him in the corridor and ran away."

Glenna crouched down. "Anne, what are you talking about? Who left—?" The crowd's gasp drew Glenna's attention.

Tavish was walking back toward her, his arms cradling the body of Iain Douglas, his form no bigger than that of a child's outside of his mountain of covers.

"Da," Glenna breathed and left Anne on the floor.

"Bring some benches," Tavish ordered. "Set them before the king's table."

Two benches were pushed together and Glenna sat on one end while Tavish laid her father's head on her lap and then stood to address the king.

"My liege, Iain Douglas of Roscraig."

Vaughn Hargrave shot to his feet again. "I demand he be taken away, at once. He's a commoner, and nearly dead, besides. What good is a silent testimony?"

"Not silent!" Harriet shouted and strode forward, her hand sliding into her double-fronted apron, from which she produced a sheaf of pages, rattling audibly with her trembling. "It's here! In his own hand." She held the pages toward the king, who only stared at her, then to the crier, who did much the same; and then back to the king. She was panting with nerves. "It's all here," she said again. "What I was tryin' to tell you, Your Majesty."

James motioned to the crier after what seemed like eternity. "Let it be read," he said at last.

Harriet backed up several paces and sank to the bench at Iain Douglas's feet. Tavish stood behind her.

The crier shook the wrinkled pages smooth and then cleared his throat again with a frown for them all.

* * * *

"I was a servant in the house of Lady Myra Annesley, given to the family by my parents when I was six years in order to escape the feuding of Carson Town. My duty was as a page until I reached my majority at nine, and Lord Tenred decided that I was to be educated in order to be a companion protector to his only son, young Thomas, four years my junior. I made my home in Roscraig village while the family was away, and in the Tower when they were in residence.

"After the lord and lady died, Thomas did not return to Roscraig until the spring of the year 1427, when I was a score and two. He told me his betrothed had been killed by her father, and the woman he traveled with was escaping that same man, by name, Lord Vaughn Hargrave.

"He bade me grant Meg sanctuary, and oversee the Tower until he returned with proof of his innocence. I agreed. I did not expect that a fine, educated lady such as was Margaret could ever love the likes of me. But we married, and she gave birth to a daughter, our own Glenna.

"Vaughn Hargrave arrived at Roscraig when our bairn was only a fortnight old. He claimed Margaret was his runaway servant, and that if she did not return to her position in his house, he would have her and our bairn jailed. If she went with him willingly, and if I never told, he would leave the gel with me and would let us be as long as Thomas Annesley did not return. I begged Meg to refuse—she had warned me that if Hargrave ever found her, he would kill her. But now that she was a mother, her only thoughts were for keeping our daughter safe. And so she left with him. I never saw Meg again.

"A terrible illness took over the village upon their leaving; nearly half the villagers died, and so I said that their lady had also succumbed. I was called laird from that time forward—the Annesleys were by then forgotten, by all save for me. I never forgot my friend Thomas, who had delivered to me the love of my life.

"I know Vaughn Hargrave killed my wife, Margaret Douglas. He is a monster. But the Tower belongs to and always has belonged to Thomas

Annesley, and now his son. I beg mercy for my daughter, Glenna; and also forgiveness from her. Her mother was the greatest lady I have ever known.

"I swear it on my deathbed before God and Harriet Cameron.

"Iain Douglas

"Tower Roscraig

"June, 1458."

The hall was silent for several moments until the king said, "Iain Douglas, is this the whole of your testimony?"

Glenna cradled her father's head as tears streamed down her cheeks. He tried to nod; drool ran from his gaping mouth, his chest heaved with each breath.

Then his curled arm lifted from his chest, his good eye rolled toward the chairs, and his emaciated wrist hooked toward Vaughn Hargrave.

"Mon-ster," he slurred and then gasped, and his eyes rolled back in his head.

Tavish went to Iain's side, and he looked to the king. "My liege, we should return him to his bed."

James nodded and motioned to his guards. "A moment, though. This man has risked his life to be in this court today, and so it is only just that he remain the last few moments to hear my judgment." All eyes were on the king when next he spoke, and it was as though everyone in the hall held their breath.

"It cannot be disputed that Tower Roscraig has rightfully been bequeathed to Tavish Cameron," the king said. "And as I can think of no lawful reason to deny him his birthright, I declare that he is laird of Roscraig, recognized fully by the Crown."

Glenna looked to Tavish and he smiled when Harriet gripped his shoulder.

"However," the king continued, "I cannot in good conscience declare that Glenna Douglas's claim is without merit, considering the trials she and her father have suffered in the years since Iain Douglas took guardianship. The loss of a mother, a wife; of livelihood and community. Therefore, in reparation for the damage done to her reputation in the preceding months, and to condone in the eyes of the church the relationship that has perhaps already been begun, I decree that Tavish Cameron and Glenna Douglas shall be married." The crowd gasped. And then the king added, "Immediately. Call for my priest. Hurry, man—Douglas is fading."

"What is happening?" Glenna asked as Tavish pulled her to her feet and Harriet took her place beneath Iain's head.

"You can't refuse," Tavish murmured, bringing her to stand before the table. "The king commands it."

"I object," Hargrave's voice rang out. "What of my investment? Thirty years of taxes that went into your coffers!"

James sighed. "Very well, Hargrave. If I grant you a boon, will you leave my presence?"

Hargrave's face mottled. "If the amount is sufficient."

James shot to his feet and roared, "*Whatever I determine shall be sufficient!*" He reined his temper and sat as the priest approached Glenna and Tavish. "The equal of five years' taxes. Do you agree, Cameron?"

Tavish nodded. "Aye, my liege."

"But, my liege," Hargrave began in a cajoling tone, "only five—"

"You were never under obligation to Roscraig, Hargrave," the king said, cutting the complaint short. "Consider yourself fortunate to recuperate anything at all, and that I have no evidence to bring charges against you this day." James looked away from him and flicked his fingers at the priest. "Go on."

In moments, Glenna was answering the priest numbly, listening to Tavish respond in kind. There was a blessing, and polite applause rose in the hall.

"Is that all?" she asked him. "Is that really it?"

"Are you disappointed?" He smiled into her face. "Because I'm not."

"I have spoken my judgment," the king said. "You're all dismissed. I'll return to Edinburgh at once where the madness is of my own making." He stood from his chair and quit the room, leaving the audience to bow at his passing.

The guards appeared. "Should we take him now, milady?"

Glenna nodded and pulled her hands from Tavish's. "Aye. Follow me."

* * * *

Iain was tucked into his bed at last, his color gone now. Glenna knew he was at last slipping away. But his voice called to her, a groan, a click of tongue. She leaned close.

"Dubhán," he whispered.

Glenna felt her face crumple. It truly was time, and he knew. He was at last asking for the monk's blessing.

"I'll go," Tavish said. "I would have Hargrave's coin in his hand and send him on his way before I truly do kill him."

Iain moaned. *No.*

"Lenna."

"All right, I'll go," she agreed, leaning down to lay the side of her face against his sunken and bony cheek. She closed her eyes. "I'll go now, Da. Right now." She pressed her lips to his temple.

Glenna rose and swept from the room, Tavish at her heels. She heard him call to the guards to bring rope, and they loosed two horses from the king's party tied beyond the bridge and raced up the cliff path. Dubhán appeared to have been waiting for them, and Glenna began calling for him before she had reined her horse to a halt.

"Dubhán, Dubhán," she sobbed and slid from the saddle.

He walked toward her calmly. "What troubles you, Lady Glenna?"

"It's Da," she said, falling into his arms. Dubhán, who had been here as long as she could recall, watching over the graves, watching over her. "He's asking for you at last. I don't think he has much time left."

Dubhán cradled her face in his smooth palms, the sweet smell of him filling her disoriented senses. "Praise to him," he said with a smile and kissed Glenna's forehead between her eyebrows. "At last."

"Take my horse," she said. "I will follow with Tavish."

Dubhán nodded serenely and went astride, his stained slippers dangling outside the stirrups. He turned the horse easily and disappeared into the trees, passing the pair of riders bearing the rope for Tavish's descent. She felt a sprinkle of rain on her crown.

"Hurry, Tavish," she urged as he was lowered over the side.

It seemed like he was gone for ages, but it was only moments later that she heard his shout and the guards began to pull him up. He carried the trunk easily, and when he gained the solid ground in the dampening clearing, he hurled the trunk toward the graves with a roar, where it burst apart against a stone in a shower of splinters, empty.

Glenna's stomach turned.

Hoofbeats sounded in the clearing, and Glenna turned to see Hargrave arriving with an order of the king's men, including the priest who had married them. The old cleric looked around the clearing with what appeared to be pleasant surprise.

"Where's my coin, Cameron?" Hargrave demanded with a smile.

Tavish charged him, causing the horse to shy. The king's men dismounted and pulled him away, but Tavish shook them off. "You took it! You knew it was gone the entire time!"

"My dear man," Hargrave said in mock offense. "I'm sure I don't know what you mean. I've only come for what pittance your foolish king has determined is mine. If you do not pay me, you must declare forfeit." He looked to the guards surrounding them. "I'm fine—he'll not harm me.

I'll grant him a grace for the time. You may leave us. That's right—go on, go on. Leave us."

The soldiers reluctantly gained their mounts and turned to the cliff path again, leaving only the old priest behind to wander through the grave markers some distance away.

"I told you this on the occasion of our first meeting," Hargrave said to Tavish when they were alone. "Accuse me all you like, but I never lower myself to perform all the base acts you would accuse me of. No, no," he denied. "They are beneath me. You doubt my power. But perhaps you will not after today."

He looked to Glenna with an expression of indulgence on his face. "You ignorant little slut. Your mother was not my servant. She was my *whore*," he said with a smile. "Just like the bitch who couldn't keep her feet at court. Only…prettier. A whore, though, whom I took a fancy to in London. I bought her."

He leaned forward in the saddle. "From a whoremonger. And I took her to Darlyrede and dressed her in pretty clothes and taught her how to speak. She tutored my daughter in the day and I fucked her at night. She was well trained, and she bled so very well. But the bitch bit the hand that had pulled her by her scruff from the gutter. And so after she whelped you, *I hunted her down and I put her back in the gutter.*"

Tavish rushed the man again, but he stopped as Hargrave pulled a small arquebus from the voluminous folds of his cape and rested it across his forearm, leveling it directly at Tavish's chest.

Then he leaned back, and his face resumed its mildly amused smile as he looked once more to Glenna. "Her grave on this hill is empty. She died screaming. And if it weren't for your idiot king's protection, you would have died screaming, too." His smile broadened, and Glenna saw the insanity in his eyes. "You may yet."

"You did kill her," Glenna choked.

Hargrave chuckled and leaned over the arquebus balanced on the front of his saddle as if preparing to deliver a wonderful joke. "You've heard nothing I've said, you stupid bitch That's the best part—I actually didn't kill her. But I confess, I did want to." He began to turn his horse. "I shall see the pair of you again."

He sped into the trees just as the king's priest approached them; his face wore an expression of bemused pleasure.

"Who has been caring for the old hermitage?" he asked in delight. "It's marvelous—some of the stones are very old. Likely the bones of a saint are buried somewhere here. We thought it had all collapsed into the sea years ago."

"Dubhán, the monk," Glenna stuttered inanely, running her hands into her hair. "He's…a Franciscan."

The priest's mouth turned down a bit. "Not to refute you, milady, but I am a Franciscan. There has been no one missioned to the cave in two score year."

Glenna frowned. "You must be mistaken, Father," she said, and Tavish left her side to begin walking toward the vined hermitage. "Dubhán was— Tavish?"

But he was pushing the door open, walking inside.

In that moment, the years of Glenna's youth bubbled up around her, conversations, warnings from her father. Snippets of Dubhán's strange way of speaking. She began walking toward the cottage.

Tavish emerged just as she reached the doorway, and the sweet smell that always surrounded the dark man bloomed from the cottage. Tavish caught her by the shoulders.

"Glenna, no," he said. "Don't."

She pulled away from him and entered. But then she staggered back with a strangled shriek.

Frang Roy's body was tied to a chair at a table, where a meal had been laid; over the hearth hung a crucifix, its corpus defiled. And along the stones of the chimney were laid row after row of human bones, the corners topped with grinning skulls and decorated with bundles of dried roots and herbs, pouches like the one still hidden behind Glenna's wardrobe.

Before the edifice, a square in the floor was shifted slightly off angle. Tavish reached down and pulled the square away, revealing a dark tunnel and ladder, and the hush of waves whispered from the blackness.

He looked up at her, and she knew what he was thinking, but all she could say was, "Tavish, Dubhán is with my father."

* * * *

Dubhán walked on silent feet into Iain Douglas's chamber. He hadn't been inside this room in the daylight for nearly thirty years. The old man lay on his bed, a pretty maid and the fat Harriet at his side.

"Oh, Dubhán," the old woman cried, "thank God you've come."

He smiled at them all. "I should always come when duty to my lord calls me. Will you give the laird privacy to confess his sins?"

They left so easily. So mildly. He slid the bolt after them, without a whisper of sound. He had the gift of silence, after so many years being surrounded by bones and ghosts.

It gave one a greater appreciation for the screams.

He approached the bed, his hands already outstretched. He had waited so long to fulfill this, his final duty. Then his debt would be paid. It must be paid.

Iain's eyes opened. "Dubhán," he slurred.

"Hello, old friend," he said in a singsong. "You called for me and I came."

"Tell," Iain said. "Meck."

"Meg?" Dubhán repeated with interest. "Of course. Meg. So lovely. My favorite." He smoothed the blankets over Iain's thin form, creased them, caressed the dying man's hairless head. "I kept her the longest, you know. I made her last. Her skull—ah! So finely turned! It has a place of honor. The lord has used my talents well."

"Har-cray."

"Aye. He was my savior from the slave market. The white men would have used me as a tool; Lord Hargrave taught me how to make tools. And poison. Poison that can be masked as a sacrament; sickness that can be blamed on plague." He caressed Iain's head again. "I was supposed to have killed you long ago. But I wanted you to come to me. I knew you had to know. And I knew that, if I was very patient, you would ask. Now I can tell you."

Dubhán leaned down to Iain's ear. "She lived for almost a year after the lord gave her to me," he whispered, his words so quiet he could barely hear them himself. "Meg. Meg. Meg. I love her name. I love saying it. Sometimes I would chain her to the gravestone that bears her name and let her watch the Towe—"

Dubhán felt a hot pinch in his diaphragm, and he leaned back to look down.

The time-worn hilt of an old dagger was protruding from his abdomen.

Iain Douglas was looking directly into his eyes.

Dubhán tasted the blood filling his mouth, but it wasn't unpleasant to him, and so he relished it for a moment longer.

Yes, now at last he would be free.

* * * *

Tavish rushed ahead to open the door to Iain's chamber. But it was bolted from the inside. He threw his shoulder against it twice until the door burst inward and Glenna ran past him.

The floor was covered in blood, and Dubhán was sprawled atop Iain. Glenna screamed and ripped the monk away without a glance for him, and Dubhán tumbled to the floor easily, his eyes wide, the hilt of a blade like a mast in the evil hulk of him.

"Da!" Glenna sobbed, her hands going to Iain's face. "Da." She turned her head to look at Tavish, and the pain in her face pierced him. "Dubhán killed him. All these years, he never would see him, and now I know why, and he killed him."

Tavish went to his wife's side and turned her into his embrace while she wept, but he looked at Iain Douglas's face and knew the truth right away.

"No, Glenna," he soothed. "Dubhán didn't kill your father—your father killed Dubhán. Look at his face, princess. Look at his beautiful face."

Glenna raised her head, and they both looked at Iain Douglas's upturned face, his eyes dull but centered. His lips upturned evenly at the ends and pressed together as if about to say *Meg*.

Tavish leaned toward Glenna's ear as she placed her palm along Iain's still cheek; he whispered fiercely. "He will be remembered as the greatest laird Roscraig has ever known."

Glenna's breath hitched, and she nodded. "He cannot be buried on the hill."

"No," Tavish said, pulling her closer. "No. We will make a new place. And they will be together."

Glenna nodded again, her chest heaved on a hiccoughing sob, and then Tavish held his wife tightly as her keening sorrow welled up and filled the room. Through the window, the clouds over the Forth began to part.

Epilogue

They burned Dubhán's cottage to the ground, making it his crematorium. The king's own priest presided, insisting on driving out the evil spirits before sealing it with a funereal ceremony.

Iain and Meg Douglas were laid to rest together in a section of land carpeted with summer flowers, just beyond the village. Bagpipes' full, haunting strains filled the warm air, glowing with sunshine as if the whole world were made of nothing but light.

They found Tavish's coin buried in what was supposed to have been Frang Roy's shallow grave on the cliff, and he grudgingly sent a good portion of it south, in care of Alec and the king's sergeant at arms, to what Tavish once considered faraway Northumberland. Now, he thought there was no place far enough on the earth he would feel was a safe distance between Glenna and Vaughn Hargrave and the dark mysteries that still lay buried at Darlyrede.

They walked back to the Tower together, hand in hand, after the funeral. They were tired, in both body and heart. Mam left them in the entry corridor, bustling toward the kitchens as Anne approached with her old double apron. Tavish reached out a hand to stop to her, but Glenna took hold of his arm.

"Let her go, Tavish," she said. "You have given her the freedom to do anything she chooses. Let her be who she is."

He leaned down and kissed Glenna's lips gently. "How does a princess become so wise?"

"I was taught by a prince," she said lightly.

They continued up the stairs of the east tower toward their chamber, streams of bustling servants flowing around them as they passed the entry to the hall.

Glenna glanced to her right at the business afoot preparing the hall for the evening meal—the aproned servants spreading the cloths, the younger girls sweeping the floor. A man in rough clothes and a cap stood before the hearth, likely laying the wood for the fire. Glenna looked up at Tavish and smiled as they climbed on. She was eager to be alone with him, warm and safe and bare in their private room, where the ugliness of the past could never reach them again.

Where she could at least pray that it would never reach them again.

* * * *

The old man before the hearth turned his head slightly, a feeling of warmth drawing his attention to the corridor. But it passed, and he looked up once more at the portrait hanging on the stones, his eyes filling with tears at the years that spanned such a short distance between his old fishing boots and the boy in the feathered cap.

The blade lent to Iain Douglas was returned to the sheath on his belt, and so now he reached up to lay the double-barred brooch on the mantelpiece— carefully, reverently—his mouth pressed into a hard line.

The first part was over. And yet his journey had only just begun.

Tommy turned away from the portrait and left the hall.

Printed in the United States
by Baker & Taylor Publisher Services